A.I. CONFIDENTIAL

A <u>LIQUID COOL</u> CYBERPUNK DETECTIVE NOVEL

Book Six

AUSTIN DRAGON

Published by Well-Tailored Books, California

A.I. Confidential
(Liquid Cool, Book 6)

978-1-946590-59-6 (paperback)
978-1-946590-53-4 (ebook)

http://www.austindragon.com

Book cover design by Leslie K.

Printed in the United States of America

CONTENTS

PART ONE | IT AIN'T EASY FOR A P.I. IN THIS TOWN 1

Chapter 1 | Mrs Wilford Jr. 2

Chapter 2 | Wilford Jr. 10

Chapter 3 | Perl, Isis, and Go-Go 14

Chapter 4 | Shift-ee 25

Chapter 5 | Officers B-and-B 30

Chapter 6 | The Ladies 32

PART TWO | THE MAN 37

Chapter 7 | Punch Judy 38

Chapter 8 | Phishy 44

Chapter 9 | The Shoemaker 47

Chapter 10 | The Man 57

PART THREE | MR. CANDY 61

Chapter 11 | G. 62

Chapter 12 | Quix 66

Chapter 13 | Compstat Connie 71

Chapter 14 | 8-Ball 79

Chapter 15 | Brackets 94

Chapter 16 | Sharp 99

Chapter 17 | China Doll 108

Chapter 18 | Wil 114

Chapter 19 | Wilford 118

Chapter 20 | Polygon 123

Chapter 21 | Run-Time 128

Chapter 22 | Tiki 134

PART FOUR | SOME SERIOUS VIOLENCE 143

Chapter 23 | IT 144

Chapter 24 | The Mick 152

Chapter 25 | Phishy 154

Chapter 26 | The Ex-Wives 160

Chapter 27 | Nobody 165

Chapter 28 | G. 171

PART FIVE | HE'S THE BAD GUY 181

Chapter 29 | Dot and Jr. 182

Chapter 30 | PJ 191

Chapter 31 | Quix 195

Chapter 32 | Phishy 199

Chapter 33 | Venn 202

Chapter 34 | Wilford G 212

PART SIX | WHO'S MR. CANDY? 218

Chapter 35 | Prima Donna 219

Chapter 36 | Phishy 222

Chapter 37 | Exe 229

Chapter 38 | Connie 236

Chapter 39 | Wize 241

Chapter 40 | Bite-Size 245

Chapter 41 | Wize Gal 249

PART SEVEN | THE CONFIDENTIAL 253

Chapter 42 | Sly 254

Chapter 43 | Exe 263

Chapter 44 | Chief Hub 268

Chapter 45 | Venn 271

PART EIGHT | A.I. ROBOT VAMPIRE ZOMBIE APOCALYPSE 276

Chapter 46 | City Hall 277

Chapter 47 | The Kill Crew 281
Chapter 48 | The Cavalry...286
PART NINE | SWAN SONG 291
Chapter 49 | AI Robot Zombie Vampires...................................292
Chapter 50 | The Rescue Crew...300
Chapter 51 | Venn Daemon 307

PART ONE

It Ain't Easy for a P.I. in This Town

CHAPTER 1

Mrs. Wilford Jr.

"Every day is Seattle." That was a common saying. I didn't know the origin of the phrase, but you said it when the rain was particularly relentless. However, I never let it dampen my style or my spirits. I was a busy detective, and I had work to do.

Where was I? On Metro Public Transportation. It existed—grimy, grungy, and nasty. It was also known as the transportation of choice for the Free City set, those Metropolis city dwellers who didn't have the necessary discretionary funds for a decent, or at least operating, hovercar. I was here because I needed to keep as low of a profile for as long as possible, and driving around in my bright red Ford Pony wasn't going to help me do that. I had become too recognizable—a string of high-profile cases made me a bit too "famous" for my tastes. I could have been shuttled around the city in style, courtesy of my best friend, Run-Time, in a premium hovertaxi, or even hoverlimo, but I wanted to do it this way. I had said many times I wanted to stay close to the streets like an average private detective, not those high-end, booshy, silver-suited ones that worked at upscale investigation firms that had more employees than all the tenants of my apartment mega-tower. Seeing how the Average Joe and Jane lived, who depended on public everything to survive, would do me good.

We called it the hoverrail, but it wasn't the real hoverrail, which was the supercity's ancient monorail system. Hovertrains served the entire city; the real hoverrail served only limited districts, one of which was Downtown Metro, so the politicians and their staff could get around conveniently. Regardless, all of it was grimy, grungy, and graffiti-ed. I did have my germophobic condition to deal with, but I had a nice, tight, frubber turtleneck top under my coat, had my second-skin gloves on, and never stopped chain-chewing immune support gum. I'd live.

The hoverrail had made its stop, and I stood up to let an elderly lady, who had gotten aboard, take my seat. I knew she was a senior citizen from her silver hovertrain ticket (70 and older) not her appearance—she didn't look "elderly" at all. She smiled at me as she sat. I held onto the handrail, turned so my back was always to the windows. I didn't need to look out. I'd seen it before, and there was nothing to see. It was the passengers I kept my eye on. I always needed to be on the lookout for any suspicious characters.

There was one. I was watching him, and he was watching me. He didn't like it; I didn't care. He was in a silver hoodie and wearing yellow shades. I observed his earrings and glowing tattoos all over his neck. It was the neon tattoos that made people look like they were some kind of android—glowing blues and greens with hard edges were the most common. His was a blue-black. The train made its next stop, and there they were, four more "youth" strolling onto the hovertrain, all dressed identically. I was in no mood.

"Hey!" I yelled. The four of them stopped. I pointed to their comrade in his seat. "You! Get up! All of you catch the next train."

"Why should we listen—?"

I pulled my omega-gun from my jacket.

He instantly did away with the attitude and smiled. "Yeah, I see what you mean, sir. This train is way too crowded."

He turned and all of them—the fifth jumping from his seat to follow—left. The doors closed. I looked around. The elderly woman, and everyone else, was smiling at me. The punks could have been legitimately riding the train, but more likely, they were scoping for victims. The first kid on the train was the scout looking out for police, other gang members, or Alphas like me that could turn their "easy" score into more trouble than it was worth. Not on any hovertrain I was riding!

"Thank you, young man," the elderly woman said. "If Metropolis had more of our youth like you, we'd have such a great society. We all travel the hovertrain to our games every Tuesday and Thursday."

I had noticed the car had a lot of elderly people. "Oh, you're all going to the same place. Games, you said, ma'am?"

"Yes, we're part of the same card club."

"Cards. What do you all play?"

"Strip poker."

Of course, I wanted to end the conversation immediately and dematerialize off the hovertrain. She kept smiling, so before she could ask me, the young man, to join their senior citizen two-day-a-week "card game", I said, "Too bad. My wife has forbidden me from playing that game anymore."

She laughed.

I was actually off to City One in Downtown Metro, but not City Hall, across the street to the Metro Municipal Courts. I had added another line of specialty to my private detective business—civil investigation. With all the cases there were in the supercity of Metropolis, with its 50 million plus people, the courts never had enough city investigators to gather evidence for trials, so they contracted with civilian ones like me. It was steady boring work—perfect! Unlikely I'd get shot at by anybody and a guaranteed paycheck—even better. Simple cases, no more "save the world" mega-cases. I had my fill.

I winced at seeing someone wearing a Liquid Cool T-shirt and made sure the kid didn't see me by quickly, but naturally, tilting my head down. In the rain, he probably wouldn't have recognized me anyway. Again, I was in no mood to be friendly with any "fans."

When I first visited the Metropolis Municipal Court Building sometime last year, I had never seen a building more like an endless maze. As chaotic as the Criminal Courts were, the civil court system was worse, but I learned that as long as you knew your floor and room, you could (and should) ignore all the rest.

I never had cause to set foot in the building, but now as a contracted investigator, I was a regular. There were far too many staff members for even me to remember; the faces were always different when I showed up. I never knew what clerk, attorney, or attorney's aide I'd be meeting. Either I was picking up the files for a new case or dropping off files for a case I closed. For some strange reason, a testament to the efficiency of government, I could never do both in the same visit. I'd give my name at the lobby desk, and they told me where to go.

"Floor 76, Cruz," the huge, tan man with a bleached-blond crew-cut said to me. "Room 4-6-A."

Out the elevator I went and the hallways were always jam-packed with people. I made my way to my room to pick up my case. I never knew what the case might be ahead of time. It was whatever case was available when I walked through the door.

"I'm Cruz. What do you have for me?" I asked when I walked up to the counter. There was a slender woman in a dark suit, wearing glasses looking at her desk computer.

"ID." I already had it ready and placed it on the counter for her. She picked it up and passed it over a scanner in her keyboard. "Mr. Cruz."

She handed it back as she looked at her display screen. "You do sex and violence?" she asked.

"No and no, but what is it?"

"Attempted sexual assault case—female on male, but with a counter-charge. Both have records."

"Okay."

"Witness statements for both parties. Both have lengthy criminal records. Total of 25 people. Do you want it?"

"Witness statements only, right?" I asked.

"That is all the associate D.A. needs."

"I'll take it."

She began typing and, in a few moments, popped out the disk file from her computer and handed it to me. She placed paperwork in front of me on the counter to sign.

"Deadline?" I asked.

"They need it all by week's end."

"Okay." I signed the assignment forms.

She took them from me, glanced at them quickly, then gave me another form. "Thank you, Mr. Cruz."

"Thank you."

Simple. Now, I was on my way.

As I left the Municipal Court building into the rain, I was already looking out in the distance for the next hovertrain. Not at all convenient, but you'd never have to wait more than 20 minutes during peak time. Depending on what part of Metropolis the subjects were, I'd decide if I could stay on the hoverrail or would have to head back to the office to pick up my vehicle.

My mobile rang, and I recognized the number. I stepped back out of the rain and walked to the side of the building as I flipped it open.

"Hi Mary," I greeted.

"Cruz. How are you?"

"I'm fine, just trying to stay dry."

"Yeah, same here."

"Is everything okay?"

"I need a favor, Cruz."

"Sure, what is it?"

"It's Wil. I need you to find him."

I had tried to find a private place to talk, but there was no such place on the sidewalk around the building. "Mary, let me call you right back."

"Okay."

When I first became a detective, one of the things I did to research my new profession was to read every book I could find from past and present private detectives, especially in Metropolis. The one who stood out from all the others was Mr. Wilford G., who died at the young age of 92. There were many books out there, but his 60-page book titled, *How to be a Great Detective with 100 Rules*—not the 1000-page tomes or 400-page non-fiction fiction—became my Bible. I quoted it often and considered the book brilliant. Mr. Wilford G. was my posthumous mentor, and I liked to think I used every bit of his 70 plus street-wise career to make me a better P.I.

He had a son—Wilford G. Jr., and "Junior" was a police veteran. Metro PD was the largest and most formidable police force on the planet, 500,000 members strong, and Wil was also the head of the Metropolis Police Union. I met Wil on my first major case, and we were basically friends ever since. He was one of the youngest officers ever to run the Union, but he was a solid guy. To hear from his wife that something was wrong concerned me. Wil Jr. didn't fold under pressure of any kind; he wasn't made that way.

I had to walk a bit to find someplace private and safe to call Mary back. I was on the third floor of a parking bay looking out to the street.

When I dialed her back from the vid-phone display, she looked like she'd been crying.

"Hi, Mary."

"Thanks for calling back, Cruz. I'm sorry to bother you, but I didn't know who else to call."

"No, it's okay."

"You always have to be careful about things like this. Things can get political so fast because of his position. I don't want someone to try to take advantage of the situation or try to twist it into something it's not."

"Mary, what's happened?"

"Wil hasn't been himself. You know they all work cases off-duty from time to time. That's what I thought he was doing. He's very good at keeping the work away from home, me and the kids, but this was different. First, he seemed paranoid then obsessed."

"Did he tell you what he was working on?"

"He wouldn't tell me. He said it was nothing, but I knew that wasn't true."

"Do you think he's in danger?"

"No, nothing like that. I think it's more obsession than anything dangerous. He's just not right."

"What happened for you to call me?"

"He called in sick—two days ago. But he's not here. I don't know where he is. I called the job, and they told me he called in sick today, but he's not home. I didn't even know he called in sick the first day. Cruz, I need to know that he's okay. Can you find him?"

"Okay, do you have an idea where he might be? You're a police wife, so you're part detective yourself."

She smiled. "I guess I am—we are. I called in a favor. The mobile he used to call in sick this time was not his regular one. It was a private line, but we traced it."

"You have an address?"

"I have a square radius of where the call came from."

"Okay, hold on; let me get something to write with."

"Cruz, you can type it right on your mobile."

"No, I'm old school and I've always found that rude—tapping my fat fingers on the display on your face. Give me the coordinates and I'll head over and see what I see."

"Thanks, Cruz."

CHAPTER 2

Wilford Jr.

I decided to call a hovertaxi. If I was going to be looking for Wil, then arriving in a bright red hovervehicle wouldn't exactly fall under the category of staying under the radar.

The district was in Neon Ya, a residential and commercial area, with a majority population of Vietnamese, Philippine, and Malaysian. It was in a Let It Ride hovertaxi, but I asked for an undercover one. Metro police weren't stupid, and Wil was at the higher end of the intellect scale. They knew Let It Ride's CEO was my best friend, and I was already wearing my trademark tan fedora and slicker.

"Do you have a spare slicker, Jax?"

"Sure do," the driver replied. He reached into the passenger compartment box area and pulled out a vacuum-wrapped folded plastic.

"Oh, thanks," I said, taking it from him.

I stepped out into the rain with my new gray hooded slicker. I was in front of a 24-hour noodles and coffee shop with a large front glass window of neon glass that changed colors. The crowd was light—people in gray, brown, and black outerwear, wearing visually-enhanced colored shades. People with hoods, some with umbrellas, some wearing pointed

Chinese bamboo hats—all normal. Neon Ya was a typical working-class neighborhood, like my own Rabbit City.

Mary had given me the four coordinate points of where Wil Jr.'s call came from, so I'd slowly walk from corner to corner, surveying the area. I was somewhat familiar with the area and started to put together a theory as to where Wil Jr. might me if he were here. This was the second time I had walked the perimeter, and I returned to hotel offices for rent in one of the towers. I stood across the street and looked from the third-floor level right up into the overcast sky to the top 200th floor enshrouded by clouds.

Outside the main lobby entrance were a group of Asian men standing around, smoking glowing cigarettes, and wearing glowing yellow or blue shades under a large awning. Some of them had dark hair, some blond, and all in the same white shirts, rolled up sleeves, and black pants—they were building employees. No one was talking, just enjoying their smokes outside.

"Hello," I said as I walked to them. They looked at me with complete indifference. "I'm looking for this man." I showed them Wil's picture on my mobile display, passing it by each of their faces. "I'm a legitimate detective, and I'm trying to find this guy." I put my mobile back in my pocket. "Who wants cigarette money?" I held some plastic currency in my hand.

One man put his cigarette in his mouth and held out his hand. "56th floor. Room D." I gave him the money.

The memories of those that worked the room rental business of any kind bordered on the freakish. He probably knew Wil's full name, when he checked in, what he had for breakfast, lunch and dinner. Two hundred floors and they probably knew everyone on them.

When I exited the elevator capsules, I pulled down my hood and walked to the door. It was already open. There was Wil Jr. seated at a desk on the room's vid-phone. He was Caucasian, tall, slim but very muscular, and dark hair.

"Yeah, he's here now," he said. "No, you don't have to call the police. I know him. Thanks."

I chuckled. "They take my money down there, and then call you up here to tell you I'm coming."

"What did you think they'd do, Cruz? Come in and close the door."

The desk was filled with paper, files, and disks, but the room was neat. Wil obviously hadn't shaved in days, but he didn't look distressed. He leaned back in his chair.

"Mary, was it?"

I walked to the open balcony and looked out at the view. "She's a police officer's wife."

"I knew I was stupid the second I hung up using the private mobile."

"What's going on, Wil? At least I didn't find you up here with another woman or something."

He looked at me. "Tell Mary you found me and I'm fine. I'm simply working a case on my own time."

"Calling in sick—two days in a row."

"I needed more time to wrap things up."

"Mary used the words paranoid and obsessed."

"Mary over-exaggerates. I'm fine."

"Wil, unless you tell me what's going on, I'm not going anywhere."

"Did my wife hire you for that?"

"Yes, she did."

"No, she didn't. She asked you to find me, which you did."

"What's going on Wil? You know your wife won't leave you alone until she knows what's going on. And Mary is not the over-exaggerating kind."

I glanced around the room.

"What are you looking for?" Wil asked, nervous.

"I'm looking for a clean place to set myself down, since I'll be here awhile."

"You have to go. I came here to work, not be bothered by anyone."

"Get away from the wife, kids, and the world."

"Yes. Surely, you can relate to that these days."

"Oh yes, I can. Cruz Jr. is quite the menace to society in his hoverchair now. He's discovered a new principle of physics—speed."

Wil laughed. "Cruz, go away."

"I'll compromise with you. You go home to see Mary and tell her yourself that you're fine, and I'll hold the fort here for you, since you don't need my help. I can watch all your secret files until you get back."

"Maybe I do need help." Wil looked distressed and placed his hand on his forehead.

"Are you going to tell me what's going then?"

"How much do you charge for services?"

"Wil, just tell me and I might not charge you anything."

"No, you know I can't get any services or work for free because of my position. I'd have to hire you."

"Hire me to do what?"

"It's an identity theft thing."

"Okay, but why would you get involved in something like that?"

"The identity they've stolen is Dad's."

"Dad? Your father? Wilford G?"

"Yes, so it's personal. And I think I know who—or at least, I've narrowed down the suspects to three people."

CHAPTER 3

Perl, Isis, and Go-Go

I sat down in another chair. Wil Jr. had my undivided attention. Wilford G. was his father, but if some grifter had stolen his ID to use for whatever illicit deeds, that was an act of war.

"I'm waiting Wil. Some mutt is using Wilford G.'s identity? Doing what?"

"It looks like it may have started a couple of years ago."

"What are they doing? Running up credit debts? What are they buying?"

"Cruz, they haven't bought or charged anything."

"Then what did they steal his identify for?"

"My father had a lot of property around Metropolis. He loved storage units. When he passed, he left ten of them to me. It took me and Mary over a year to go through everything. A lot of the memorabilia he collected was worth some serious money. I always thought he had more units."

"Why?"

"My father also collected guns."

"They weren't in the storage units?"

"No. Nor the ones he left to my mother or the ones he left to his ex-wives."

"Ex-wives. Your father had ex-wives?"

"Cruz, my father died at 92; what do you think? Yes."

"What are you saying? Someone stole your father's identity to get into storage units."

"Yes. They knew about them and have been trying to get at them. Maybe, besides the guns, my father had money stashed in them."

"Wil, that doesn't make any sense. He would've put all that in the will for you and his family."

"I know I don't have all the pieces yet. That's why I've been working this on my own time."

"What tipped you off on this?"

"The security company called me awhile back and said someone had gotten access to some of the storage units, mine, using Dad's old access codes. We never changed them, and the company forgot to delete them. I got the access logs and saw that someone had accessed mine a couple of times, and it wasn't me or Mary."

"You said you know who it is, though."

"Who else could it but the ex-wives?"

"Or—"

"Be careful, Cruz."

I stood from my chair, walked to the other end of the room, turned and said, "Or your mother."

"Cruz, I told you to be careful. I played American football in college and the academy. I was the quarterback. I can throw my computer and hit you from here."

"What are your next moves then?"

"Come on back over here. I can't hear you from over there."

I returned to my chair. "What's the move?"

"I'll hire you to investigate."

"Investigate who?"

"Cruz, I don't need you to investigate my mother. She would never do this."

"Then I can rule her out, just like the police do."

"You better tread carefully around my mother."

"Do you care if I tread carefully around the ex-wives?"

"Them, I don't care about."

"Was that the real reason you decided to hide out here in your new hotel office headquarters—to spy on citizens?"

"I'm not spying. I'm investigating."

"Investigating people who you have a connection to from your late father, and that connection isn't a positive one. Wil, what's wrong with you? If they found out, the trouble you would be in—suspension, you'd be booted out of your union president job. No, you're turning this over to me—all of it. Mary is right about you. Go home, Wil. I'll handle it."

He reluctantly began to stand from his desk. "How do I pay you, hire you?"

"Don't worry about that. I'll have PJ call you at home. She's very good at collecting payments."

"I heard that."

"Is any of this password protected?"

"No."

"Again, is that the Wil I've grown to know, who's a stickler for information security? Get out of here. You're useless."

Wil grabbed his black slicker from the back of his chair and put it on. "Thanks, Cruz."

"Don't thank me yet. We haven't found the mutt who's using your father's identity yet, but you're welcome."

Old Harlem was the site of two separate, but connected crimes that I solved, launching my detective career. The district was a mostly Italian enclave now and had more historical landmarks than any other part of Metropolis. It was known these days more for its clubs and restaurants, and especially because of an establishment called Joe Blows, as the center of the cigar aficionado world.

It also had a small residential area. The buildings in Old Harlem were not tall at all compared to the rest of the supercity, and neither were the residential towers. While the neighborhood's hipster clubs and restaurants catered to younger crowds, the residences were filled mostly with the elderly. It was here I arrived in another hovertaxi.

Since Wil was probably never planning to speak to his mother about this situation, even though she had to be considered a possible suspect, it meant I would talk to her first. I buzzed her apartment, and she wasn't surprised when she saw me on the vid-phone display.

"Come on up," she said.

It was an ancient building but well-kept and well-maintained, with a nicely dressed doorman watching over things. I got on the elevator and went straight up to the penthouse floor, which in this tower, was the 50th floor.

As soon as I came out of the elevator, I saw her at the end of the hall waiting. She was a petite brunette in a sharp one-piece crimson dress with matching shoes. In her generation, such attire was considered normal casual gear at home. She would have been in her seventies, but had I not known that, I would have sworn she was decades younger. My wife had told me many times we had entered the age that, once you reached your forties, you would "be in your forties forever"—and people lived easily into their hundreds, except if you were hovertrain-riding, strip poker maniacs. "Hello, Mrs. G." I extended my hand.

"I haven't been Mrs. G. for some time now, Mr. Cruz." She shook my hand, and I said nothing.

She led me into her place. It was very prestigious-looking—lots of white, original paintings on the wall, plants and flowers all over the place.

"Your paintings?" I asked.

"Actually, yes," she said as she led me to the sitting room. "I've been dabbling in the craft, as they say, for half a century."

"Impressive."

"Some agree; some have even parted with large sums of money to get one for themselves."

She sat and gestured for me to sit when we got to the chairs in one of the many rooms on the single level of the apartment.

"Have you been in touch with your son?" I asked.

"I'm sorry. My manners. Do you care for anything to drink?"

"Oh, no. I already have, but thanks."

"I've already eaten. My son? No, I last spoke to Wil two weeks ago, I think."

"You said you're not Mrs. G anymore."

"It's Mrs. Starr. But, please, call me Perl."

"Perl, Wil believes that someone has stolen the identity of Wilford G."

"Is that so?"

"Beside the storage units that he willed to the family, was there anything else he might have not included in the will?"

"No, Mr. Cruz. We each got 10 units—me, Wil, his other two ex-wives; that was all. There was his office, but he had the landlord handle that. Bank accounts, there were two. Half went to me and the other half was split between the other two wives. There was nothing else. Why does Wil believe there might be something else?"

"Guns."

Perl smiled. "Yes, men and their guns."

"I've met quite a few women who like guns too—a couple of them shot me."

"Yes, I imagine you do meet a more sordid group in both sexes. They're probably in another storage unit, and when the lease is up, they'll call us or whoever is still living or the next generation in line if we're not around. Simple oversight on my ex-husband's part. You're allowed to forget things at 92."

"That seems like a very logical explanation. However, there is more. Wil said that someone other than the family used your ex-husband's old access codes to get into the storage units."

"All my storage units are empty. I know the ones of the other wives would be too. Tell Wil to stop procrastinating and empty the ones he has. Then whoever it is won't matter. Is any money involved?"

"No."

"There it is then. Someone wanted to steal whatever was in the storage units, probably an employee of the storage unit company. See which units haven't been accessed in ages and knew my ex-husband had passed."

"May I ask you a question, Perl?"

"Of course, Mr. Cruz."

"How did Wilford G die? It's funny I don't know. I've read his book like a million times."

"Yes, Wil told me you're that one person who bought his book. He died in an explosion doing the very thing he loved more than me or anyone else—the business. He was investigating a case at the time. They said he would have never felt anything; death from the blast would have been instant. The crooks he was after had booby-trapped their residence for the police. They were supposed have gone in to arrest the crooks the day before, but the paperwork got held up. They said the blast wouldn't have done a thing to the police with their body-armor, but to the average person, another matter altogether."

"I'm sorry."

"Why sorry, Mr. Cruz? Not your fault. That's life. We had been long since divorced, though we remained friends."

"Was there a body?"

"Yes, not much, but enough for DNA to confirm identity and to bury, well, cremate. The guns?"

"It's the guns. That's all. Wil feels that because they're unaccounted for, there may be a lot more storage units, and that's what the thief or thieves are really after."

"Wil seems to forget that we were never wealthy and Wilford didn't have a secret fortune stashed away anywhere. Tell my son not to upset himself. I can look around and see if I have anything that would tell us where my ex-husband's gun storage unit might have been."

"That's the best thing to do. He actually is upset about it. He thinks someone is sneaking around with his father's identity."

"They were close, so it must be upsetting. I'll see what I can find, and I'll call him tonight."

"Thanks, Perl."

"Thank you, Mr. Cruz. Please don't tell me you're going to speak to the other two."

I laughed. "Ah, yes, I am, but only to cover all the bases. Standard procedure according to Wilford G's *How to be a Great Detective with 100 Rules.*"

"You really have read it a million times. It's a waste of time, but you have to do what you have to do in the business."

"Thanks for seeing me, Perl." I rose from my chair.

"Thanks for helping my son." She stood too and then led me back to the front door.

"I'm off to see Isis."

"Oh, the cold one," Perl said in a very disapproving tone.

After Wilford G. divorced Wil's mother, he married Isis. She was a shapely brunette with blue eyes and lived in Elysian Heights, which meant I could stop by the Hell Spawn's (my wife's parents) place, if I were ever possessed by the Devil to do such a thing.

However, that's not where I went. I went to ex-wife number three's place in Silicon Dunes, which was one of the most expensive areas of the supercity, even more than Elysian Heights. Go-Go was blond, brown eyes, and, I believe, the same age as Wil.

When I buzzed her apartment—an apartment didn't have a doorman but, instead, a security detail of four cyborgs in the lobby, I wondered why it was audio only and why it took so long for her to allow me up.

She finally did after 15 minutes, and I rode the elevator capsule alone to the 285th floor. I came out and was greeted by a barking white poodle.

"Precious, get back here!" I heard a woman's voice yell.

In these buildings, the elevator typically opened right into the apartment itself. Go-Go was behind a center counter in the kitchen, and I could smell the aroma of food being cooked.

"Mr. Cruz, a pleasure to meet you. Please don't mind Precious. She barks at everyone until she gets to know you. You can have a seat. I'm warming up the food the maids prepared this morning. I won't be long."

"In the living room?"

"Yes. I've been so scattered lately. I'm on a new diet to get all this fat off.

"If you don't mind me saying, you're not fat."

"Mr. Cruz, if it jiggles, it's fat."

I knew better not to continue that line of conversation. The woman probably had zero fat over her entire body. The only thing that could possibly jiggle was her fake chest or butt. I walked up two steps to the elevated living room with holographic walls. The couches were made of that material that, once you sat down you had to wait to see just how far you would sink.

"I hope my visit didn't inconvenience you at all."

"Not at all. I had to quickly make the place presentable. The maids are at the market right now, leaving me to fend for myself," I heard her call out from the kitchen.

Staring at her mobile, she didn't notice I had returned to the kitchen.

"Is it Ms. or Mrs. Go-Go?" I asked, startling her something good. She almost dropped her mobile, and her dog instinctively started barking at me again.

"Precious, shut up!" The dog quieted down. She looked up at me.

"Are we waiting for someone?" I asked. She didn't know what to say. "Who are we waiting for?"

"No one."

"Ms. or Mrs. Go-Go, I'm armed. Anyone comes in here after me that I don't like, I'm going to shoot them, shoot you, and shoot your dog."

"I'm not saying anything unless I have an attorney present."

"What? I'm not a police officer. Why would you need an attorney?"

"I mean, I'm not saying anything more."

When I pulled my gun from my jacket, she went white, and with her complexion, she was white enough. I gestured for her to sit in the living room. She did exactly that, after she picked up her poodle. I stood with my back against the holo-wall with a frown and a bad attitude. We waited.

Thirty minutes later, we heard a beep. I could see Go-Go want to jump up and run to the coming elevator, but she stared at the gun in my hand and settled back down. The elevator arrived.

"Go-Go! Why didn't you answer your mobile?" a voice called out, but I heard two sets of heeled shoes walking.

The two women appeared in the living room and froze.

"Well, look at this. I know who the other one is, so you must be ex-wife number two, Mrs. Isis. Why don't you two join your friend with the poodle. Come on, Perl, smile! Sit down, ladies."

"There is no cause for you to brandish a loaded weapon in this residence," Isis said to me. She was the only one of the of trio who was panicking.

"I like to brandish things. It makes me feel important."

She wasn't amused. Go-Go was in almost a trance, and Perl didn't make any eye contact with me at all. I stared at the three women on the couch.

"Wil was right," I said.

"Wil was right about what?" Perl asked.

"Well, he was partially right. He suspected that you and Go-Go were up to no good, but his mind wouldn't include you. But I don't trust anyone, so I included you, Perl, from the start. No wonder he divorced the three of you!"

"Wait, one minute!" Now, Go-Go was back from the beyond, mad and ready to fight me verbally. So were her two friends.

"You don't know why we divorced," Perl yelled.

"The three of you are crooks!"

"Mr. Cruz," Isis said, without any emotion whatsoever. "We're not crooks; we've committed no crime."

"You haven't?"

"But—" Go-Go had leaned over to say, but Isis held up a reassuring hand.

"Mr. Cruz doesn't know anything, and as long as none of us says anything, he'll continue to know nothing at all. Remain silent and I'll do any talking that needs to be done. But nothing needs to be said. Ladies, we are leaving."

Isis stood first, and the other two slowly stood, too.

"Perl, I'm going straight to Wil's house—" I began.

I could see the look of panic return to her face, but Isis grabbed her. "And tell him what, Mr. Cruz?" Isis snapped. "Tell him nothing. In fact, Mr. Cruz, let's make a wager right now. Rather than try to emotionally blackmail Perl, you tell us what you know, and if it's correct, I'll tell you everything."

I stood there with a smirk. Isis was the leader of this crew, and she was good. She correctly called my bluff and smiled to herself as I put my weapon back into my inside jacket holder.

"You're right, Isis. I know nothing at all. All I know is that the three of you are involved in a conspiracy related to Wilford G. That's what I'm going to tell Wil."

"No!" Perl yelled, but Isis restrained her again.

"Let him," Isis said to her. "Let him do whatever he wants. He'll talk to Wil, then we'll talk to him."

"You'll talk to Wil? Good luck with that," I said. "In the state he's in, he'll never speak to any of you ever again." I began to walk to the elevator, but I stopped. "You do know that Wil is the head of the Metro Police Union. All he has to do is make one call and you'll have 500,000 police officers following every move you make."

"You don't scare us, Mr. Cruz," Isis said. "We haven't done anything, and we're a lot smarter than you."

"I've had a lot of criminals tell me how smart they are," I said.

"We're not criminals!" Perl interjected.

"But all those criminals who thought they were smarter than me are dead or in prison here in Earth or Up-Top. I'm still standing. I'm going to talk to my friend Wil. He won't like it that his mother is involved in a conspiracy, but as you said yourself, Perl, he and Wilford were close. Enjoy yourself, ladies, because you're about to have two very determined men after you—and it will not be to get your phone number. Bye."

CHAPTER 4

Shift-ee

When I called Wil at home, he had a very uninviting look on his face. I'm glad it was a tiny face on my mobile viewscreen.

"Wil, I'm not going to tell you what I uncovered because it may set you off in such a way you'll want to throw your mobile out the apartment window and then Mary will blame me. All I'll say is it's not two suspects; it's three."

"Cruz, I'm hanging up." And he did.

I had concluded my case.

There wasn't a lot of time to get my 25 witness statements for the courts, but I had been under tighter deadlines before. I had a hovertaxi drop me off in one part of town, where it seemed most of them lived. Tomorrow, I'd be back in my vehicle to finish the rest. I wanted it all done in two days, with plenty of time to spare.

Whiskey Way wasn't a good part of the supercity anyway, but I was in an especially bad part. I had my bag of recording equipment in one hand and my other hand in my jacket pocket as I walked to my next apartment mega-tower.

I had my secretary calling the witnesses beforehand, so they'd know who I was and why I wanted to interview them. The courts often did the preliminary work of telling them that an investigator would contact them, so it almost always went smoothly. Only one person wanted to reschedule for another day—apparently, they had been arrested for something and wouldn't be home until next week. I used to think this was only a Free City thing, but I had learned this sort of thing was as prevalent in the upper-scale neighborhoods, too, making me wonder how many criminals, ex-criminals, and about-to-be-criminals there were in Metropolis.

The apartment tower was a dirty mess of a building. It looked like the carpet hadn't been vacuumed in decades. The walls looked like they were coated with grime from when I was Cruz Jr.'s age, and most of the ceiling lights were dim, about to go out, or flickering. The only good thing about the place was there was no graffiti.

I had rung the doorbell. I stood at the side of the door, but knew I was being watched though the above-door monitoring camera.

"What do you want?" a man's voice came over the intercom.

"It's Cruz. My office called about the witness interview and recording."

"Hold on." The man took forever to respond and forever to open the door. He was a stick of a man in an A-shirt, messy sandy brown hair, mustache and goatee. What I didn't like is that he was wearing his boxer briefs and bunny slippers. "You got ID."

I showed him my government-issued court ID with photo. "Is this a bad time? I can come back if it's more convenient. I just happened to be in the area."

"No, man. It's good. Come in."

I couldn't tell if he had been sleeping or had been doing drugs. The inside of the place sure didn't smell drug-free to me.

"Where do you want me to set up? Someplace where we can sit comfortably for the interview."

"How long will this take, man?"

"I don't think very long. It's really based on what you saw."

"What I saw?"

"Didn't the court call you?"

"Oh, yeah, that. What I saw. You can set up at the dinner table."

The apartment was a mess—clothes everywhere, empty beer cans, empty bottles, food boxes, pizza boxes. I bit my lip because, if I saw even one jumbo roach, I'd have run out of there faster than Rocket Man.

The man pointed to the dinner table, which wasn't exactly clean, as he stood there biting his fingernails. I took out a napkin, wiped down the table thoroughly.

"Have a seat here." I wanted to sit with my back to the wall.

"No, man. I want to sit with my back to the wall," he said.

"Okay, have a seat here." I was still going to move my chair. He sat but didn't look happy.

"What do you want me to say?"

"Answer the questions truthfully. This is for the Court. What you saw and the particulars. I'll walk you through it all."

"I don't like any of this."

"It'll be fine. Answer the questions, I record it all, and then I'm off on my way."

"I should be paid for this."

"It's our civic duty."

"What if she finds out what I said?"

"It's not just you. Everyone is going to say what they saw."

"How many people, man, besides me?"

"I don't know but more than you."

"I don't know about this, man. I don't want her to do to me what she did to that guy. He was going to testify against her, you know."

This was the only downside to this kind of work, the interviewees trying to pull you into their situations.

"Okay, let's start the interview."

He jumped from his chair. "You didn't answer me!"

I remained calm, but I did not like him screaming at me. "Sorry, did you ask me a question?"

"What if she does to me what she did to the other guy?"

"I'm going to tell you again that the Court sent me here to record your statement. I don't know what your conversations have been with the Court. The Court told me you're ready to record your statement and that's why I'm here. Should the Court not have sent me here?"

He began biting his fingernails again. "No, I'm ready for the statement."

I returned to taking the recording device from the bag and then he bolted away, disappearing around the corner.

"Sir," I called out. "Where are you, sir?"

I dropped the device back in the bag as quickly as I could and reached for my gun. The only thing I was going to do at that point was get out of the apartment and out of this building.

I tip-toed, head down, out of the kitchen, looked to the main door on the other side of the living room. The problem was I'd be completely defenseless on the way to the door. I ran and reached for the doorknob—locked. I set the bag down on the floor and tried to unlock the door, but nothing worked. I stepped away from the door.

All I heard was laughing at the other end of the apartment.

"Sir, you need to open this door so I can leave the apartment." No response at all, so with my left hand I fished for my mobile in my pocket. It was one of the only times in my life that there was absolutely no signal, which meant the apartment had some kind of illegal jammer. As far as I was concerned, it was a kidnap situation.

I put my phone back, knelt, and listened. What he probably didn't know was that I was the king of the stake-out. I could wait for hours, even days if I had to. I made not one sound, didn't move a muscle, with my eyes closed for nearly two hours. I heard laughing again, then after a few moments, I heard more noise.

"Hey man, are you still there?" I heard him ask, walking down the hall. "Are you still alive?"

I rose and shot him once in his chest, then turned the gun and blasted both the lock and door knob to pieces. I kicked the door out and ran. As I did, I heard a lot more commotion from within the apartment. I ducked around the corner, stopped, and crouched.

I heard not one but multiple footsteps approaching, and when I peeked around the corner, I saw three armed men after me. I opened fire on all of them. They never knew what hit them as they dropped to the ground.

I listened. Nothing. I reached into my pocket for the phone again. Now I had a signal and simply pressed one button for the police. I dropped the phone on the ground and waited to be rushed again, looking around the corner and then behind me. I heard the 911-voice answer, but I said nothing. It kept talking, but I was busy watching all around me. The police would be sent to the scene whether I answered or not, and they would trace my phone, so they'd know it was me.

After this incident, at least, all I would need to get was 24 more witness statements.

CHAPTER 5

Officers B-and-B

When Metro PD arrived on a scene, they made sure everyone knew about it. I waited until the absolute last minute to put my gun back in my jacket, raise my hands, and yell to them who I was, as they stormed out the elevator.

A lot more officers arrived, and I had to wait in the building's lobby, while two officers watched me. The coroners had arrived, and the four bodies were being taken away on hovergurneys.

Two seniors walked to us. I recognized them as Officers Boot and Bus, who I'd met a few times before. Boot was the bigger Russian one, and Bus was the Italian. They were known even among their fellow officers as "B and B."

"Tell me, Cruz," Bus asked. "Why does everyone like you so much?"

"I'm sure you already called the Court, so you know they sent me. I'd like my weapon back, and there's Court recording equipment up in the apartment, so I want that back too. Then I can be off on my way."

"Four dead people and you don't care?" Officer Boot asked.

I looked at him. "No, I don't. I came to do a witness statement, not play Rambo with real guns."

"It seems you've solved a few crimes," Bus said.

"What do you mean?" I asked.

"A few court investigators have disappeared in the recent past. One four months ago, another ten months ago, and it looks like one from a year ago," Bus informed me. "Their bodies were found in the apartment."

"Looks like they wanted to add you to their collection," Boot added.

"Unlucky for them," I said. The more I thought about it, the angrier I got. "How could this have happened? Didn't anyone know they went to their apartment?"

"Follow me," Bus said.

The officer walked me to the main door with the directory of tenants. Bus pointed to the very button I had pressed hours ago. I leaned forward to look at it. I looked at the rest of the board. There was another 33C. I did what probably everyone else had done: pressed the first 33C I saw. I looked at the top one again and peeled off the fake letter and number.

"When our officers investigated, we'd go to the right tenant, not the fake one," Bus said.

"After they did what they did, they'd come down here and do what you just did," Boot said.

I looked at them. "Bring those four gurneys back inside, so I can shoot them again."

CHAPTER 6

The Ladies

I didn't know what angered me the most. The fact that I came to do a routine municipal court witness statement recording and could have been gunned down and buried in some psycho gang's apartment, or that they did so to three other innocent people with families like me.

I was so mad and told the officers that, if there were more of them, I wanted the whole gang taken down. I'd help if needed. Officer Bus said to me, "Cruz, if there is a gang, tomorrow there won't be." I knew it would all be handled.

The head of the Municipal Court operations division personally called me at home to thank me for solving the disappearances and bringing the perpetrators to justice. I had already turned in 11 of the witness statement recordings, but he told me the job was done and I'd be receiving a bonus.

The call was welcome because my wife, Dot, and I had confiscated Cruz. Jr.'s hoverchair. He only wanted to fly around, rather than learn to walk like a normal person. Both our parents warned us, but we didn't listen. So, Cruz Jr. resorted to trying to break the Guinness Book of Galactic Records for a toddler who could throw the longest tantrum of crying and screaming. We resorted to confining him to his crib in his room alone with no toys.

I made sure I'd kept the full details of the shootout and the police finding the bodies of the missing municipal workers. I didn't want to be confined to a crib in a room all alone too, even though it wasn't my fault.

My secretary called me while I was on the way to the office. Instead of coming in, I was redirected to a Silver City restaurant for an impromptu meeting. Silver City was the center of robotic production for Metropolis, and I had a few unpleasant incidents happen there on cases. I had hoped that the meeting would change my perception.

I actually didn't know Silver City had a restaurant section. It apparently was an open secret among foodies, and when I sat down at my table, I saw why: All the chefs in the kitchen were robots. The wait staff were all human, but I'm sure that was only for political reasons. The restaurant was all glass and silver everywhere.

The ladies—Perl, Isis and Go-Go—sat across from me. I was still in a bad mood from my latest shoot-out, so I said nothing and simply folded my hands on top of the table.

"Mr. Cruz, I want you to know that I'm not a crook," Perl said, "and I need you to tell Wil that."

"Why would I need to do that? He's your son."

"Thanks to you, he's not talking to me."

"What did you say to him?" Isis asked.

"He already knew you and Go-Go dancer were up to no good. All I told him is that it was a trio not a duo."

"I've never been a go-go dancer," Go-Go snapped.

"No one is up to no good, as you put it, Mr. Cruz," Perl said.

"Okay, nothing is going on. Why am I here then? Why did you want to meet me? I should leave."

"Mr. Cruz, you can save the performance," Isis said. "Do you want us to explain everything or not?"

"Honestly, Isis, I don't care. You work it out with Wil, and I'll go about my life."

"We want to hire you," Perl interjected.

I laughed out loud. In fact, I laughed for a bit. It was too ridiculous for me. "Is that how people are going to try to soften me up or try to fool me? I'll hire you, Mr. Cruz. But I want to hire you, Mr. Cruz. I'm not interested in your game."

"This is not a game," Perl said. "There's a very good reason why we did what we did. It's because of Wil."

"What about Wil?"

"It's how he might react," Perl said.

"React to what?"

"Wil didn't tell you the truth," Isis said.

I smiled. "Isis, you're good, but I'm better. I don't trust you, so anything you say, even if it's the truth, I won't believe it."

"Then I'll tell you," Perl said. "The access codes into the storage units. What if it wasn't someone who had stolen Wilford's identity?"

"Meaning what? Is that why we're in Silver City? The robots did it?"

"I'm not making a joke, Mr. Cruz," Perl said. "Wil didn't tell you the truth. He suspects himself, but can't face it. It's why he hasn't been himself. His wife can tell you. We created this ruse so that he'd suspect us of something illicit, like trying to find some secret fortune of Wilford's."

"We planted that idea in his head," Go-Go said.

"The truth is—" Perl began.

"Are you all telling me that you think Wilford is alive?"

"Yes, Mr. Cruz," Isis said.

"That's ridiculous."

"How would you know?" Perl asked. "You didn't even know my ex-husband existed back then. You weren't even a detective."

"You built hovercars for a living," Go-Go said in a dismissive way.

"I'm not playing your games," I said and stood from the table.

"Wait, Mr. Cruz," Isis said. "You don't want to believe us, fine. But you trust Wil. He believes it too."

"Why would your ex-husband fake his own death? How could he? You all told me the DNA confirmed it was his body in the explosion."

"Take a look at who the chief coroner was," Perl said.

"What does that mean? Most people don't know this, but it's the computer that identifies bodies, not the coroners. The machines tell you who it was; the humans sign off the report. Wilford hacked into the Metropolis Morgue and CSI computers? Ladies, stop it."

Isis held up her hand. "We will pay you for one day of work. We have it written down here. Wilford was a very clever man. He only pretended to be this folksy, good ol' street detective to his friends and families. Wilford was smarter than me."

She knew admitting that statement would pique my interest for real. I knew Isis prided herself on her intellect. She didn't wait for me to talk myself out of helping them.

"Here," she said handing me a paper. I took it. "We wrote it all down. Those are the leads. Either there is truly someone out there masquerading as Wilford for some unknown reason, or Wilford isn't dead."

The women watched me for any sign as to what I might do. I didn't know, myself.

"Don't tell Wil, though," Perl pleaded. "We need to know for sure, either way, before we say anything to him."

I read what was on the paper. "I don't know why I'm doing this."

Isis held up a reassuring hand again. "We will call your office. Pay for one day of work and stay away from Wil until we hear from you."

"I don't know how I get into these situations. Okay, I'll look into it for a day. But if I find out that you three are trying to scam me, throw me in a wrong direction while you're up to something criminal, I'll find out."

"Yes, Mr. Cruz, that is your reputation," Isis responded.

PART TWO

The Man

CHAPTER 7

Punch Judy

I was glad to be back in my vehicle. People had their black, gray, and dark blue hovervehicles; I had my sleek, bright red, classic Ford Pony—high-performance, super-charged, advanced nitro-acceleration hydrogen engine that still made the average person gawk and grabbed the eye of the genuine hovercar enthusiast and collector alike. I had found the shell in a junkyard when I was a kid in middle school, and it took me a few years to build and restore it, spare part by spare part. I'd been upgrading it ever since, especially now that I was a bona fide Metropolis street detective.

I flew into the business district of Buzz Town to my Liquid Cool office on Circuit Circle, known more commonly as simply the Circle. My office was on the 100th floor of the tower, and it, too, was in a constant state of upgrades of the security kind, courtesy of my one full-time employee. My deadly run-in with the man I learned went by the name of Shift-ee and his crew was a stark reminder of how dangerous this job was—actually it was more dangerous than even being a police officer or fireperson. At least my own office was the fortress it needed to be because sometimes the criminals didn't wait for me to get to the streets to take a shot at me, and sometimes, the criminals were the very clients trying to hire me.

Punch Judy was her street name because her first name was Judy, from Neo-Paris, and she liked to punch people, though she had reformed her ways ever since becoming my employee. She had short crimson hair, a simulated mole on her face, a dot, above her lips, loved her sleeve-less tops—to show off her bionic arms—and her heeled boots. To me and all her friends, she was P.J.

Before I knew her and she became a tenant in my building, when she was back in France, she was a soldier in the punk-posh gang, Les Enfants Terribles—a gang that prided itself with haute-couture designer clothes, fashion-matched combat boots, knuckle-studded, leather, half-gloves, and Devo-style half-helmets on their rainbow colored, punk hair. That was then; the gang didn't exist anymore. I had hired an ex-felon, but besides being able to punch a 300-pound cyborg through solid concrete and steel, I couldn't be happier she was my second in command. She ran the Liquid Cool office and did so exceptionally well. I was often in the field, and she was always here to manage the front-end, client-contact operations.

She was also quite the interior designer and had turned the reception-waiting area, the first thing you saw when you entered the office, into a shrine to all my high-profile cases, including a picture of me shaking hands with the Mayor of Metropolis (we hated each other) and another of me with Wilford Jr. (one of my favorites). PJ had become a master at chatting up potential clients with these pictures, and through her tour of Liquid Cool history, she was able to weed out the legit clients from the looky-loos and crazies.

"Boss, the Metro Court sent the bonus check," she said, smiling to me from her desk behind the receptionist wall, as I walked through the front door.

"Good."

"And I have even better news."

"What's that?" I stopped at her desk.

Her French-language old punk rock music was always playing in the background on an infinite loop. Her work area had psychedelic posters on the wall, her fancy "modern" glass desk with see-through glass drawers, and a boom box on top along with her own mobile computer. All of it was her metal barrier, but it didn't look like it with its new decorations of French action movies—previously she had simple posters of French historic sites.

"Mr. Grumpy is ready to sell."

That's what she called our next-door office neighbor. The man hated me. I couldn't blame him—we had had real shoot-outs in the hallway with bad guys, more than one criminal had been killed by me, a killer cyborg had been punched through the door by PJ and shot out the window by me to his death 100 stories below. For Mr. Grumpy, I'm sure it was a bit too much excitement for him. Last year, I asked if he'd be interested in selling his office lease to me; he told me go do something obscene with myself. I thought that was the end of it, but apparently not.

"What did he say?"

"He said he's ready to sell. 'Tell that Cruz that I'm ready to sell,' he said exactly. We can expand the offices!"

"Let's not get too excited until I know all the terms."

"He said call his office to set up a meeting, but I already did that for you. Tomorrow morning at 10 a.m. sharp. Be here."

I looked at the office, already imagining the larger office space.

"If we get the other office," she said, "you won't even need to hire contractors. I can just punch all the walls out. I'll save you a lot of money, but I want a bonus."

I looked at her a laughed. "Okay, PJ. Whatever you say."

"And that means staff. I want an assistant, so I can be the boss too."

"What do we need an assistant for?"

"You need an assistant too. Put both of them on the computer. Your assistant will do your criminal research, so you don't have to do that. My assistant will do the potential client background checks—make sure they're not criminal maniacs."

I started laughing. "You have it all figured out." I started walking to the door of my private office, with the neon LIQUID COOL. It was the other thing people saw when they came into the office.

"That's one of your favorite words—maniac. So, I'll keep them away and grow the business. You close the cases. You should think about having your own firm," she called out

I was in my private office looking and stacks of printed messages on my desk. They were arranged the PJ way—the "hot" pile, the "hold" pile, the "hell no" pile, and a few other miscellaneous ones.

"I don't want a firm. That means a whole bunch of junior detectives running around doing who knows what, half of them building a client-base so they can steal them from you the first chance they get to go out on their own or get an offer from a competitor. I don't want the headache. High quality cases are all we need and we'll be fine."

"You didn't tell me the whole story about the shootings." PJ stood at the doorway of my private office.

"PJ, it's a damn, dangerous world out there. Lots of crazy maniacs."

"I said that a long time ago." She disappeared to return to her desk.

I grabbed the messages I wanted, a few gadgets from my desk, and I was ready to get back in the field.

I was back at PJ's desk. She was typing at the speed of light with those bionic fingers of hers. To this day, I don't know what she was always typing.

"I got a task for you," I said.

She stopped typing and grabbed her electric steno pad from the top of her desk. "That's more like it." She was smiling with stylus pen ready to begin writing.

"Wilford G."

"Wilford G.? Your Wilford G.?"

"Yes."

"What about him?"

"When he died, he willed ten storage units to his son—"

"Wilford Jr.?"

"Yes, and ten to his first wife, ten to his second, and ten to his third."

"Is this a mathematics quiz?"

"No, but more interesting. How many storage units did Wilford G. have and how do we find all of them?"

"Oh, this is an easy puzzle. Criminals try to hide things in storage units and bank safety security boxes all the time. The government doesn't really allow people to be anonymous when renting them but is okay with people thinking they can. This is easy to find out."

"How much illegal hacking are you going to have to do?"

"Lots, but—"

"I don't want to know."

"The wives—it was those women I had you meet?"

"Yes. Perl, Isis, and Go-Go."

"Okay, I'll get on it. Where will you be?"

"I have some other leads to follow up on."

"Leads? What's the case?"

"Someone's stolen Wilford G's identity to get access to the storage units."

"Cruz, what's going on? Is your mentor alive? You're always reading that one book."

"No, but maybe he did have a lot of valuable stuff hidden away in storage units and people want to get at it. PJ, if Wilford G wanted to fake his death and had, why show up now and blow it all by doing something as stupid as using his access codes to gain entry to a storage unit. Wilford G wasn't stupid. It's someone else. Probably one of the ladies, or they've hired someone off the street to throw us off the trail. Nope, this is about simple greed—money."

"Secret money in the secret storage units."

"Exactly."

"Okay, I'm on it."

CHAPTER 8

Phishy

There were so many betting clubs in Metropolis that there was no one that was bigger or better than the other. They used to be called parlors, but they were really restaurants bars these days. Many times, the main considerations as to which one you went to were what music and food you liked and what kind of people you wanted to hang out with. There was a betting club for everyone, and if you grew to dislike where you were going, all you needed do was hop in your hovercar and fly down the street to another.

Governments had long since given up on trying to regulate or ban them; there was too much money involved, so as long as they got their cut—oh, taxes—they didn't care in the least. People could bet on anything and did. The only law there, which was more imposed by the market, or the "street," was you couldn't bet on a team you had any direct connection with. Owners and players couldn't bet on their own teams; if you were friends with, related to, married to, or divorced from anyone on a team, you couldn't bet on it. This code seemed to work well because cheating scandals were rare. The penalty was too severe—not prison, people could handle that—lifetime ban from the entire betting industry. People had committed suicide, rather than face that punishment.

I strolled into the Crystal Cactus in Smoky City. There were lots of sidewalk johnnies outside and a lot of low-level dons in cheap suits and their hustlers inside. Lots of booze and the walls were covered in viewscreens of every possible sports game on the planet. Everyone had bets in on something.

I saw who I was looking for in the crowds and walked to him. A lot of the patrons inside recognized me and nodded. I nodded back or waved hello. Smoky City was right next to Buzz Town, so I figured I might be known in these circles.

There were a handful of people in my immediate circle—my wife, Dot; PJ, my secretary; my best friend, Run-Time; and Phishy. Phishy's trademark look was dark colored vests and pants, with some off-white colored, long-sleeve shirt extravaganza with colored fish all over it. In here, like everywhere he went, he was the life of the party, strutting around, saying hello to friends, slapping a high or low five as he went around.

He was a street hustler—a little non-narcotic running here, a bit of courier work there, whatever scam he could get into to bring in some cash. Nothing illegal enough to get him a solid prison stint, but always at the level where, if he got caught, he'd get no more than a mere misdemeanor situation—pay the fine and be on his way, not even a blot on the record. The police and courts couldn't be bothered with street hustlers working non-violent, low money scams. They had real criminals to deal with like the four who tried to gun me down and killed innocent municipal workers for no reason at all.

Phishy saw me and began his chicken dance, which is how he greeted me. But this time, I couldn't wait for him to amuse himself and tire himself out. I ran and grabbed him.

"Oh, no not this time, Phishy," I said. "You can do your dance jig another time. I got a job for you."

"You do, Cruz? Do we need a confidential place to talk?"

"Over in the corner here is fine."

There really wasn't a quiet corner or space anywhere in the club, and outside was worse, so I moved to a spot near the bar where he could at least hear me above the sports commentators and the noise of the patrons.

"What do you know about betting on greyhounds?"

"I know a lot."

"Older clientele, right?"

"Oh yeah. Not a lot of younger bettors like the sport. They like a faster sport and more action. Robot greyhound racing never did catch on because everyone thought it was rigged."

"Since there's not a lot of people betting on it, if I were looking for someone who liked to bet on it, could I find them?"

"Find them in person?"

"Find out when they last bet on the sport."

"How long have they been an active bettor?"

"Eighty years."

"Seriously, Cruz? That'd be a long paper trail."

"Can you find you find out if I gave you a profile."

"Cruz, it would be easy. There's records of everyone, but that long of a time and the greyhounds—that's an easy search job."

"Okay, then you got the job."

He gave his wide Phishy smile. "Great, Cruz. I knew I could help you."

CHAPTER 9

The Shoemaker

The clue about the storage units was from Perl. She had known Wilford G. the longest and had been there at the beginning when the Metro P.I. legend—my term—was perfecting his craft. Wilford didn't believe in data storage, but most of those of his generation grew up during the Crash, so that made sense. To them, the only thing that was real was what you could touch and feel. Their generation was the one that returned Earth to analog technology, while Up-Top continued with new digital. Perl would have the best sense as to what Wilford G would have accumulated over 70 years of a private detective life. I didn't trust the woman, or any of the ex-wives, but I agreed that Wilford G probably had a lot more than 40 storage units around Metropolis. Hopefully, PJ could find out for sure.

Wilford G. married Perl in his 50s, Isis in his 60s, Go-Go in his 70s—seemed like he was making up for lost time. Go-Go was the one with the lead about the greyhound racing betting. She had accompanied him most times when he'd make the rounds placing bets, watching and cheering races, and either collecting winnings or cursing losses. It was a good hunch on her part. Not a huge sport, but those involved tended to be lifers.

Isis was who I was betting on. She was the smartest of the three. Her lead was—shoes. Wilford wore custom-made, fancy black and white loafers. The factoid intrigued me because I wore my unique tan fedora and slicker. Wilford, too, had a trademark "uniform." Isis gave me the name of Wilford G.'s shoemaker at the very outskirts of Old Harlem, the complete opposite end of where Perl lived.

These kinds of shops were the gems of Metropolis, not relics of the past, classics from the past like my shop, Harry's Haberdashery, in Woodstock Falls, where I now frequented to buy new quality hats for others as gifts becoming a kind of a hat connoisseur. I was already a hovercar connoisseur; maybe I could add custom-shoes to my list of classy expertise.

I had set the Pony down in the street parking lot at the farthest end and watched the shop. I was thinking about how I'd play it—act as myself or pretend to be someone else. Then I noticed someone step out of the shop. It was a man in a black slicker holding an umbrella with a glowing white handle. I wasn't positive yet, but it looked like he was looking straight at me from my view of him in my rearview mirror. I reached for my gun without hesitation.

The man then started to jog toward my vehicle to the passenger-side. He came up, I could see him clearly and he tapped the glass. I rolled down the window.

"Yeah," I said.

"You're too early," he said.

"What?"

"You're a day early. Come back tomorrow, same time is fine."

"What?"

"Thanks." He then jogged back to the shop.

I sat there not quite knowing what had just happened. He didn't threaten me or say I couldn't come into the stop. Did he know who I was? The more I sat there, the more questions filled my head.

"I'll just come back tomorrow," I said to myself. It was the easiest course of action to take, and I started up my vehicle.

Now what was I going to do? This shoemaker had upset my whole universe of plans. I didn't want to go back to the office, and I didn't want to go home—I wanted to do my detective work! I ended up pulling into an all-night diner to get some coffee and look through PJ's messages. There had to be something in the stack that I could handle, something relatively close-by, because in a supercity of 50 million, nothing was really "close-by."

I was following a hovercar two lanes up in traffic. This job was not a spouse following a spouse, but a parent wanting me to follow a child, child being daughter—these kinds of cases were not unknown to me. This was what I called a pre-intervention case, catching the person before they officially crossed over into the dark side. Following kids was always easy—they drove fast and erratic. Real drivers or mature ones never had to slam on their airbrakes because they never tailgated. Kids were neither. Mainly, all I had to do was follow her brake lights as I coasted along in the sky traffic.

She zipped into valet at some mega-club. I bet every girl in a slinky dress was under 18 and every guy was over 30. It was that kind of a place, but again, Metro PD had to prioritize their crimes. They did do the occasional sweep, but club owners factored that into their entrance prices as the cost of doing business. She exited her hovercar in a tight dress with a red waist-high slicker and with her too-tall heels hobbled into the front entrance.

My video-phone rang. I pushed the button and there was PJ. "I was going to leave a message. You're still working. That's good."

"Yes, PJ."

"I couldn't find the other storage units, but I looked at the prices of the ones that we know of."

"And?"

"He was paying the bulk price rates. Based on that, he had at least 100."

"Good work, PJ. So, there are definitely others out there."

"Oh yeah."

"Do you think the wives would have figured that out too?"

"If they're looking for money, absolutely."

"How can we find the units?"

"If he was clever, we never could. All he'd have to do is take the credits and transfer it to another person and then that would take it out of his file and put it another person's private file. Then they could give the credits to someone else, and so on. "

"He makes it so we'd never find them."

"Yeah. We know they exist, but finding them would be a miracle. The only way would be if their lease ran out and someone got into them that way. But people buy leases for 20 years, 50 years, a century."

"Okay, at least we know we're onto something. Thanks, PJ."

"Bye."

She hung up and, unfortunately, I had to go to valet too. It was one of those clubs that was purposely constructed so you couldn't walk to the club. I was tempted to park elsewhere and then call a hovertaxi, but I didn't want to wait in case my target was actually sneaking out the back.

I was glad the girl had a red slicker, because it was truly the only possible way I could have found her. There were others in red but not a lot. The inside of the club was dark, on three levels, and each one was the twice the size of an American football field. However, I didn't go to the dance floor or the bar—that's where the "good" kids would be. I looked for where the "bad" kids would be.

She was jumping on and off a spiky haired guy, I guess horse-playing. I stood off to the side in the shadows to watch them. There was a line of other couples waiting in front of some door in the corner. While they were waiting, they were kissing, smoking, drinking or talking. The door opened and some guy in shades waved the next couple in. The next couple walked in and the door closed. The wait was almost 30 minutes and then the door opened and the same guy waved the next couple in, but the previous one didn't come out.

I stood trying to figure out what could possibly be going on in that room. I laughed because I could think of a lot. My target and her boyfriend were next, so I decided to wait. Thirty minutes passed and the door opened again and they were waved in. They disappeared through the door, giggling, or at least she was.

I glanced at the time on my mobile and I counted to myself. "One one thousand, two one thousand, three one thousand....five one thousand." I was ready.

I walked past the waiting couples to the door, aimed, fired my gun, blowing off the door knob, and walked through. It was pitch black. I heard yelling. "Who are you?" Someone yelled. I threw a stun flash grenade ahead. It exploded, and I saw not just the man who was opening and waving people through the door, but two other thuggish guys. As they were rubbing their eyes, now temporarily blinded, I brushed past them to the open room.

"Oh, we're making naked movies, are we? Get your clothes on," I said. I was already dialing the police.

I stood guard at the front of the room until the police arrived to take charge. The arrival of Metro police of any kind was purposely meant to instill fear—what the residents of the supercity demanded—nothing else could stop the kind of criminals we had. They had the word PEACE in big bold white letters on their chests, but they could kill you in an instant if you did the wrong thing. They wore silver-and-black body-armor uniforms and visored half-helmets. The man who ushered the kids in smiled and he stepped forward. "Officers, there has been a misunderstanding here. We were having a party, and this man barged in shooting a deadly weapon."

"I shot out the door, fearing for the safety of an underage minor, whose parents hired me to follow, fearing she was being blackmailed."

"Blackmailed?" the man asked.

"Cruz, did you use some kind of stun grenade on them?" an officer asked me. I didn't answer. "We'll talk about that later."

"Sir," the officer said to the man. "We're going to take everyone down to the station."

There was a loud groan from everyone in the room, some fifty kids in some form of undress.

"No crime has been committed here," the man said to the officers. "What are we being charged with? There is no alcohol. There are no drugs. You can see for yourself that no one here is being held against their will. It's a party."

The officers looked at me.

"Naked movies. Underage minors. Do they have written releases from the parents?" I asked.

The officers looked at him. The man was turning as red as my client's daughter's jacket.

"Okay, everyone," an officer said. "We're all going down to the station." More groans from the room.

The girl walked up to me. "You tell my parents that I'm never coming home!"

"Okay."

"Never. I hate them!"

"Okay."

"I'll be out in an hour."

"How do you figure that?" She looked at me, thinking. "You're a minor. Your parents have to come get you. Your parents aren't going to come to get you. They'll come and get that hovercar in valet. They'll get that, because it's there, but you? No. You're soon to be a proud participant in the Metro Child and Family system. I'm sure you're going to have lots of fun and lots of parties, too."

"I turn 18 in 6 months, copper."

"I am not a policeman. I'm a private detective. And six months will be plenty of time for you to be scarred for life by the city's foster care system. You have a good night, miss."

"You dirty copper!"

She tried to spit at me, kick me, and punch me. She would have, but the police restrained her and picked her up and out of the room.

"Cruz, you do your work so well," an officer said to me.

"I aim to please my clientele," I said and began to make my call to the parents. Hopefully, I'd have the balance of their payment first thing in the morning.

I purposely didn't go home. I returned to that diner and rented a mobile computer to do some Net searches. I was preparing for tomorrow, but really, the only thing on my mind was the shoemaker.

When I did arrive home, Dot was asleep. I made sure I was in ninja-mode because Cruz Jr. had developed superhuman hearing of late and could hear a pin drop. If he was asleep, you did not want him waking up before morning. If he wasn't sleeping, then neither would anyone else in the apartment.

Before I came home, I had texted Dot not to wake me and I would come by Eye Candy for lunch. Even as I lay in bed, I was thinking about the Shoemaker and his "come back tomorrow" line. As long as he didn't plan to shoot me.

The next day couldn't come fast enough. I knocked out four separate cases before noon. All I wanted to do was get to the evening. I was glad that Dot did most of the talking at lunch. Eye Candy was rolling out a new line of beauty projects inspired by—extraterrestrials. That was from my last major case. PJ, of course, was very pleased. Clients paying bills always made her happy.

I flew back out to Big Bang Cobbler's in Old Harlem an hour early. I couldn't wait any longer. I still didn't know why I even listened to the man. I assumed he was the owner, or an employee of the place, but I didn't know.

A video-call came in. I pressed the button. "Wil."

He looked like he either woke up or was trying to sleep. "Hi Cruz. I think we're the only two in the known universe who would care about the significance of this day."

"What happened today?"

"If my father was still alive, he'd be 95 today."

The revelation made me stop. "Then happy birthday to Wilford G."

"Happy birthday to Dad."

"I'll call you and Mary. We should all go out for lunch or dinner."

"Sounds good. Good night, Cruz."

"Night."

I sat there staring out at the shop. This time I had landed not with the back of my vehicle to the shop, but the front facing it. I didn't like people coming up from behind me.

Through the downpour I stared...95 meant something, and it was more than simply being Wilford G.'s age if he was still alive. But I couldn't remember what. I thought I caught the flash of light inside as if the front door had opened and closed. I kept looking. Was someone standing there? I could make out a figure. Whoever it was wasn't in a black slicker and holding an umbrella with a glowing white handle. The person stepped forward into the rain and moonlight, wearing black and white loafers!

I jumped in my seat and reached for the door. The man had turned right and was walking down the street. I jumped out of the Pony, closed the door, and I actually started running. I stopped and realized I had to get a hold of myself. This was exactly the kind of situation that got people killed. I took a breath and moved onto the sidewalk and close to the building. The man was gone, but I walked at a fast pace in his direction.

When I turned the corner, I quickly peeked around the corner and could see the man. He had already reached the other end of the alley and was about to turn. When he did, I started running after him. It didn't take me long, and then I stopped. Wherever I was, I could see and hear the pedestrian traffic. At least, it wasn't some deep, dark, secluded street. Lots of people, clad in slickers and wearing their colored shades, hoods, and umbrellas galore. I felt confident stepping forward, but I still had my hand on my gun and crouched a bit.

The man was standing there waiting for me. I stood slowly as my mouth started to drop open. I started to laugh, but my legs started to buckle under me. He grabbed me to keep me from falling.

"Good God, man. You're laughing and falling down on yourself. Make up your mind."

"You're alive."

"What are you going to do? Stand up, man!"

"You're supposed to be dead. Did you just shoot me? Is that's what happened? I'm dead."

"No, Cruz. You're not dead."

"You're alive."

"Yes, I'm alive."

"I'm fainting."

"Cruz, man, you're a hard-boiled Metro street P.I.! Hard-boiled Metro street P.I.s don't faint. Stand up, man!"
I fainted.

CHAPTER 10

The Man

There was something quite heavenly about a warm bed when you were exhausted. I lay in my bed, half smiling at the crazy dream I had. I normally didn't remember my dreams, but the one I had was a doozy.

This isn't my bed!

I looked at the wall. It was different. I smelled smoke and sat straight up in the dark. There was a crack of light coming through a door that wasn't completely closed. Looking around, I saw I was on a twin bed, and it was a small room. In rich neighborhoods, it would be considered a closet.

When I came out of the small guest bedroom, there he was, kicked back on a couch with his feet on a faux-wooden table watching a sports game on the wall TV, a glass of alcohol in one hand, a cigar in the other. The Man. Tan, rugged, salt-and-pepper hair, cut very close on the sides, slightly taller on the top. His shirt was unbuttoned and open, wearing boxer briefs, his pants were draped over another chair, and socks with flip flops, a combination that always bothered me.

"What are you wearing?" I asked.

"Sleeping beauty awakes. Come on, Cruz. Clearly you've seen a grown man with his boxer briefs on before."

"Not that. Why are you wearing a Liquid Cool T-shirt?"

He laughed as he was exhaling his cigar smoke. "How many people get to wear the gear of a student after death."

"I can't believe you're wearing Liquid Cool T-shirts."

"Only kind I wear nowadays. Besides there was a bulk sale."

I looked around the apartment. It was some kind of martial arts dojo, or had been. I sat in a one-seater adjacent to Wilford's couch. He was watching a competitive martial arts match.

"Wilford—"

"Cruz, there's plenty of time for the third degree. I want to enjoy my cigar, saké, and match in peace. Besides, I'm not sure I'm talking to you anymore."

"Anymore?"

"I expected you to be at the hard-boiled, steel-grip detective level by now. Instead, you're giggling and fainting in front of me."

"Says the man with no pants." He chuckled. "Maybe I'm not talking to you, Wilford! This is a downright evil thing you did!"

Wilford put the cigar in the corner of his mouth. I knew his fingertips were bionic—he had a few inorganic parts in his body like a lot of people—but they looked real to me. He turned off the wall TV with the in-armrest remote. "Looks like I'm not going to get any peace."

"You brought me here."

"Would you have preferred I left you on the wet pavement? You have quite a fancy weapon. Where do I get one?"

"You get nothing. You're supposed to be dead. Your son, daughter-in-law, and your ex-wives were at your funeral."

"I don't care about the ex-wives, but Wil is different."

"I'm glad you agree. What's this about? Why are you back from the dead? Why are you sneaking around in the storage units you left them in the will? Sneaking around your old shoemaker, leading me down dark alleys?"

"Cruz, am I supposed to be taking notes? That's a lot of questions, and you're still going."

"I'm just getting started."

"I had to come back from the dead. I became dead for a reason, and I'm back for a reason."

"What reason? And today's your birthday. You know your son called me. You really are a bum, doing that to your son. He's still upset."

"Wil's the head of the Police Union so he better toughen up. I didn't raise him to be any other way. Hopefully, he's not given to giggling fainting spells like you."

"How exactly does one act when you see someone who's supposed to be dead?"

"You were happy to see me."

"My brain wasn't working. Why are you back, Wilford?"

"Oh, don't say my name like that. You sound like Perl or Isis. It was so annoying."

"Why are you back?"

"I'm back because I've gone as far as I can go on my own. Today, my file goes into mandatory archive, so I'll be an invisible man for a while. We can move."

"Mandatory archive." I was thinking, trying to remember. "It has to do with turning 95."

"At 95, the Metro central computer moves you to their archive files."

"What? Why is that important? You're dead."

"I don't need to be dead, Cruz. I need to be invisible."

"Invisible? To who?"

"Not who. It. Cruz, man, I came back for you."

"Me?"

"Yes." He smiled, almost as wide as Phishy. "We're going to break wide open the biggest caper in Metropolis history!"

PART THREE

Mr. Candy

CHAPTER 11

G.

The Police Watch Conspiracy Case. The Blade Gunner. NeuroDancer. The Electric Sheep Massacre. My E.T. Case. My posthumous mentor came back from the dead with a case bigger than any of those?

"Wilford, what are you talking about?" I asked.

"Cruz, only my wives called me that, and it was always to annoy me. Call me 'G.' That was my street name for the non-criminal."

"I haven't decided if I'm talking to you yet."

"You don't want to hear about the greatest criminal case in the history of the world? I can disappear again. You didn't find me at Big Bang's Cobblers. I left a trail of breadcrumbs for you to follow. I know you got people looking into my storage units and greyhound racetrack betting. Cruz, I've been at this before your father was born."

"Okay, so you've been around the block a couple of times. What's this all about?"

"Then you are talking to me."

"Only until I find out what this is about."

"Sit down, then, man."

I sat back down on the chair adjacent to his couch. He moved closer.

"Put on some pants," I said.

"Cruz, when you get to a certain age, you let things be free. The clothes I have on are for your benefit."

"I don't even want to think about the fact that you just told me you walk around the apartment naked."

"My wives didn't mind."

"You're divorced—times three."

"Not for that."

"Please, forget about that. Tell me what you're going to tell me. Your wives are going to kill you."

"No, they're not. They're trying to find my secret stashes."

"You do have secret money stashed."

"Of course, didn't they tell you? I never used banks. I don't believe in them, never have. They always knew I had more money than what I left them lying around. They probably told you that dumb story that they suspected I had other storage units because I didn't reveal my gun stash to them or Wil. They're not getting the guns and not getting my money, even when I'm dead for real."

"What about Wil?"

"Okay, that I agree with you, but it was for a reason. I told you. Are you going to let me tell you about it, or are you going to keep scolding me?"

"Scolding you. I need to get it out of my system."

"Hurry up then. We have a lot of work to do starting tomorrow. We have to have our plan ready, and we start bright and early at 6 a.m."

"Starting what?"

"Cruz, be quiet! I can't tell you about the biggest crime caper in history if you keep talking."

"It? What's 'it'?"

He smiled. "That's more like it. You're letting your detective senses do their thing. I'll fill my drink." He stood from the couch and went to the kitchen area of the room. "I don't suppose you smoke."

"Absolutely not."

"Cruz, where are your bad habits?"

"I don't need any."

"I'm glad you're not into that anti-hero, tortured soul nonsense, but real people need bad habits. If you don't have natural ones, you need to manufacture a few. You got to be more human, man. That's going to be on your list of homework. Get some bad habits like a real person, and I don't care you could have been a lunar Bubble Boy as a child. You're a grown man now. You've conquered your germophobia. I saw you lying on that dirty floor when you first got your Liquid Cool offices."

"What? How did you see me lying on my office floor?"

"When you first got it?"

"How? How did you know about that?"

"I'm your guardian angel, Cruz."

I saw him pouring from a bottle into a new glass and he returned to sit back in his place. His cigar was lit again.

"How did you know about my office?"

"Connie told me."

"Connie! Compstat Connie?"

"Yeah."

"How do you know Compstat Connie?"

"Cruz, I dated Connie for years before Perl. I talk to Connie all the time."

I stood from my chair and had to pace around. "Connie knew you were alive?"

"Cruz, lots of people do. Sit down! We have work to do."

"I'm mad at her now."

"You can tell her when we see her. She's one of the stops we have to make tomorrow."

"What is this hijacking my life? I do have my own life and business to run."

"Your life is on hold, Cruz, and this is your only case until we solve it. We're going up against the most dangerous criminal you've ever faced and against the most malevolent entity you've ever battled."

"It is the source of all evil in the world, Cruz. I.T."

"I.T.? The I.T. department."

"Yeah."

"The information tech department?"

"Yeah."

I burst out laughing.

CHAPTER 12

Quix

We had left his dojo apartment and were in my Pony. I had forgotten all about it when I remembered that my vehicle was left unguarded on the street, and it sent me into a panic. The Pony was fine and then Wilford G wanted me to play chauffeur.

It wasn't even dawn yet when we set out. He sat in the passenger seat and was smart enough to know not to have a lit cigar. It was bad enough that he wore Liquid Cool T-shirts, but now he added a black fedora to his attire. He knew it annoyed me, like wearing socks and flip-flops, rather than either/or.

"I'm going to have to call Dot. I didn't go home at all, and she's going to think something's wrong," I said as I coasted into another sky lane.

"Not allowed out on a school night."

"I am a man of routine. If I'm out, I call. Besides I do have an infant son, which I'm sure you can relate to with Wil Jr."

"Wil an infant? My memory doesn't go back that far."

"But you can remember back to when you dated Compstat Connie."

"That's different. My memory goes way back to the dinosaurs in that area," he said, grinning. "Cruz, you're way too uptight for a youngster."

"Youngster?"

"You need to, to coin a common phrase, 'be cool.'"

"My agency is cool. I wear a cool hat. I have a cool vehicle. I am plenty cool already."

"Not act cool, Cruz, or have cool things. 'Be' cool. There's a big difference."

"I have no idea what we're even talking about. When are you going to see your family?"

"That'll have to wait. We're going to a joint called The Fubar."

"Joint?"

"Yeah, in Whiskey Way."

"That isn't a very nice part of town."

"We private street detectives rarely frequent the nice part of town, and when we do, it's because we're after not-so-nice people."

I smiled. "You really do talk like you write in your book."

"Well, I did write it. Thanks for the sales, by the way. You bought my book. I bought a T-shirt. You should have Cruz hats next."

I couldn't believe what he had just said. He was now channeling PJ or Phishy. "I'm a detective agency, not the local market. What's in Whiskey Way?"

"Some people I know."

The name Fubar said it all. It was a very seedy dive bar of ex-military. Outside the main entrance, there were a half-dozen big bald guys talking and drinking—I didn't know if they were customers or bouncers, but they were blocking our way. Wilford G. was unconcerned and said something to them in another language, then suddenly, they went from looking like they'd kill us to exchanging handshakes and fist taps.

"What language was that?" I asked as we entered.

"Czech."

All the bionics I saw drinking and joking in the dim, smoky, noisy bar were not for cosmetic purposes at all, hence, the amount and variety of odd-looking cyborgs. Wilford G. strolled in without a care in the world. From the time we left his place, and now, I was noticing his snazzy two-color loafers. The man had some cool shoes on his feet. He waved to one of the bartenders behind the counter, a huge man with a fat cigar in the corner of his mouth. The man pointed to a corner, and Wilford G moved in that direction.

"Hey Quix," he greeted.

The man seated at a round table on a stool immediately stood. "G." He was another cyborg—short, bald, muscular, big leathery hands, an earring in one ear, part of his jaw and neck were metal, and he was wearing glowing yellow shades.

"Got it all."

"Got it."

"We're driving a cherry red Ford Pony."

"Got it, G."

I was smiling. "Cherry red? The official color is Miami Vice Red, thank you."

The men laughed.

As we got back into the Pony, I watched Quix exit the Fubar.

"Where are we going now?"

"CIC."

"Metro PD's Crime Information Center?"

"That's what CIC stands for."

"Where's your friend?"

"He's going to follow us."

A loud, gaudy black hovercar pulled up behind us. I was not pleased that it was so close to my vehicle with all its noise. "Is your friend a bodyguard?"

"He's actually an ex-Marine, or I should say a Marine. You're never an ex-Marine, or Special Forces."

"Can you be ex-Army, Navy, or Air?"

"Of course, I am."

"I didn't know that. Which one?"

"Navy."

"Why would you want to be stuck in a steel can in the Great Oceans on a planet where it's always raining?"

"I was your age back then, so I wasn't that smart."

G always had me smiling. "You should have been Air and Space."

"Cruz, back then Air and Space was a damn dangerous thing to be in. Why do you think the government military got out of that division?"

"Because Up-Top made them."

"Because they were happy to have Up-Top make them with people getting accidentally spaced all over the place."

"What? I never heard that."

"Oh yeah, Cruz. The media never hid the real news from the people. Yeah, that never happened ever. The media always tells the whole truth and nothing but the truth."

"G, I learned something."

"What?"

"You're as cynical about people as I am."

"The only way to stay alive in the private detective business."

"Why is your friend following us then?"

"He's going to wait for us when we go see Connie. Then give me my tools of the trade when we come out."

"Guns? Your friend is holding guns?"

"No respectable Metro private street detective goes anywhere without his guns. You got your fancy, foo-foo, Up-Top guns. I have my real man's guns."

I laughed again. "Foo-foo? My gun is not a booshy Up-Top gun. And ask all the bad guys I've blown away if they thought it wasn't a real man's gun."

"Oh, I'm not criticizing. Men with smaller hands need a smaller gun. That's all I'm saying."

"You better be careful how you talk to me. I have an ejector button for the passenger seat you're in."

He chuckled. "Let's go see Connie."

"Connie, who knows you're alive. That bartender knew you were alive. Your friend Quix."

"All my people know I'm alive. That's why they're my people. Let's go see Connie."

I flew the Pony into the sky traffic, with Quix on our tail.

CHAPTER 13

Compstat Connie

I f Wilford G. had been my posthumous mentor, Compstat Connie was my current one. Metro police officers always got a kick out of seeing me show up for a few hours every other week to see her. I was her thirty-something intern. Actually, I had taken it upon myself to know everything she knew before she retired. I had been impressed with her encyclopedic knowledge of Metropolis's criminal class when I was a real police intern back in high school; I was even more impressed with her now. Megacorporations had machines that knew all there was to know worth knowing. Metropolis had Connie, a human computer, but were too stupid to take full advantage of it.

Metro's CompStat (Computer Statistics) Division was where all the city's crime data was collected, collated, and analyzed. Compstat Connie was in her late seventies and ran the multi-hundred-million-dollar division from her subterranean offices. Her division drove everything that the police did—deployment, budgets, resources, and personnel. The stats made it into every government press conference, all the way to the Mayor. The City Clerk's office had a prominent place in the main city towers, but her Crime Information Center (CIC) was in the basement levels of Downtown Metro. The Clerk's office had guards and other visible security; CIC had nothing, which always puzzled me because it was such an important office for the police brass.

When we entered Compstat Connie's office, she looked up, wearing fashion bifocals, immediately at Wilford G. from her seat behind a desk. She wasn't surprised.

"So, he was telling the truth," I said.

"Yes, Cruz, the man is alive."

I began to start shaking my head and G. immediately cut in. "Cruz, if you're going to begin lecturing me again, I'm going to put you out in the hall and lock the door. Hey, Connie."

"Hey, G. Looking well for a dead man, as always."

"How long did you know?" I asked.

"Well, I didn't know when they buried him, if that's what you're asking me."

"What's the significance of the day after his 95th birthday to start running around Metropolis like he owns the place, even though he supposed to be dead?"

They both looked at me. "G., are you sure about partnering with Cruz?" she asked. "He's one of those kids that you assign the first chapter, and he reads all the chapters, answers all the quiz questions, and is already on book four before you know it."

"I'm sure," he said to Connie.

"You call me a kid," I chimed in. "He calls me a youngster."

"Have a seat, Cruz. Connie can explain her part better than me."

I sat in the chair in front of the desk. "Connie, I think G. has gone mental. He was babbling about a secret plot by the IT departments of the world taking over. He called it the biggest caper in human history, bigger than all my other cases. He obviously doesn't know my big cases."

"Oh, he knows."

G. had closed the door and grabbed another chair from the corner of Connie's office and set it next to mine. "I've been monitoring you closely, Cruz."

"Why me?"

"I'll tell you later. We're working the case, Cruz. You need to focus." I laughed. "What's so funny?"

"That's exactly what I say to Phishy."

"Oh, your sidewalk johnny gun-dealer friend."

"How do you know about Phishy?"

"Cruz, I told you. I've been monitoring you over the years. Connie, get a hold of your intern's attention."

"I can see the two of you are going to get along famously," she said.

"And just so you know, Cruz," Wilford said, "we're not on chapter one yet. This is the introduction, and you need to pay attention. Because in this story, if you jump ahead to another chapter before you've been prepared, you can get shot."

"What does that even mean? That analogy makes no sense. Now *you're* talking like Phishy."

"You're what we used to call a figurer. You're always figuring out things, even when you're not supposed to. I know you found it amusing when I said that I didn't use banks, but that's how my parent's generation was, and they passed that mindset down to the children. My Pops and—"

"Pops? That's what I call my dad."

"Yes, all us old geezers use that word."

"I—am—not—old."

"My Pops was bad, but my Gramps was even worse. He literally kept his savings in the mattress. And he and my Grannie had those real nasty laser rifles to protect it. Yeah, all those generations after The Crash were like that. All of Earth was digital tech until The Crash. Up-Top would have you believe they were more enlightened and went a different, better way, but the truth is they were just as terrified. They were forced to keep digital because you can't run a cable from a space station to the moon and back."

"I know the history. The hackers hacked everything."

"No, Cruz," Connie began. "If it was a matter of hacking systems that could have been countered. No, the cyberpunks were moving far faster than cyber-security. The cyberpunks didn't hack into all the world's systems; they were able to pass through all of it as if it wasn't even there. Firewalls, passwords, redirects, any and all security was erased. They stole everything, shut down everything. They crashed the entire world, because the entire world was digital. The only people who were able to function were the off-Grid survivalists. Their ancient analog tech became the foundation for the rebirth of all Earth's analog tech."

"Ever heard of the Great Depression of the ancient times?" Wilford asked me.

"Yes, of course," I replied.

"That's how it was for people. No food, no money, nothing. No society whatsoever. In a situation like that, humans become worse than animals, become so bad that the animals run away from the people."

"That's why there's no such thing as anarchist hacking anymore. Analog tech is not as fancy as Up-Top, but we Earthers will take it over theirs any day of the week," I said with pride.

"Well—" Connie began.

"Well, what?" I asked.

"I told you already, Cruz. I.T."

"Wilford—"

"G!" he corrected.

Connie laughed. "He hates his first name."

"G., my last major case was a whole lot of people paranoid about 'Them.' Them watching, Them abducting them, Them in league with aliens to take over humankind."

"Oh, yeah, the Alien Case. Good job, man. Wrapped that one up nicely."

"What about I.T.? What I.T.?"

"Let Connie tell you her part. Then I'll tell you my part and what led me to fake my death and return."

"It'd better be a good story, because if I don't think it is, your son won't either. He'll probably still want to punch you."

"I'm sure he'll want to shoot me, but forget about that. We're on the case, Cruz. We need to keep our heads in the game."

Wilford G. really did talk the way he wrote, which was a source of endless amusement for me. He was a walking relic of the past, and he was working a case with me. The only problem was I had no idea what the case was, but here were the three of us gathered together in Connie's cubby-hole of an office.

"Cruz, if you were to describe me to someone, as far as my skills and qualifications, what would they be?"

"Compstat Connie is a human computer, and as much as the CIC computers can compile and analyze data on all the criminal activity in Metropolis, her analysis is of a predictive nature. She can see what the computers can't and never will be able to because their analytic ability will always be reactive."

Wilford G. did a pretend clap. "Wow," Connie said. "You need to tell my boss that so I can get a proper raise."

"And out of these offices," I added.

"Oh no, Cruz. These offices are where I want to stay. Don't be fooled by the apparent lack of security in this section. If there's a disaster, this is where you want to be."

"Why did you ask me the question?"

"Do you think I'm unique in government?" she asked me.

"Yes, without a doubt."

"What about the megacorps? Do you think they have someone like me?"

I had to think for a moment. "They may have people who think they are at your level, but it's all focused on defeating the corporate competition, getting more money, increasing stock value. I have no idea what increasing stock value means, but I'm told it's a megacorporate thing to say, so it's not really comparing apples to apples."

"What about organized crime?"

She had stumped me. "Are you telling me the criminal gangs have their own Compstat Connie? The person can't be all that great with all the deaths and arrests in the supercity."

"They are great, Cruz, because you don't even know they exist."

I looked at Wilford G. He smiled at me. "He's trying to figure, Connie," he said.

I grinned, but ignored him. "This would go a whole lot faster if you simply told me and stopped with the trying to make me guess game."

"Yeah, he's right, Connie. Cruz and I are on the case. We have to get to work." He turned to me. "Cruz, every detective has *the* case. This one has been mine. I've stumbled in and out of it for decades. I had to be patient. I've even had to fake my own death, but we're going to close it. Close the case and close in all the bad guys."

"What's the crime?"

"Everything and nothing."

"Everything and nothing?" I looked at her. "Help me, Connie. Wilford G. has gone mental."

They laughed. "I am 95, Cruz. A little mental is expected at my age."

"Let's hope not, G.," Connie said. "You could live another 20 years."

"Don't remind me," he said.

Connie had been glancing at her computer screen on her desk from time to time during the whole time we were talking. Messages from her department and Metro PD flashed on her screen all day long. Most she could ignore for her staff to handle, but she had to see all of them.

"Cruz, did you ask Metro PD to start scanning even law enforcement upon entry?"

I thought it a question from left field. "Yeah, why?"

Connie and Wilford looked at each other.

"It's nothing," he said to her.

"How do you know?" She looked at me again. "What prompted you to do that?"

"My last case," I replied.

"The Alien Case?"

"Yes, I found out that the Up-Toppers can make androids that look so human that they can actually fool us. But with the scanners, that's over. Again, why?"

They both seemed worried about something.

"It's not your fault, Cruz," Wilford said to me.

"What's not my fault? I didn't do anything."

"I.T. might suspect."

"I.T. again. What might I.T. departments around the world suspect?"

"That we're on to them," Connie answered. She looked back at Wilford. "Assume it knows. Forget suspects. Act as if it knows."

"If it knows, it'll be waiting," he said to her.

"If it knows, G., it'll come after you," she corrected.

I raised my hand and waved. "Hello. I'm here. I still don't know what's going on."

Wilford G. stood from his chair. "Cruz, time to go. We have to alter the plan and skip a few chapters after all, but we're Metro street detectives, so it goes with the business."

He had already opened the door and was walking down the hallway.

"Connie." I looked at her like an upset child. "What about your evil counterpart?"

"He'll tell you, but not here."

"Why not here?"

"*It* could be listening."

"Connie!"

"Cruz, I not mental."

"Cruz!" I heard Wilford yell out. "Come on, young man, you're moving far too slow for a youngster!"

"Go on." Connie stood and pushed me out of her office.

Wilford wasn't in the hallway. I had to sprint after him. He didn't even hold the elevator for me. When I exited the elevator into the main lobby, there were plenty of people walking to wherever they were going in the building, but Wilford wasn't one of them.

He was in the parking bay next to the Pony, smoking a cigar.

"You move too slow, young man."

"We came here to see Connie for a meeting. A meeting where I would be specifically told about your supposed case, why you faked your death, what this great I.T. conspiracy is, and why we still haven't gone to see your family. None of those things have happened. Why? Why did we run out of Connie's office like frightened little rabbits? Is I.T. going to get us, Wilford?"

Wilford huffed out some smoke from the corner of his mouth. "You can get wound up, can't you? And don't call me Wilford. Let's get in the vehicle and stop down the street, so Quix can drop off my gear. I can't function when I feel naked. I don't have my guns, so I feel naked. When I have them in hand, whether we drive to our next stop or pull off to the side, I'll explain it all. I don't know why you're so impatient. You just got to the party. I've been waiting to break this case for 50 years."

CHAPTER 14

8-Ball

We were like the corner dope daddies or street corner captains of some seedy criminals-are-us part of the supercity. I held the Pony hovering inches from the ground with Wilford G. looking out the open passenger window. Quix's hovercar dived, inches from my vehicle, with the driver's window open. Normally, I'd be terrified at the thought of any driver maneuvering so close to my vehicle, but he was military and I had watched his driving skills when we first left the Fubar. He was a real driver—precise turns, never slamming on the air brakes, coasting rather than hopping into lanes. He reached in with a huge duffel bag.

"Thanks, Quix," Wilford G. said as he grabbed it. "The tools of my trade."

"I took good care of them for you, G."

"Never a doubt crossed my mind."

"Glad you're back in action, G. Call me if you need me or any of the boys. Jobs haven't been as frequent as we'd like. Harder to find ones that aren't outright illegal, and we're tired of only working for the megacorps."

"We'll sort it out. Besides, I have my man, Cruz, here. He's famous, so I'm sure he'll be able to send some jobs your way."

I said nothing as Quix looked at me. "I threw in some goodies, too," Quix said to G.

"Goodies? You know I like goodies," Wilford answered.

When Quix smiled, I could see that his teeth looked enamel for the bottom half, but the upper were metal. "I knew you would. Go get 'em, G."

"Thanks, Quix."

Quix's hovercar ascended, disappearing, as I pulled out. Wilford lightly shook the duffel bag, smiling. He opened the zipper and sniffed inside. "Nothing like that new gun smell."

"Hopefully, we won't get lucky and have the police pull us over with your goodie bag."

"No chance of that," he said as he closed the bag. "The cops are your friends. Every single one of them must owe you favors for the duration for all the bad guys and plots you've put down for them."

"G., I've solved a handful of high-profile cases. They have to solve cases every day that are every bit as important, if not more. I come and go, they have to keep the streets safe every day. What I do is nothing compared to that."

"Cruz, why didn't you become a cop like Junior? You talk like he did. I tried to get him to be a detective, but he talked like you."

"I don't know why, actually. I built the Pony, and life went in another direction."

"Well you're a detective now. That's what we need to bust this caper wide open."

The thing about smokers is, even when they weren't smoking, they were fidgeted around, with their hands especially, as if they were.

Wilford G. was finally telling me the story as we drove to the other end of the supercity.

"Back when I was younger than the youngster you are today—"

"Cruz, Jr. is a youngster."

"Cruz, Jr. is a baby, Cruz. You're a youngster. When you get to your 90s you'll be calling everyone a youngster. You'll see. Back then, Metropolis wasn't a supercity. It wasn't one huge city; it was a bunch of them all spilling into each other. It was a mess. Dozens of municipalities, hundreds of police forces, millions of gangs. People have no idea what you all missed out on. Back then all this area was the final frontier, the undiscovered country, the Wild East. There was so much murder and mayhem that none of you today could have imagined it. You probably don't even know where they got the name Metropolis from."

"I do. The Dark City."

"No, Cruz. They didn't name what became the new supercity after a fictitious city of shadows, bats and grown men and women running around in tights, a bunch of super freaks. They named it after a fictitious city of lights. In that story Metropolis was a beautiful, shimmering city of flying cars and machines. When everything was centralized, they called it after that Metropolis, not the other one. Ironically, that story gives us the first clue of this story. In that Metropolis, they had robots too, and one robot that was indistinguishable from a human being."

I glanced over at them. "Like Up-Top."

"Forget Up-Top. The plot is here. It always has been here. I had just become a detective myself. This was before I even met Perl. I don't think I was dating Connie yet. Back then, the cops wanted us to get into shootouts with the criminals. Back then, freelance corpse recovery was a huge business. People were getting rich contracting out with the Morgue to pick up bodies all over the place—cops shooting bad guys, bad guys shooting innocent bystanders and cops, detectives shooting and getting shot.

"Back then, even after the Crash, there were still people expecting that one day someone would figure out how to transfer a person's mind into a computer—A.I. Immortality. It was a big, big scam. Scammers taking people's money so they'd be the first to be transformed into the coming new world of existence. There was also the on-and-off again Transhumanism Movement. Being a cyborg was one thing. That's just replacing body parts with machine parts, but these Transhumanists messed with people's brains, including their own. That's why all that was banned. Cranial compartments, brain wires, a lot of disgusting crap. Criminals were the ones leading the movement, because after the Crash, they couldn't do their illegal activities on the Net anymore without the police catching them, so the era of data couriers was born. That didn't last long; electronic lobotomies were so common that it was becoming a crisis. Criminals went even more retro—forget data couriers, just put it on a simple briefcase, give them a squad of cyborg bodyguards, and do it like it was done in the pre-hovercar, old gangster days. Force the cops to come out into the light and chase you."

"They don't even have to do that anymore," I said.

"No, they don't. They stay put in their crime towns and let the suckers come to them. Well, The Crash was still on people's minds then. Hackers weren't exactly a popular species of human. I met this ex-hacker who hired me to be his bodyguard. It wouldn't be for another 20 years when I gave up that part of my business, but then I was a tough guy. I wanted to get into shootouts. I was stupid and hadn't gotten shot by my first bullet, or laser blast yet. When you're a youngster, you think you're invincible and immortal all rolled into one.

"This ex-hacker wasn't like other jobs. He was part of some underground cyber-group. He actually wasn't an ex-hacker of the criminal kind but an ex-hacker who had worked for the government; his friends were current and former corporate. That's when I first learned of the plot."

"When you were—in your twenties?"

Wilford G. was thinking. "I had just crossed the big 3-0, so yes, I was a bit younger than you now. In your last major case, you had to deal with extraterrestrials."

"Fake extraterrestrials."

"During the case, did you ever believe in them?"

"That question is irrelevant. I was and am agnostic. I neither believe nor disbelieve. You want me to believe, then prove it."

"But basically, your attitude is there aren't any E.T.s running around the universe."

"If there are, then show me. In fact, don't show me. Let them stay where they are. We have enough problems already created by us. We don't need another player on the scene adding to them."

Wilford chuckled. "You are a curmudgeon."

"Are you calling me old again?"

"You aren't just a born skeptic. You're a born cynic. Good. Means you'll have a long career as a Metro street detective. The only ones who make it to my age are the ones who trust no one, not even the priest."

I laughed. "You forgot to add that line to your book. 'Not even the priest.'"

"You can add it for me when you do the updated version."

"I appreciate the Metro history lesson, but I still don't know anything. I also don't know why we ran out of Connie's office and the building."

"What are your general feelings on A.I.?" he asked in a serious tone.

"Fiction or reality?"

"In general."

"Personally, I wish the phrase was abandoned. The word that should be used is 'programming'. A.I. is—nonsense. It's all simple programming. You program the computer or machine to do something or react to some internal or external situation. People have been using the word A.I. to mean programming. A new phrase to mean the exact same thing as the old one. No machine, robot and androids included, have ever gone past their programming—ever."

"If they could, that would be true A.I.?"

"It would be, and you might even get me to consider using that other word the evangelists like to throw around—sentience, but how could you prove it?"

"Cruz, you do understand. Connie told me you were far smarter than the average street urchin."

"Urchin?" I laughed. "What's that? Sounds like a kind of isopod."

"Old word for youngster."

"Not that again."

"You restored a lot of hovercars in your brief years of existence, which means in addition to being a builder, you're a programmer too."

"I never thought of it like that, but yeah."

"You got programmers in this city with fancy degrees, making obscene amounts of money, everyone calling them 'whiz kids' and not a one of them could build a hovercraft on their own, let alone when they were a kid, like you. You and I focus on the job, and we use the best tools to get that job done. They are in love with the tools and go searching for the job to do to justify their existence.

"What do you know or remember about Deep Machine Learning or the Sandbox Project?"

"G., you're leading me down a path, but we still haven't gotten to this case or plot yet?"

"Humor me."

"Teaching, or allowing machines to learn for themselves, solve problems that their human inventors couldn't solve. That has never been impressive to me. Machines are following their programming, they travel a path to the end, solve a problem, because that's what they were programmed to do. Was the Sandbox the project years ago where the scientists let these A.I. programs run wild and create their own virtual reality world?"

"Yes."

"More media hype. Did the programs create the world independently of their human creators or do exactly what their human creators programmed them to do within the vast parameters given? It's the same as the 'which came first, the chicken or the egg' question. The answer is irrelevant, because the answer is based on what you believe, not on what you can prove or what you can prove to those on the opposite side."

"Cruz, fifty years ago, someone created an AI program to take over Metropolis."

"What does that mean 'take over'?" I asked. "All kinds of people use that phrase. It can mean anything."

The desire of an AI running human society was not a new one. A fair amount of people were intrigued by the concept or outright desired it, but it was never the masses, who like me, thought the whole idea was foolish. Unfortunately, through the years, people tried violently to make it happen. I had to tangle with probably the most formidable of these AI-worshipping cults ever to exist in my Blade Gunner case. They were so insane that even their own founders had to run from them and eventually led the effort to destroy them.

Free City, where the poor of Metropolis lived—those not fortunate to have their own legacy (free housing for life)—never once hatched a world domination plot, nor did any member of the working-class neighborhoods, like Woodstock Falls, or even my own Rabbit City. It was always from the children of the wealthy classes, kids who were born knowing they would never have to work a day in their life. Whether they were 20 or 120, they would never want of anything. It was always these people who came up with these discredited, foolish, and often dangerous concepts, and had the means to try to make them reality, no matter how illogical or insane. Crime was bad enough in the supercity, but then we had to deal with crazies who wanted to control society for no other reason than to do it.

"Take away all human control of the government, megacorporations, even organized crime. It would control everything," Wilford continued.

"Not possible, G. Humans wouldn't tolerate it."

"Really? Isn't that what Up-Top is? The Founders control everything, don't they?"

"Earth isn't Up-Top."

"You're being sentimental. You, more than most, have seen this city on its knees. People are not as brave or independent-minded as all that. But you know that—so does the AI, especially if it has the ability to create androids of people."

"What?"

"You'll probably be able to figure out why we were concerned that you had Metro PD change its protocol to scan all law enforcement coming into the premises, even on duty. It will have surely taken notice."

"Create androids?"

"The only people 'It' felt could stop it was that ex-hacker who hired me 50 years ago. That ex-hacker was Connie's first husband. He was part of a group in the government that almost killed it before. The AI learned from that experience. It learned, when no one knows you exist, then they won't come around looking to kill you. The AI has been waiting for all the people it thought could stop it to die off. There were sixteen of them in all. Connie's first husband was the last of them. He died four years ago. I faked my death to go underground. Connie and I are the only ones left who know, who were here at the beginning. It knows that. That's why we needed you."

"You haven't answered *the* question. Why? Take over Metropolis to what end?"

"You forget one question, Cruz. Who? The AI was created by the children and grandchildren of the same anarchists who gave us The Crash."

"But the original anarchists—weren't they all killed or died in jail?"

"There were 34 of them. The original anarchists that created The Crash did so to destroy the world by destroying their technology. The descendants created this AI to destroy the world because it destroyed their grandparents."

"How do you know this? I never heard any of this before."

"I know because of Connie's ex. He always suspected the AI hadn't been destroyed and was waiting."

"Wouldn't another Crash would be impossible with our current tech?"

"Why do you think that? Our core tech is analog and decentralized, but they still need to talk to each other. Your local diner still has to talk to your bank that you bought your coffee and muffin. Your hovercar has to talk to your secure parking lot and so on. We're still vulnerable. Not in the same way but a different way.

"Cruz, this is my pro-bono case. I never did any in my career, but Metropolis has been good to me in this life, so I owe her. This is the case where the people of Metropolis are the client, and they don't have to pay me; they don't even have to know that I'm working to save them. Because they've already paid me over a great career of over 70 years.

"This is the greatest caper in human history because it's against humankind. The crime is to destroy humankind. You and I, Cruz, are the only ones who can stop it. And I do mean that; you can't tell anyone—not your wife, kid, your sidewalk johnny friends, your cyborg secretary, your best friend, the cops, your Up-Top cop friends, no one. It's just you and me against the machine. I'd bet on us, even though I'm sure, before all this is over, it's going to try to kill us in ways neither one of us have ever faced in our lives."

We had arrived. I'd never been in this part of Metropolis before, probably because I didn't like the names of the districts. This was Pigstown—a flashy neon place, but all the lights couldn't hide the fact that it was a seedy, low-life area. It didn't have sidewalk johnnies hanging around or punks; it had thugs in cheap, shiny suits guarding their turfs: bars, night clubs, hotels, parlors, whatever the business. I had landed in the open parking lot on Fat Street. My eyes were watching any and everyone anywhere near us, but I could multi-task and kept talking.

"Why do you think that?" I asked.

"It killed a dozen of the last 16 men—accidents. Not Connie's ex, though. He and a few others were too careful. And before you question me, Connie says the accidents were suspicious, and you've worked with her long enough to know if she says something isn't right—"

"Then it's not right. Okay, what else? Because you do realize that you've already blown your own AI theory out of the water."

"Yeah, I know." Wilford G. reached into his jacket for a cigar. He knew better than to light it, but would as soon as we stepped out of the vehicle. "It means that a human element is involved."

"Because a machine could care less about the passage of time. It would just let you all die of natural causes. Machines don't get impatient."

"We're not wrong, Cruz. This case is my big 'save the world' case. You've already had more than one. This one is mine, and I've been on it in some way for 50 years, even when I didn't know it. The AI is real. Maybe, the human programmer is still alive too. There's only one of the original descendants left from the Crash cyber-anarchists. Maybe, I already know who he is."

"You know who he is?"

"We have another question to answer: is the AI controlling the man or is the man controlling the AI. But we'll answer that question in due time." He opened the door of the Pony and stepped out. Already he was lighting his cigar.

"And the first question we have to answer?" I stood there, impatiently.

"Cruz, I would have thought that was obvious. We have to prove the AI plot is real."

"I thought you already did that."

"No. You said it yourself. We have to prove it."

"Prove it to who?"

"You, Cruz. We have to prove it to you. Come on."

I wished it was raining because the streets were filled with the lowest low-lives I had seen in a while. I was used to a higher-class of low-lives in my part of Metropolis.

"This is one of the older parts of the city, isn't it?"

"Yeah, Cruz, it is." Wilford had been leading the way through the crowds of people, thugs lining the sidewalks in front of the business establishments. "Most of my detective career was working Old Metro."

"You can't possibly miss this."

"Actually, I do. One day, Rabbit City and Buzz Town and all the places you frequent will be Old Metro. All this will be new again, so you better get to know it."

We stopped at what looked like a pool hall bar. There were no neon signs telling you the name, which meant it was a place for insiders only. Outside were all these thuggish men in front of the door. Wilford spoke to them in another language and in moments they were all laughing and exchanging fist taps and handshakes. He led me through the swinging double doors.

"How many languages do you speak? And which one was that?"

"Cruz, that is the one deficiency you have. How can you work the Metro streets and know only English?"

"English is the official language, so why should I?"

"Keep telling yourself that and see how far you get. I was speaking Persian, to answer your question."

"Persian? How do you speak all these languages?"

"Yeah, I know. You're still mastering English."

I didn't know what it was with places like this and their aversion to a well-lit interior like normal people. It was dark, and all I saw were glowing shades everywhere surrounding sunken pits. In the center of the pits were high-stakes pool games. No one had to tell me, but these were those marathon competitions between two people that literally could go on for days. Winners could become rich, and losers could lose everything. It was that kind of game. The battle pitted a skinny guy with a purple pool stick against a short college-kid-looking female wearing a skull cap and platform heels. Her pool stick was translucent, and she had been hitting shot after shot from the time Wilford stopped for us to watch.

We moved away from the action to the private viewing rooms to the back of the establishment. This was where the people who had real money riding on games watched. Plush seating, lots of expensive booze, lots of scantily clad waitresses and buff waiters. They had both giant hoverscreens and holo-interface, for those who wanted to wear their VR-shades and "stand" right next to the pool table to watch.

A bald man saw us as soon as we entered and stood from his chair. Another bald man with a thick mustache appeared next to him.

"Here he is. The G-Man returns."

"8-Ball," Wilford said, when he stopped in front of the man.

"I told everyone I knew you weren't dead. I asked, 'Is there a body?' They said no, it was blown up. I said, then he's not dead. He'll be dead when I can go to the grave, dig him up, and take a piss on the corpse."

"I'll be cremated, 8-Ball."

"Isn't it against some kind of laws to fake your own death, G-Man?"

"No. No life insurance was involved."

"You giving people ideas, G-Man."

"Someone with brains has to."

"Who's your girlfriend?" 8-Ball's sideman asked.

I didn't wait for Wilford to answer. "The name's Cruz. And call me girlfriend again, and I'll wait for you outside and run you down with my classic Ford Pony."

"Cruz?" the sideman looked at 8-Ball. "Boss, the detective guy." 8-Ball had no idea who I was. "The Blade Gunner Case. The Alien Case."

Another man stood from his chair. "The NeuroDancer Case."

8-Ball perked up. "Oh yeah! That detective. You did it, didn't you?"

"Do what?" I asked.

"Killed her? You were the one. They said it was the cops, but she died from one shot. That had to be you. If it were the cops, she would have been Swiss cheese. That's how the cops kill you."

They were all watching me, but I said nothing.

"I knew it!" 8-Ball declared. "She would have killed you, you know. That was the most dangerous person I ever met, and I've met a lot of dangerous people. She was always thinking. Even when she was smiling and dancing on the stage, she was thinking. Thinkers are always dangerous. Isn't that right, G-Man? You're a thinker too. But you're also a softy. I still see you're spending all your money on shoes like the ladies."

I didn't even see the motion. Wilford G. kicked 8-Ball in the face so fast, no one had time to react. 8-Ball was on the ground on his back. It was like a delayed response when 8-Ball's bodyguards drew their weapons and pointed them at Wilford. My formerly-posthumous mentor was unconcerned.

"8-Ball, it's been only a few years, and already you've forgotten all the lessons I taught you over the years. You insult me, and I don't talk—I react."

8-Ball held his bleeding nose. "You broke it."

"You'll get another one." Wilford looked at me. "See, back in the day, 8-Ball here used to annoy a lot of people. He annoyed the wrong person, and that gangster bit his nose off and swallowed it. 8-Ball had to get a whole new nose."

The gangster was helped to his knees by his men. "Lower your guns!" he yelled at them. "You're not shooting anybody in here. Yes, G-Man, he did. I heard that someone cut him open like a fish to see what else he might be storing in that stomach of his. When they finished checking, they decided to walk away and leave him as is."

Wilford G looked at me. "8-Ball wants you to believe he killed the man, but I know it was someone else."

"I did—"

"What's that 8-Ball? Were you about to confess to a homicide?"

8-Ball chuckled, holding his nose with a handkerchief from one of his men. "G-Man, I missed you. These chats always made my day. Why are you here?"

"I have business to discuss."

"Discuss it then. My original ears work fine."

"I need an introduction to the Shadow Market."

"Why?"

"I can pay."

"Why? Am I your new friend in your new back-from-the-dead life?"

"I'll pay *and* give you a piece of information."

8-Ball lowered the handkerchief from his nose. It was still a bloody mess, but he didn't care.

"I don't have all day, 8-Ball. Yes or no?"

"What's the information?"

"The identity of the spy in your crew."

The look of surprise on 8-Ball's face wasn't what concerned me. It was the look on the faces of his side-man and bodyguards. As my Ma would have said: 'I know you did something you weren't supposed to do from that look on your face.' I kept my eyes on everyone, but in my mind's eye, I was recalling how many steps to the exit and anything around us that could be used as a shield.

Then the shootout began.

CHAPTER 15

Brackets

I was in Wilford's domain now. He knew the people, places, and everything else. I watched for his lead, and when 8-Ball drew his laser pistol from I don't know where—one minute his hand was empty, the next minute this weapon was there blasting away—Wilford G stood there as cool as ice.

People in the room had dropped to the floor for 8-Ball to "retire" his entire bodyguard crew, including that sideman.

"Which one was it?" 8-Ball yelled.

Wilford was puffing on another cigar. "One of them, I'm sure."

"What's that supposed to mean?" he asked.

"8-Ball, yes or no to the money for the introduction? Looks like you'll need that money to hire another crew."

8-Ball pushed his laser pistol back up the sleeve of his jacket. He had a contraption similar to my pop-gun. "Yeah, yeah, I'll take it. When?"

"As soon as possible. Tonight."

"Not possible. I can get you in there tomorrow. I'll find out the time."

Wilford reached into a jacket pocket and pulled out a roll. 8-Ball was more than happy to take that roll of money off his hands.

"Use the exchange to get me."

"Yeah," 8-Ball answered.

Wilford turned and walked out of the room, with me following. As we neared the entrance, the main area outside was unaffected by the shoot-out in the room. Everyone was glued to their restive pool pits with their shades on. I got the impression that, if the place was on fire or we were receiving Up-Top flying saucer laser fire, they'd still be standing, watching like frozen statues.

"Come on, Cruz. You walk too slow for a youngster."

As soon as I stepped outside, I was hit by stinging rain. "That didn't last long." The rain was back, and I lifted my collar and tightened my jacket around me.

Wilford was already halfway to the Pony when I started walking. I saw two men quickly come in behind him, but they hadn't seen me. One was already pulling a weapon from his jacket when I fired my main piece into his back. I saw from the corner of my eye another fast approaching figure. I turned to see another thug about to blast me, but I flicked my left wrist and blasted him first with my pop-gun. I heard multiple gunfire, quickly turned my head, to see Wilford standing over the third man, gun in hand.

"Cruz, there's more!"

I looked down the street, where the man had come from and there it was. A dark hovercar began to rise. I aimed to shoot and stopped.

"Shoot it!" I heard Wilford yell.

"Just because the hovercar is leaving at this moment doesn't mean it has anything to do with these killers!" I was so certain of my logical position when machine gun fire from that hovercar almost cut me in half.

Wilford was shooting his weapon at it. It was some kind of gun that every bullet made a strange metallic sound. "Enough of this," I said, aimed and fired. One round from my omega-gun and that hovercar started to descend to the ground fast. It hadn't even crashed yet, when someone jumped from the back seat.

I didn't wait. I took chase after the man, who turned and started shooting at me. I dropped to the ground to avoid the shots—the nasty, slimy, concrete in the rain. I gritted my teeth; I was mad.

"Cruz—"

"I got him!" I jumped up after him, running.

"I got the driver!" Wilford G. yelled just as I turned a corner after the man.

What I was doing was one of the most dangerous things for anyone to do—chasing someone who was armed down dark streets. The man obviously knew the neighborhood; I was the visitor. I had a new gadget on my omega-gun, and now, I was going to be able to test it. I had already locked the man into the weapon's targeting. I stopped running, aimed— the man was nowhere in sight—and squeezed the trigger. A special electronic bullet flew away, then another, and another. They raced out of view, and all I heard were yells.

I casually walked to where the yells came from and there, around the corner was the man on his back, writhing in pain.

"You shot me!"

"That's what you get for trying to shoot people," I said and kicked him in the side.

"You can't kick me, copper."

"I'm not police!" I kicked him again.

"Help! Call the police!" he yelled.

You never knew what street pedestrians would do at the sight of violence—watch or run away. This group seemed to be of stronger mettle and watched. If the men really expected someone to call the police, he'd die of natural causes before then.

"Why were you trying to shoot G.?" I yelled at him.

"Who?"

"G-Man!"

"None of your business. Who are you?"

"G-Man's friend."

"G-Man's partner, Brackets." It was Wilford walking up to us. "Why is it, Brackets, that every time I see you, you're lying on the ground after someone's shot you. You need to find another line of work. Doesn't seem like you're well-suited for contract hitman work."

"Go to hell, G-Man! You should have stayed dead."

"Who sent you, Brackets?" Wilford asked.

"Go to hell, G-Man."

"Cruz, let's drag Mr. Brackets into the dark alley over there for privacy, shall we?"

I grabbed the man by the legs and pulled him along the ground, as he yelled and cursed at me. It was a dark alley all right—it also was flooded with crate covers and other assorted garbage along one side of the wall.

"Perfect spot for you, Brackets. If we need to throw you out as garbage, we don't have to travel anywhere. Who sent you, Brackets? I will find out."

"Then find out."

"This will not turn out well for you, Brackets. Remember, I'm dead. Dead men can't go down for homicide. Tell me who, and we'll let you go, then you can at least try again. Right now, you've been paid money to do a job, and the job isn't done. Your friends are all dead but not you. What do you think your employee is going to do? He's going to hire more men for me, for sure, but not before he hires them to take care of you."

"I'm not talking."

Wilford reached down, picked him up, and threw him against the wall, shattering one of those crate covers. Brackets began to scream. I knew Wilford was still strong for a man a nickel away from the big 1-0-0, but he didn't throw him so hard against the wall to cause Brackets bodily injury.

I saw them!

Wilford turned, and I was nothing but a distant figure in the distance.

"Help me!" Brackets yelled. His body was crawling with isopods!

CHAPTER 16

Sharp

Superman had Kryptonite. I had isopods. Every hero had a weakness; that's part of the contract. Clinically, I was a recovering germophobe. To go from almost having to be sent to a bubble colony on the Moon, to being able to live and thrive in Metropolis was real progress, but I was still "recovering." That meant certain things could trigger an attack. Even if I wasn't a germophobe or recovering one, I could not and would not deal with isopods. Jumbo roaches, rats, and isopods were my own personal trinity of terror.

"Isopods were the most terrifying. People always say that science fiction can never create something scarier than what already existed in nature. Biologists say isopods are crustaceans—part of the same family as shrimp and crabs. I'd say that those biologists are big fat liars. Shrimp and crabs are cute animals that deserve to crawl around on the sea floor or grace a person's dinner plate. Isopods are space alien creatures deposited on our planet and deserve nothing less than total extermination. Some biologists are at least trying to be honest in saying they're related to woodlice! That means they're blood suckers. But Metropolis doesn't have any real wood anymore, so that means the blood sucking would be an invasion of the body snatcher, vampiric kind. To this very day, I remembered a documentary where an isopod infested a fish and literally took the place of the poor fish's tongue. That meant the isopod would eat the fishy's food before the fish could eat it, before it could even get to its stomach. What a way to die. The alien parasite takes over your own body part. That's what isopod infestation is, and there is no science fiction scarier than that—because they're real. The very whisper of these alien creatures could bring me to the edge of an attack. But seeing a live one, or a horde of them, means a full relapse.

"Their bodies protected by a rigid, exoskeleton comprised of overlapping segments, their bodies segmented—fused from head to tail, large beady eyes, not one but two pairs of antennae, thoracic legs arranged in seven pairs, multiple sets of jaws, ability to breathe underwater as easily as on land. The Alienists were right! We have been invaded by space aliens! It's Them! It's the isopods!"

"Mr. Cruz!" one of the CDC orderlies yelled.

I started to run again. "I'm infested!"

The orderlies tackled me to the ground as another ran to me and jabbed me with a needleless injector to sedate me.

When I walked out of the Metropolis Centers for Disease Control building, I realized that I had left the Pony in Pigstown. I had left my prized classic hovervehicle in a district called Pigstown! But there it was in the parking lot, with Wilford G. leaning against it. I was wearing borrowed facility clothes, which meant they were white, oversized, and were hanging all over the place. Every piece of clothing I had on before, including by prized tan fedora, I had incinerated. I was still rolling up my sleeves, no coat, no hat, walking down the steps to him.

Wilford G. had a cigar in the corner of his lip. "The people here must love you," he said.

"How did you find me?"

"I know things."

"Know things?"

"About you."

"How long have you been waiting?"

"Not long, it usually takes you a couple of hours for your gel pool bath."

"You know too much about me. That is not cool. Metro Disease Control hates me, because I know things most of the people in Metropolis don't: access to Decon is free."

"Decon? Cruz, are you going to have an attack like this again?"

"Are we going run into an isopod infestation again?"

"I'm glad Brackets thought the same thing as you because he spilled all his secrets to get those critters off him. But he didn't need me to bring him to any Decon."

"Decon is—"

"I know what Decon is, Cruz, and what they do. Decon is for real biological and chemical contamination, not what you imagine in your own mind. Cruz, are there any other medical conditions I need to know about, real or imagined."

"I don't have any medical conditions."

"Cruz, you are one slow walker, but when you were running out of that alley in the pouring rain, I swear you set a human speed record; that's how fast you were running."

"I don't do isopod infestations; that's all."

"Well, I'm going to remember that for next time. What about your OCD thing?"

"OCD thing? I don't have an OCD thing."

"Cruz, if we're going into battle with the bad guys, I don't want to turn to see you having to zip up and unzip your jacket five times or have to spin around three times or some kind of other weirdness."

I laughed. "My shoes don't have laces, the only spinning I do is on the dance floor with my wife, and my OCD is history."

"But not the germophobia."

"It's gone, too, but not when faced with an isopod infestation! Did you scratch my vehicle?"

Wilford G. grinned and threw my Pony's keys to me. "You're welcome."

"I'm going to see my wife and son. You didn't think I'd stay on the road with you on this phantom case of yours without seeing them."

"Cruz, you can see anyone you like. We both can now. I simply said you can't tell them or anyone about the case. We're working a case; that's it."

"How did you get my spare keys?"

"Cruz, I'm a detective. Give me some credit."

I got in on the drivers' side, and he got in on the passenger seat. I was soaked, but I didn't care. He saw that I wasn't going to drive until I got the answer to my question.

"Flash gave it to me. I called your friend Flash to let me into the vehicle, since you had kindly left me stranded."

"Sorry about that." I started up the Pony.

"I had to hold down the fort by myself. Watch Brackets. Watch your vehicle. Wondering if more hitmen were lurking in the shadows."

"Yes, I'm sorry about all of that." We were in the middle of the sky traffic congestion in no time. "I can't believe how much trouble I'm in."

Wilford G. laughed. "Your mommy-wife is going to ground you?"

"My wife and son have not seen me in two days because of you."

"Me? You're the one fainting and running from imaginary isopods."

"Those isopods were not imaginary."

"They're harmless."

"Brackets and I don't agree."

He laughed. "Yeah, Brackets didn't like the critters trying to crawl down his mouth."

"I do not want to hear about it!"

"You're going to need a change of clothes. After you clean yourself up, then we better check in with your wife and son."

"Oh, thank you for the permission to do that."

"Then we have to continue with the case."

"Continue how?"

"Find out who sent Brackets. Was it really who Brackets says it was or was it the AI?"

"What? Are you really saying this program might have contracted a hit on you? That's crazy."

"We need to find out for sure. We have a lot of work to do, so if the AI is already onto us, we need to know now."

"There is no AI."

"That's the second question, Cruz. Is it the AI or a person controlling the AI? Either way we'll need to deal with the AI. Remember, I've been working this case since before you were born."

"I probably wouldn't say that out loud, since that's not exactly a testament to your detective skills."

"If an AI sent guys to shoot at you, don't you think it's something you'd want to know. I heard you don't like it when people shoot at you."

"You're right about that."

"You need to keep an open mind about this, Cruz. There was a time in this world when flying cars was the stuff of fiction, but here we are. I grant you there does seem to be a human element here, but that doesn't change the fact that Connie and I believe there's an autonomous computer program out there doing its own thing, and may have already killed twelve people that we know about. I wouldn't ruin my relationship with my son, possibly forever, if I wasn't certain of all this."

We had flown into the Rabbit City, but I pulled off to the side. "Let's wrap up the Brackets thing now."

"Are you sure?" Wilford asked me.

"After I take my super-shower, get in clean clothes, and visit the family, I will be in no frame of mind for bad guys. I'll be out of commission for at least a day. So, either now or two days from now."

"Now then."

"I have spare clothes in the trunk. Where am I going?"

"Another part of Metro I'm sure you haven't been to before."

"What is it this time? We were in Pigstown before. Is it Rats-ville this time?"

"Close. Snake Eyes Junction."

I came to learn that a lot of Wilford G's life revolved around the professional sports and gambling world. We were in another seedy area, old as time, the people looked like it, no matter how young they were, but this time it was a cyborg boxing match. Whether it was legal or not depended on if anyone in the ring, including referees, got killed.

Wilford G. got us in by speaking another language. He told me it was Tagalog. I was beginning to believe he was actually some kind of linguistic genius—I could build hovercars from scratch; he could speak every language on the planet. He didn't just speak the language; he spoke as a native of that language.

The difference between the inside of this dimly lit establishment was there was one ring, and from the time you crossed the threshold inside, you could smell the perspiration in the air. It almost made me gag and wonder why everyone in audience would be sweating so much, when they weren't the two fighters in the ring trying to pummel each other to death. After five seconds, I realized why. There was no air condition in the place. We were told it was broken again, and maintenance was working on it.

Wilford G. came in behind his man like a ninja and got up right behind him. He had a brawny bodyguard on each side who saw us and turned around. The man in the center didn't.

"G-Man," he said.

"Sharp."

"What brings you here, G-Man? Got any money riding on the fight?"

"Maybe we should talk outside."

"Why is that, G-Man?"

"I don't need you to explain to me about the hitmen you sent after me. Obviously, I know you sent them, and obviously, they failed. I need to know what led to your decision to send them now. It's for another case I'm working."

Sharp turned around. All his hair was silver gray, which matched his silver-gray suit. He apparently loved silver—necklace, bracelets, an earring, a bow-tie that looked to be made out of metal.

"It's noisy in here. Outside we can talk in peace," Wilford continued.

"In peace." Sharp smiled. "I thought you were resting in peace."

"But here I am."

Sharp lifted his chin, gesturing to his men, and the three of them followed. I followed behind them, and I glanced behind me. Literally, the entire section Sharp was sitting in had gotten up and was following me. I turned my head to the front, but I had already done a quick count: More than 50 men were behind me, and none of them looked friendly.

I strolled outside, and there was Wilford G. lighting his cigar. Sharp faced him with a glare. The bodyguard on each side and the army of other men flanked them, forming a half-circle facing us.

"Sharp," Wilford G. began. "As far as I'm concerned, I don't care about the hit. I know that may seem unlike me, but I am after bigger fish than you. The hit...was it your idea alone or did someone get you to do it?"

"Why would I need someone to get me to do anything against you? You killed my father and brother. Most of my family and crew is in jail because of you."

"Sharp, that's because you and your family are vicious animals preying on innocent people, and you need to be put down. Are you going to help me out here? Answer that question and we're gone. You'll never see me again. I'm getting soft in my elder years. I want this big fish I'm chasing. I could care less about you. I'm forgiving and forgetting this time around. You'll have to be someone else's problem."

"You come into my turf with one man. You act as if I'm intimidated by you."

"Sharp, don't work yourself up here. You don't like me. I don't like you. But this has nothing to do with that. I'm not here for you, only information."

"G-Man, I'm going to do what I've been waiting for all these years to do. I'm going to kill you and your man here. Then, since you like to fake your own death, we're going to dump the bodies right on the steps of Metro PD, so there won't be any doubt this time."

"Sharp, why did you go and say something like that? Do you know who this man standing next to me is? This is Cruz, the Metro street detective. The one who brought down Blade Gunner, the Trix Gang; since you like contract killers, he took down Neck Muncher, Crossbow, Church Lady, and Pipsqueak by himself. He killed the Ripper. He killed the Alien. Sharp, I ask you, do you have enough men?"

G. did my private detective history well. I had rarely seen a gangster with a look of fear, but that's how Sharp looked. But I wasn't reassured because all the men were now all laser-focused on me, and all I saw was a lot of twitchy movement. One of them was going to draw on us. It was inevitable.

Wilford tried one more time. "Sharp, did you put the contract out on us by yourself or did someone put you up to it?"

"I did it myself! You stupid fool. One of my men was let out of lock-up and saw you walking out of Metro PD, which seemed strange since you're supposed to be dead. It took nothing to find you!"

"Thanks," Wilford G said and shot him.

CHAPTER 17

China Doll

Wilford G. later told me how Sharp got his street name. He liked to throw razor sharp shurikens at people and was quite good at it, able to bury a dozen in your head and chest in less than ten seconds.

Once Wilford blew him away, the other men simply stood there.

"Two ways we can play this," he said to them. "We can have the shootout and we kill all of you. Or you can walk away, and the next one in line can take over all his businesses, money and interests."

The men seemed very nervous by my presence. Law enforcement and the criminal world had one thing in common—they knew guns. With a glance, they could recite everything about a weapon—its manufacturer, how it performed in the rain, capacity, type of rounds. They were all watching my omega-gun, and none of them could place it, which was what was making them nervous. The fact that I had a new glowing tip on it didn't bolster their confidence.

One of the men stepped forward, smiling. "We'll take care of the body, G-Man. You have a good rest of your night. You too, Mr. Cruz.

Thanks for killing that Ripper, VL serial killer. My little children were having nightmares every day until you took care of that beast."

"Glad I could help on the parenting front," I said.

Wilford and I walked back to the Pony, as the late Mr. Sharp was picked up off the ground by his former men.

There was no greater home remedy for a germophobic attack than my super shower. I had one in my old apartment as a bachelor. I had a bigger and badder one (meaning better) in my new apartment as a married man. Lukewarm water shot out of the main floor and ceiling vents, and side nozzles blasted out waves of hot steam. My super-sauna shower. I apologized to Wilford in advance as I would be in there for more than 90 minutes. He didn't mind because he had multiple sports games to catch up on. I didn't even know how to do that on my own TV, but he knew how to set it so he could watch two boxing matches, one mixed martial arts match, and a greyhound race all at the same time. I wondered how much money he bet on the games.

I realized I would have to pay a visit to Harry's Haberdashery, because the only tan fedora I had was one that didn't fit my head right. But that's all I had, so with my formerly-posthumous mentor following, it was time to "take my medicine" and face the wife after two days without a call.

At least we'd be in my neck of the woods and not in some no-name, scary part of Old Metro. Instead, we'd be going to where the beautiful people came and went—my wife's salon in Paisley Parish. No chance of any isopods there.

Eye Candy Image Salon was a high-end establishment packed with customers from the time it opened until its late-night closing. But with my "fame" and people finding out my wife worked there (and she was already famous) and my "little" stunt in my last major case of landing a real Martian flying saucer right in front of the salon, they had more clients than they could handle. People came from every corner of Metropolis to be made to look like movie stars with its "fashion police" of makeup artists, hairdressers, manicurists, pedicurists, skincare techs, tattoo artists, wardrobe stylists, and even dressers to assemble their wardrobe, if needed. Everyone who worked there, including my wife, had advanced degrees in beauty and skincare, fashion and style arts, health, and nutrition. Prima Donna, the Matron Queen of Metropolis fashion, started Eye Candy decades ago.

My wife's public name was China Doll, and she was Prima's number one and the boss in her absence. She went by China Doll, but women clients called her China; male clientele called her Doll. Only her family and I called her by her real name—Dot. It was always a personal treat to see what Dot's attire would be any given day. As the consummate fashionista, every piece of clothing, every accessory, and every piece of jewelry was the trendiest and the most stylish. I walked into the packed establishment and saw her in an amazing two piece white and silver sleeveless Chinese dress, white silver bracelets, and neon yellow heels. She hadn't seen me yet.

The interior of the salon was designed in a beehive design, and every section was visible, due to transparent walls, to every other section, except the break room, full body baths, and the bathrooms. Eye Candy was nothing but carefully coordinated chaos—women sitting on chairs getting their hair and makeup done in one section, their nails and toenails in another, facials in another, tattoos in another (always temporary to change according to current fashion trends), skincare consultations in another, and style analysis wardrobing in yet another section.

No one noticed me yet either—I spoke too soon. Prima Donna stood there with her mouth slightly open. But she wasn't looking at me. She was looking at the man behind.

"G."

"Prima," Wilford answered.

I looked at him, then her, then him. "How do you know Prima?"

"We dated."

"Dated? You dated my wife's boss, too?"

"I dated a lot of people you know, Cruz."

"What? What does that mean? Who else?"

"Exe."

"Exe! You dated the head of the Police Watch Commission?"

"I dated her before she was the head of the Police Watch Commission."

"G, I'm starting to wonder when you ever had time to investigate cases with all your dating activities."

Wilford smiled. "Hear that, Prima? The youngster doesn't approve."

"He'll get over it. Can't say that I'll get over seeing a dead man walk into my salon."

"I'm working a case."

"A case that caused you to deceive your family."

"Yes, Prima, it did. But I'll square it with the family."

"You really shouldn't have come here, G."

"Why is that, Prima?"

I truly felt that, sometimes, the cosmos purposely allowed things to happen to kick you in the gut. Dot was standing looking at me, and it wasn't the 'happy to see you, honey' look, but that was not what I was looking at. It was the person standing next to her, who Dot had been working on. Wilford and I were looking at Mary—Wilford's daughter-in-law. The look on Mary's face was a combination of tears and rage. She had temporary rollers in her hair and was wrapped in a clear smock over her clothes. I heard Wilford swallow hard. Mary marched right up to him and slapped him across the face.

"How could you?" she yelled.

She marched out of the salon, crying.

Wilford stood there frozen. I had had it. I took out my mobile and dialed.

There was Wilford Jr. staring at me on the tiny display. "Cruz."

"Are you sitting down?" I didn't even say hello.

"What?"

"Are you sitting down?"

"Has something happened to Mary?"

"Mary is on her way home right now, and she's going to tell you something. I thought I should tell you first. No one has died, but it'll feel worse than if someone did."

"Cruz, tell me!"

"The fact that you're yelling means you already know."

"Tell me!"

"I'm standing here in Eye Candy with your father. Mary was here. It's why she's not here and is on the way home to you."

That's as far as I got. I heard a crash, and the line disconnected.

"What did young Wilford Junior say?" Prima asked.

"I don't know because—I think he just crashed his police cruiser."

Some of the people who heard me gasped.

"G, you're a real bastard," Prima said and walked away from us.

"Wilford, do you think you should take care of your family issues first?"

"I told you not to call me that." He turned and stormed out.

"Oh, that's the behavior of an adult!" I yelled. "At least, when I run away, it's from shooting bad guys or nasty isopods! Why are you running from talking to your own son?"

I turned and there was my wife, standing with her arms folded in front of her, and some of her colleagues.

"There he is. Wilford G., my posthumous mentor, isn't posthumous, and he's a bum!"

Wilford G. was gone. I had no idea where he went, but it was fine. Dot and I went to the break room and all I wanted to do was sit down and relax.

"Who has Cruz Jr.?" I asked.

"My parents do. Cruz, what's going on?" She sat down at my table after she placed a plate with a sandwich in front of me. I had already gotten a can of sparkling water from the dispenser.

"I wish I knew. I think I do, but I don't know. I knew this was going happen. I should have kidnapped him and taken him to Wil, but he said he'd take care of it. Now, all we have is a big mess."

"It's not your fault. He was the one who faked his death. What a thing to do."

"He said he had a very good reason, but I'm not sure yet."

"I heard him say he did it for a case."

"Yes, he's brought me into it."

"Why you?"

"That's a good question. Why did he pull me into this? I'm going to give him an ultimatum. He'll have to get right with Wil or I'm out."

"There you go. That's the right thing to do. Did you see Mary's face when she saw him?"

"That's why I'm mad. There are other people in Metro who already knew he was alive."

"Already knew? He let strangers know he's alive but not his own family?"

"Yeah, he's a bum all right. I should burn his book I bought, but I've already studied it from cover to cover. Enough about him. I'm relaxing here for the day with you, and then we can get Cruz. Jr."

"What happened to your hat? That's not your regular hat."

I drank from my can, trying quickly to think of a way not to answer.

CHAPTER 18

Wil

Dot called Mary, and they spoke for a while on the phone. I played with Cruz Jr. in the living room. He was talking to Dot and me again, but he was still gruff after losing his baby hoverchair. I was getting him reacquainted with all the toys his grandparents and we had gotten him.

"Cruzie, I'll make a deal with you. You start walking and running around, and I'll let you fly in the chair."

Cruz Jr. dropped his toy spaceships to the ground and stood up. He was wobbly but then started running. He stopped and looked at me.

"How did you know what I said?" He smiled and started clapping. "You're a very sneaky toddler," I scolded. "That means you're going to be a very sneaky person." I pointed at him. "Your mother and I are going to be keeping an eye on you."

Dot returned from the bedroom. She had her mobile in her hand. "He'll meet you."

"Where? Can I call him?"

"He doesn't want to talk to you now. Meet him for breakfast at the City Diner tomorrow morning first thing."

"That's progress at least."

"What are you going to say to him?"

"Not sure yet."

"Why are you talking to him? Where's his father?"

"Maybe faking his death again. I don't have time for him. I'll get Wil settled down first."

"Then—What's Cruz Jr. doing? Why is he pointing to the locked closet? Cruz, what have you been saying to him?"

"I might have said if he did some walking and running that he might get a quick hoverchair ride."

"Cruz, Cruz Jr. is always walking and running. He just plays cripple when you're around for attention, and it seems to get you to get him the hoverchair. How could you fall for that trick? Are you this gullible when you're out there on the street dealing with criminals?"

I absolutely hated the Metro City Diner. It was in the center of Downtown Metro and was where most of City Hall, Metro PD, and court employees ate. It wasn't that I didn't want to bump into the mayor's or city council staff or police brass; it was because the place was a zoo. The diner was sprawled out over 100 floors and was always busy. I didn't consider the food particularly good, and though I would never be the interior design guru like PJ, the diner rooms always had an outdated government look, even though I had seen the rooms remodeled many times before.

Wil said he'd meet me on the 20th floor, and when I arrived, I saw him in the corner. He was in uniform and didn't seem particularly pleased to see me when I sat down at his table.

"Wil, how are you?"

"Mary told me the two of you strolled into her salon like best buddies."

"I didn't know he was still alive, if that's what you're asking."

"What are you two doing?"

"Working a case."

"What case?"

"I don't know all the details yet. He seems to have drafted me to tag along."

"Good for you, Cruz. Then I'll let you get on with your escapades with my father."

"Wil, I'm not trying to upset you. I was pulled into this because of you. You suspected it, and now I'm in the middle of it. I'll find out what's going on and report back to you."

"I thought you had to protect the confidentiality of your clients."

"Only the ones who are legally alive. Upon death, I have no such restrictions."

Wil managed a smile. "Okay."

"I'll kick around with him and find out what this all about and tell you. I promise. I'm also going to make it my personal mission to pester him until he makes things right with you."

"Yes, do that. He deserves as much grief as he can get."

"I'll give it to him."

"What about the ex-wives and my mother?"

"That's a bit more complicated, but I'll handle it."

"I know what they're doing. Looking for money."

"They won't find it, but let me handle it. You shouldn't have to worry about any of it."

"Okay."

"Are we okay?"

"Yeah, we're okay."

"If it cheers you up, Mary managed to give him quite the power-slap across the face."

He smiled again, longer. "Good. Then out to the streets to do our jobs."

"Yes, and next time we meet for breakfast, please not here."

CHAPTER 19

Wilford

Wilford's dojo apartment was completely empty. A tenant told me moving men came, packed up everything and moved it all out. I imagined everything was sitting in another one his storage units somewhere in Metropolis. He had vanished.

I was tempted to drop it, but I pressed on. When I called Compstat Connie's office, I found out that she was on leave. I had no idea what that meant, but when I found my way to her Woodstock Falls apartment, she too was gone.

I was not going to continue searching the supercity for a man who I now regarded as a bum. It would be back to the office for me to do some real work.

PJ's call came in over my vehicle's dashboard.

"PJ, what's up?"

"Where are you? Your place called and said you hadn't shown up yet. They can't hold the room forever."

"What place? What are you talking about?"

"The Wet Cabeza. Your client reserved it for your meeting, but you both are past the time."

"Okay, PJ. I'll be there soon."

"What client is this?"

"I'll tell you when I see you."

I realized this was how the game was going to be played. I wasn't supposed to find him. He was going to find me.

The Wet Cabeza was my favorite eatery in town. Usually, when I ate there, I had some humble pie and a cup of silk coffee. I did reading there, had meetings from time to time, or went there simply to get away. Everyone there knew me before I was "famous," so I remained one of the guys.

The inside layout was a large, open cafe, all booths and barstools at the kitchen counter, with college-kid waiters and waitresses on hover-roller skates. Upstairs were the tiny conference rooms for rent. I came in and asked which room my "client" had rented for the meeting. I walked up the stairs to Room 7, but no one was there. When I turned to walk back downstairs, there was Quix. He walked to me and handed me a card. With that, he was gone and out the door.

The name of the establishment was one that I had been to a couple of times on a previous case and had hoped never to set foot in it again. I flew up in the Pony, parked, and sat there scanning the parking lot. Wilford knew what vehicle I drove, so I figured he was watching me to see if I could figure out what vehicle he was in. I had read his book a million times; I knew he used to drive an Old Continental hovercar. For some reason, the manufacturers added "old" to mean "retro" and "hip," but the public took it to mean "stupid." They were not popular then, but they had their own rebirth, courtesy of hoverracers and restorers who loved their sturdy construction. They weren't fast but could take damage that most hovercars couldn't. For that reason they became the go-to vehicle for police departments and criminal gangsters of the past. Today, they were considered the classic hovercars for people who liked vehicles to be like flying tanks. When he "died" he surely wasn't able to keep his, so he probably would have bought a new one. I saw it at the far end of the lot, face out. Wilford liked silver cars, and it was silver. I stepped out of my vehicle, walked toward it, and angrily waved to him to get out of the hovercar. I saw a door open, and there he was laughing, and he waved. He was wearing a black fedora.

"Figurers sure can figure," he said, grinning, when he reached me.

"You're a piece a work."

"Cruz, man, this is where the case begins."

"Really."

He stopped walking and looked at me. "But before we begin, let's get something straight about my family. None of it is your business. You have a son too, but mine is an adult. When Cruz Jr. gets to Wil's age, talk to me then. All this that's going on is for him. I did this for him. He doesn't realize it, but he will. I'm doing this for my son, your son, and all the sons and daughters in Metropolis and beyond. I'll take care of things with my son; you can bet on it. But, that's not why you're here—to pretend you're my dad, scolding me for not living up to his standards again. You're here because this case is big, ugly, and I need a detective to partner with me to close it and close it hard. I don't have time for Wil and his hurt feelings. He's the damn head of the Metro PD, so he's going to have to man up and stop crying. He kicks in the teeth of punks and has shoot-outs with gangsters before lunch every day, so I don't know why he's so overly sensitive. Cruz, we have work to do. Worry about this case and not my family. We can deal with that after. If we're not focused, we're dead. Are you hearing me? Here, catch."

He threw me a block of wood. I almost dropped it when I saw what it was—a baby isopod encased in a clear, solid resin in the middle.

"YOUR DAY IS MUCH BETTER THAN HIS—OR WOULD YOU LIKE TO SWITCH PLACES?"

I didn't even know what to do. I took his point, but I was not putting it in my jacket, which meant I'd be carrying it for the day.

"It's small enough to fit in your pocket," he said.

"I'll hold it."

"You do that, but I hope you were listening to me."

"I heard you."

"Good, then that bit is closed until the case is done. Let's get on into the Skanky Squirrel."

I laughed. Already Wilford managed to make me forget that I was angry with him. "Sketchy Squirrel."

"What?"

"It's the Sketchy Squirrel, not the Skanky Squirrel."

"Whatever, the words are the same."

"The words are completely different."

"How do you know this place? You sound like a regular."

"I'm not a regular. I've met some clients here a couple of times."

"Oh, who?"

"Australians."

"Australians." He just stood there looking at me with a half-smile. "Cruz, the word is Aussies."

"Yes, that's what I said."

"You said Australians, not Aussies. Cruz, you need to use more contractions and slang."

"What? I use plenty of both."

"Whatever amount of contractions you use in speech, double it. For your slang, you need to triple it. People outside the biz shouldn't be able to know what you're saying when we talk."

I tried not to laugh again. "The point of communication is to communicate."

"No, it's not. And you need to smile less, too. We're entering the danger zone of this case. If you're watching my back, you can't be giggling and fainting."

"How did I handle Sharp and his crew?"

"There, that was a smooth piece of work. That's what I want to see from you for the duration of the case. They were scared of you, and you didn't even do anything. Because they knew you were serious, and you weren't giggling, smiling, or about to faint."

"G., I put down more than my fair share of bad guys."

"I know. Keep doing it, but again, that was all play before. This is the serious part now. We're going to see a man named Polygon. I'll do the talking; you keep your eyes open and watch my back. He's the resident expert in his field, which means he's crazy, but again, I'll doing the talking."

"He's an expert on what?"

"How to kill deviant AI programs."

CHAPTER 20

Polygon

I was back in the seedy, shady Sketchy Squirrel, where criminals and borderline criminals did their lunch meetings. Wilford walked in with his black fedora, two-tone shoes, and cigar in his mouth.

"I don't know why you're copying me with the fedora."

"Cruz, two hats are better than one. Besides, they won't know which one of us to focus on."

Of course, we were going all the way to the back with the bigger booths and more space in between them. When I first saw Polygon, I almost thought he was a mannequin of some kind with the gleaming round shades, diminutive stature, and black hair that looked like a wig. I still hadn't gotten over the last maniac I came across who wore a wig.

Wilford sat down across from him, then moved in a bit for me to sit. I didn't like how this place was designed. The man was sitting with his back to the wall, but anyone could sneak up behind us. I took out a pocket mirror from a jacket pocket. My wife gave it to me, and it didn't look too girly. I flipped it open and held it so I could see anyone coming from behind us. Polygon smiled as I looked up at him. He turned his attention to Wilford.

"Who's your friend?"

"My business partner," Wilford answered.

"I thought you were a solo operation, G-Man."

"Not this time."

"I feel after all these years that we know each other so well, Detective."

"Only we don't—know each other, that is." Wilford took his cigar from his mouth. "Am I allowed to smoke here?"

"You can smoke wherever you like," Polygon answered.

"We're going to the Shadow Market."

"Oh, good, that's very good."

"I need to know what to get."

"You believe now."

"I do."

"We should have done this years ago."

"Are you going to be helping us, Polygon?"

"I'm a behind-the-scenes man."

"I thought as much. That would mean 'no' then."

"Has your partner here been brought up to speed?"

"He has."

"What does he think?"

"Ask him. He's sitting right across from you, and he talks too."

"Are you asking me about It?" I said.

"Yes."

"I don't believe in It."

"Because—"

"Listen, Polygon, is it? My partner here thinks you're an expert. I think you're funny looking and possibly wearing a wig, which means I don't trust you. I've done programming, and with all the hype over the ages, I haven't met an A.I. program that wasn't just a regular program doing what it was programmed to do by some human. Humans do crimes, not programs."

"Actually, Mr. Cruz—"

"You know who I am."

"They called it The Crash. It's when cyberpunks were really cyberpunks—hacking the cyberverse to crash governments and megacorps—"

"And they succeeded. They sent society back to the stone ages."

"Rather than create the system of the future, we Earthers retreated to the past, regressing to the tech of the past to create a new future."

"Yeah, and you never see news stories of someone hacking into these government agencies or company systems anymore, do you?"

"We let the barbarians win."

"No, we made it impossible for the barbarians to do what they did ever again. I'm sorry, but neither of us were alive when it happened, so why are you waxing nostalgic for something you didn't experience? You want your digital? Move Up-Top. We Earthers like our tech."

"Tech of the stone ages."

"I built my classic Ford Pony in my parent's garage when I was in high school. I've restored hovercars here on Earth and for Up-Top visitors. Earth cars you want to break into you need to go to the vehicle with a sledgehammer and you still might not get in, and that's assuming the owner doesn't have mobile security around that will shoot you in your face. Hovercars with their fancy digital systems. If I couldn't hack it, and I'm no hacker, I could find a kid on the street to do it in five minutes. You keep your digital. My Great-gramps told my Pops what the Crash was like. It was no joke. People died, or don't you know that?"

Polygon looked at Wilford, smiling. "Good, he's one of us." He was playing games with me. "Mr. Cruz, we are on the same viewscreen. I have to know the positions of people before I get comfortable. The anarchist computer hackers don't exist anymore. Governments and megacorps have seen to that. Our hi-tech analog system has seen to it. There no longer exists a central Net where all our systems live. Or is there?"

I looked at Wilford. "This is your expert?"

"My partner is a youngster, so he's a bit on the impatient side. Give me the laundry-list that we need. We'll take it from there."

Polygon reached into his coat jacket and pulled out a small tablet. "It's all on here."

Wilford took it and turned it on.

"Mr. Cruz, the mission of the AI is to make humankind 'happy.' Its term."

"Is that a bad thing?" I asked.

"*Happy* is a euphemism for total eradication, Mr. Cruz."

Wilford read the list. "Polygon, how am I going to get some of this?"

"We talked about this. You don't have to get it. You only have to place the order. If it's there, it will react. We'll know for sure."

"G., what's on the list?" I kept my eye on my hand mirror but wanted to know what the list was.

"Neural scramblers, digital ROS shut-off, BCI jammer. That's the easy stuff. EMP-grenades and portable nano-tech delivery system packs."

They watched me for a reaction. I didn't give them one.

"Once you place the order," Polygon said. "It will act to preserve itself."

"Or it will do nothing because it doesn't exist," I said to him.

"The only people who might act are the police who'll want to know why a nonagenarian and tricenarian detectives are acquiring weapons that terrorists might want," I said.

"Hence the Shadow Market," Wilford said as he slid toward me. I got out of the booth and stood. He did the same when he was fully out.

"Well, G-Man, it's been a good run." He extended his hand.

Wilford G. shook his hand; his face was somber. "Yes, it has, Polygon. Hopefully, we're wrong."

"Your skeptical friend aside, we know we're not. Good luck."

"Have a great life, Polygon." Wilford G. threw a set of keys on the table in front of him and led me out of the establishment.

CHAPTER 21

Run-Time

We were in the Pony and off on our way, me at the driver's wheel.

"What happened to your Continental?"

"That hovercar belongs to Polygon now."

"You're giving away your possessions."

"Cruz, I only had the vehicle for a few months. I didn't own it long enough for it to be a possession."

"Where's Connie? I went to her place, and it looks like she's cleared out."

"Connie went where she'll be safe until this all blows over. Knowing Connie as I do, she'll fight the battle the way she knows best—with a keyboard."

"Who's Polygon to you?" I was descending the Pony into the sky lanes.

"I met him a while ago. He worked the Fringe News on Metro News back then."

"Fringe News?"

"Yeah, anyone could submit a story. It was mostly scientists. Polygon used to work at the Lab."

"The Lab?"

"Lotus Lab. That's how Connie and I came across him. He was also an assistant to Connie's ex. They all worked for the Lab. Back then, it was just a theory of Its existence."

"I looked into those accidents that you mentioned—Connie's ex and the others."

"You did all that on your day off?"

"I did. They were accidents, and I see nothing there that says otherwise."

"Except for one thing."

"Which is?"

"Connie says they weren't accidents."

"What happened that made you think your theory of the It was real?"

"When we heard about Mr. Candy."

For the first time, in all his games, I knew what this was all about. Mr. Candy was the urban myth of the crime world. They were many of them, and I knew them all, but this one had always intrigued me. The mysterious Mr. Candy was a crime lord who "owned" everyone in Metropolis—politicians, police brass, megacorp CEOs. Whether it was through blackmail, bribery, or simple threats, he could call in a favor anytime. They said he was the real most powerful crime boss in the supercity, because no one, neither law enforcement nor other crime bosses, knew who he was. Some suggested he might even be a woman, which is really how I became interested in the urban myth, because I thought it might be the late NeuroDancer.

Wilford was telling me that Mr. Candy was actually an AI program, hiding until the right people died, to make its move. I still wasn't convinced, but that piece of information made it more credible. If It existed, then I still felt a real-life flesh and blood human being was behind it all. We didn't need machines to engage in evil; we had plenty of humans to do it for them.

"We're making a stop," I said.

I flew into Peacock Hills, one of the premiere business districts in the supercity. Its monolith buildings extended, like gargantuan fingers, into space through the clouds, each illuminated in the conservative colors of white, light yellow, and blue.

The Founder, President, CEO, and COO of *Let It Ride Enterprises* was my best friend, Run-Time. We had been friends since before middle school, and while I was building real hovercars, he went from body shop go-fer to hovercar mechanic to valet attendant to hovertaxi driver to hovertaxicab owner to his own fleet by his early twenties, then launched Let It Ride. He also owned all the top car washes, hovercar body shops, hovercar rental shops, hovercycle rental shops, hovertaxicab, and hoverlimousine services in the city. He was well past being a mega-multi-millionaire, and thanks to my last major case, had expanded his services to Up-Top.

As a member of the "Who's Who" of the Metropolis wealthy elite, he was my go-to guy for anything that had to do with the corporate, finance, or political world. I was lucky he was free to see me. Wilford said he'd let me go up alone while he made calls.

Monday to Thursday, Run-Time wore his slim fit business suits and slim ties, and on casual Fridays and the weekends, if he came in, he left the tie at home. The only casual thing he wore was his trademark flat hat. You'd never see his head without it, and you'd never see him wearing it backwards.

He greeted me with a bear hug, and we sat in the client guest area of his newly remodeled—and larger—office. Unsurprisingly, it had a "stars in space" ceiling and wallpaper motif.

"The wallpaper says business is good," I said as we sat.

"You sure you don't want anything to drink?"

"No, I'm fine."

He sat with a glass in hand. "Business is better than good. How do you and Dot like being Let It Ride's first lifetime Andromeda members?"

"Hmm. Let me think for a second. Love it!"

He laughed. "What kind of case are you working these days?"

"Not sure yet. Still piecing it together, but I did want to ask you if you ever heard of a particular criminal, Mr. Candy."

Run-Time didn't hesitate. "Yes."

"Is he real?"

"He's real."

I was surprised by his response. "I thought that was a myth."

"Cruz, I'm surprised that you would be surprised. You've run up against secret megacorps and secret villains. Gidrah. The Super-Cyborgs. Mr. Viper."

"Don't remind me about them."

"Why do you think Mr. Candy couldn't exist?"

"Interesting. No one knows who he is?"

"No, but everyone I know believes he, or it, exists."

"Why did you say it?"

"It could be a gang that collectively calls itself Mr. Candy."

"What does he do?"

"Blackmail mostly for favors. Hand out bribes, have people on a secret payroll doing work for him, ransom, threats."

"Do you know for a fact that any of that has happened?"

"It's happened, and the person claiming responsibility identified himself as Mr. Candy, but no one has ever been arrested or directly tied to any illegal act. You're working a case involving Mr. Candy? Cruz, you're big time all the way."

"Is there anything unique about this Mr. Candy that you've heard? Anything usual or strange?"

"Yes, that he's immortal."

Run-Time noticed my expression. He stood from his chair to go into his office's private kitchen to fill up his glass with a beverage.

"I know what you're thinking."

"What?" I asked. Run-Time came back and sat back down.

"Mr. Candy is a machine."

"Why would you say that?"

"Others have thought the same thing. That he's a computer program."

"It's suspected out there?"

"Yes, for a long time."

"When did Mr. Candy first come onto the scene?"

"Decades and decades ago."

"I still think it probably a myth."

"It could be, but I side with the people I know who say he's real."

"Then I have to assume he's real, too."

"Cruz, be careful with this one. He used to be called the Candy Man, way back when he first started on the scene. I'm sure he didn't get much respect with that name, so he upgraded it. The reason for the name was that he could give you anything you desired to hook you, then you'd owe him a favor. But he also used the same strategy against his competition. He'd lure them into something then kill them."

"Has anyone ever been close to identifying him or catching him?"

"Catch what? It's all whispers and rumors. Look at how powerful the Gidrah Corporation was, and none of us ever knew it existed."

"True."

"And if it really is a computer program, how would you catch it? Stop it or slow it down?"

"There's always a human being behind it."

"Doesn't matter. Whether the program is acting alone or for a real person, how would you stop either one?"

"My client feels that it may do more, a lot more."

"I've heard stories like that too."

"What stories?"

"Same motivation as any other illegal criminal gang or legitimate company." Run-Time smiled for a moment. "Expansion. We're always looking to expand and take over other territories where we hadn't existed before."

CHAPTER 22

Tiki

I never went wrong when I spoke with Run-Time. It wasn't only Wilford and Connie that felt it was an AI program. The reason I was so successful in my newfound trade of private investigation was that I always assumed the worst of everyone involved (including clients who hired me) and prepared for all options to be true, even if I felt only one could be true. I had to take Wilford's theory as gospel, even if I felt it was bunk. I had to cover all bases. If Wilford and Connie were right that an evil AI program was preparing to take control of the city, and would soon know that two people (and me) were after it, what did I think would happen? As Polygon said in the Sketchy Squirrel, it would act. I had already dealt with killer cyborgs and killer robots, did I really think a killer AI would send us a box of chocolates and flowers?

"Got your calls made?" I asked Wilford G., who was in the parking bay around the Pony, smoking.

"I did. Did your friend help you out?"

"He did."

"Why don't I drive this time?"

"Why?"

"Cruz, I'm not going to scratch your vehicle."

I threw him my keys.

I monitored his operation of my Pony very carefully. He didn't look at me directly, but he was chuckling, knowing what I was doing.

"Cruz, you do know I was driving vehicles before your father was born?"

"I didn't say anything. I'm just looking."

"You're a curmudgeon in a youngster's body is what you are."

"Where are we going?"

"Mad City."

My heart skipped a beat. "Mad Heights?"

"Cruz, what did I tell you? You have to speak the lingo of the modern day. Mad Heights? Only cops call Mad City by that name. When Mad Heights was first incorporated people didn't call it Mad Heights. Slang, contractions, the lingo of the day."

"I almost got killed in Mad City."

"We'll be fine."

"That place is too dangerous, too many crazy maniacs. The last time I had cyborg bodyguards, and I still almost didn't get out."

"What are you talking about? In my day, it was madder than it is today, far worse. Metro PD wouldn't go near there."

"Yet, we're going there now?"

"Mad City is nothing now. Two street-wise, amply-armed P.I.s. Just make sure you wear your steel groin guard."

I burst out laughing. I didn't know where he came up with these things, but he was serious.

"Don't laugh. Cyborgs in Mad City like to kick you in the nuts. Getting kicked there by an unmodified person is one thing. A big, ol' bionic foot, or a bionic leg. My God, Cruz that's a kind of damage that your great, grand offspring will feel, assuming you're able to make babies ever again. Your whole gene pool will be messed up."

I was still laughing.

I lost my ability to laugh; I could see the place in the distance. When you lived in a supercity, such as Metropolis—the largest on the planet, you knew your place. You knew where your people hung out—working class, wealthy class, sidewalk johnnies, skaters, hackers, racers, whatever the clique or social class. Then there were the mean streets and all the groups that hung out there. You learned where you could go and where you shouldn't, if you didn't want a beat-down or wanted to stay alive.

Like in Hell, the criminal world had its levels of bad, then you got to the really bad, then to true evil; beyond that, you didn't even want to know. Mad Heights wasn't the hangout for the truly evil, but it was for the truly bad and the truly violent.

I didn't care what Wilford said. We were going into Mad City without the bodyguard protection we needed. My next thoughts were of my vehicle. There was no place it could be left. Five seconds unattended and it would be gone, never to be seen again.

"Cruz, you're going to give yourself an ulcer."

"G., there is no way I'm leaving my Pony in this place or near this place. And I don't know why you're driving so nonchalantly into such a seriously dangerous place. We're good, but not that good."

"You worry too much."

We were diving in the vehicle and then we stopped close to the ground. Ahead of us was a giant hovertruck and the back was open. There was Quix again, directing Wilford in. He coasted forward and landed.

We exited and stepped out the back. As soon as we did, the doors closed and two other guys locked it up, and the craft rose into the darkened sky. Then a group of black hovercars descended and landed. Out came armed men in black slickers and silver goggles. Wilford was chatting it up with them—in some other language, of course, with Quix standing next to him.

He turned away and started walking. "Let's go, Cruz. They'll watch our back. I need you to watch my front."

"What remote language do they speak?"

"You really don't have an ear for languages, Cruz."

"Never did."

"Portuguese, Cruz."

"How do you speak all these languages?"

"Cruz, I've been in this city for over 90 years. It's easy. But forget about that. It's show time."

The last time I came to Mad City, I lamented that, with my new career as a detective, I'd need my own muscle for these occasions. Well, Wilford G. had muscle. The armed men following us looked like ex-military. Last time I was here, I hired gang members as my bodyguards and they tried to leave me behind, and much later try to assassinate me. This time I felt confident. I glanced back again and noticed Quix wasn't among them.

When we turned the corner, it was like someone opened a door, and we had passed right through a vortex into another world. It was noisy and flashy; sidewalk hustlers were everywhere, with their backs against the wall in their neon suits and outfits, watching everyone who passed by. There were also lots of dope roaches—drug addicts with their morbidly skinny bodies, scales and sores, bad hair, bad teeth.

I knew about the Shadow Market, the shopping center for the criminal class. The Net version was the Ghost Market, but that was used mostly to traffic stolen information. In the Shadow Market, you bought and took your illegal goods with you at the same time. There wasn't a main Shadow Market; their "outlets" existed all throughout Metropolis, and they were constantly moving, not always successfully, to avoid the police or other criminal gangs.

Wilford moved like he was a gangster, himself. He didn't move out of anyone's way, no matter how big, scary-looking, or armed they were. All of them moved out of his way; it was all attitude—or the ex-military guards with us sporting very big guns.

At some point, it seemed like a game. Around one corner, down the steps of one place, up the steps of another, down hallways, around corners. I had no idea where we were, and I was very good with directions. What I did know was that we had been walking for quite a while. Wilford never slowed his pace and he never said a word.

Finally, we came down a hallway that ended in a large black steel double door. Wilford did nothing but stand there with his hands in his slicker pockets. I glanced back and our bodyguards stood with their laser rifles "ready to rumble" and fingers on the trigger. A door opened.

"Yeah?" a voice came out of the dark.

Wilford reached into the darkness with a card. A gloved hand took it, then the door closed again. When it opened, both doors opened. Wilford stepped into the darkness; I followed. I had quickly reached into my jacket for my night-glasses and put them on. Wilford was following a path that could only be seen with night-glasses; I assumed he had some on too.

We came through a curtain of stringed beads into the light. Immediately in front of us was a fat male ninja sitting in a hoverthrone. He even had a silver scepter in his hand. If it were just him, I would have laughed. However, all around him were other ninja suits—ninja masks, business suits, laser swords. I looked up, and though I couldn't see them clearly in the shadows, there were armed people on the next level looking down at us.

"G-Man," the fat ninja said.

"Tiki," Wilford G. Said.

"You're not dead."

"No."

"I didn't think you were dead."

"That's what people are saying. Can we do business?"

"Money?"

"Money transferred?"

He looked at his wrist display device. "What do you need?"

Wilford handed him a list. The fat ninja stared at the list for a while. He handed it to one of his men, who then handed it to another.

"Why do you need these things?"

"My business," Wilford replied.

"In all my years, no one has every submitted such a list to purchase."

"My money has always been good, Tiki."

"It has, but a seller in my position has to know if there is a need for such items in the market that I was previously unaware of."

"It's a one-off, Tiki. I doubt you'll ever see such a list ever again."

"Which brings me back to my question. Why do you need these things?"

"I pay for items, not for questions. That is how the Market works. Have the rules changed?"

Tiki turned to some of his men and snapped his fingers. "You can wait or come back in two hours."

"We'll wait," Wilford said.

"As you wish." He flew away on his hoverthrone with men following. Others pointed us back to the door. We walked back the way we came. This time, the lights were all on, into the main hallway, then the black double-doors closed.

Wilford pointed, and we all followed him to the end of the hallway, turned the corner, and stopped. He stepped back a couple of steps, put his back against the wall, and looked down the hallway to the door. The bodyguards took positions to secure the corner.

"Hope you don't mind the wait," he said to me.

"Like any other routine stake-out."

"Good man."

All of us waited without any complaints. The two hours went by slowly, but they went. Promptly, we heard a *click* and then the two black doors opened. One after another, an Asian woman was pushing a hovertrolley. They kept coming until they reached us and stopped.

The first woman walked to Wilford and handed him a tablet with a stylus. "Your delivery, sir."

Wilford moved quickly from trolley to trolley, opening the containers, checking each thoroughly; a couple of bodyguards moved with him, one as a human shield and the other in a firing stance. The other guards remained with me; one watched around the corner.

There were more than 30 trolleys, which meant it could be another hour or more to finish the inspection and be on our way. Wilford G. took 90 minutes to finish, and then he made a call on his mobile with the same head woman standing next to him. He hung up, and she dialed into her mobile. I saw her say something, then she hung up and shook G.'s hand. The women marched back through the black double-doors. Wilford powered them up, flipped a switch, and the trolley locked together like a long metal snake.

"Let's go."

Two bodyguards at the end, one on the left, one of the right, the rest with us at the front as we began to run. This was all new to me, and I remembered all the twisting through hallways, down and up stairs we did to get to wherever we were. Wilford led us back the exact same way, and I knew it would take longer to get out of the madness of Mad City. However, the adrenaline was pumping for all of us. We were extremely vulnerable, but we moved fast.

When we emerged back onto the main streets into the rain, we continued to move like an advancing military unit. The street hustlers all had their eyes on us, which I expected. Wilford ignored them and so did the bodyguards.

A man ran to us from ahead. "What's that you have there?" he yelled, and Wilford shot him point blank in the chest.

We rushed past his body on the ground. The crowds in Mad City were not the crowds of normal neighborhoods. No one was running. They stood there and watched us. Finally, we turned the corner out of the main streets into the dark alleys. I remembered what almost happened to me the last time I escaped Mad City.

"G!" I yelled, and he looked back at me.

"Last time, I was here there were people out here waiting to snatch me."

He turned around and starting yelling in another language. Two of the ex-soldiers in front reached into their jackets, and I didn't see what they tossed out ahead of us. I heard bouncing metal on the ground. We all stopped.

"Turn away!" Wilford G. yelled at me.

The explosions were photonic stun grenades. I didn't turn away but did shield my eyes. I wanted to see, and I saw them. It was dozens of people, dressed from head to toe in black, blown back and away.

"Who are they?"

Spotlights appeared on us, then all around us. The Night People were running away into the shadows as three hovertrucks descended. I heard gunfire, turned, and the bodyguards were firing their weapons. I was grabbed; it was Quix and he literally threw me into the back of the hovertruck and jumped in after me. Wilford jumped in too, with half the other bodyguards. The back doors closed, and I felt the hovertruck quickly rising into the air.

A shower of bullets hit the outside hull, but we were safe.

Wilford sat down on the hard steel ground. There was limited light in the compartment.

"Well, that went well."

"That's why I don't go to Mad City," I said.

"This was an easy trip. Always bring your protection, Cruz, and you'll be fine."

"Now what?" I asked.

"We'll see if It reacts," he said with a smile.

PART FOUR

Some Serious Violence

CHAPTER 23

IT

In my last major case, I was like an inter-galactic secret agent. I kept telling people, "I'm a street detective," but so many people weren't listening to me. In the end, I closed the case on my terms. I thought—I wished—I could've conducted this case as I wanted as I did a moving (and illegal) sky-walk (moving from one hovervehicle to another), got back on the hovervehicle containing my Pony, and I let Wilford drive again. He flew out without a hitch. The hovertruck continued forward and Wilford turned east into another sky lane.

"Dial a number of your vehicle," he said to me.

"Who am I calling?"

"Wil."

I glanced at him, as I started to dial. It rang quite a while, but it finally connected, and there stared a very disgusted Wil Jr. on my dashboard viewscreen.

"He told me to call you," I said to him.

"Junior, you can yell at me later. They're back."

"Who's back?"

"The Night People around Mad Heights. I thought we cleaned out that rat's nest for good but apparently not. There's a lot more of them, and they're bolder than ever. Call up the crew and let's make sure we do it right this time."

"When were you there?"

"We just left."

"Okay."

"Thanks, Junior."

Junior wanted to say something more but managed an "Okay" and hung up.

"The Night People are a bad bunch."

"What do they do?"

"Modern-day slavery, Cruz. You join their ranks and can never leave. They're involved in every street crime there is, but drugs and prostitution are their main business."

"How was it actually talking to your son?"

"Cruz, I know where your passenger ejector button is too."

I laughed. "Where to now?"

"Nowhere in particular. It's a waiting game now."

"My friend Run-Time told me this Mr. Candy could be a woman or could be an entire gang using the name."

"Oh yeah. In my career, I've helped put away dozens of male Mr. Candys, female Mr. Candys, Mr. Candy crews, Candy Man crews, Candy Land, anything Candy. I had Connie write a program and any case with the word Candy, I was to be notified. Yeah, I know all the stories. But it could also be the AI."

My dashboard vid-phone rang. "Looks like Wil is calling you back," I said, connecting. The display screen was a blue screen. Suddenly, there was a baby picture, followed by a progression of photos of increasing ages—it was Wilford. The final picture was of him as he was now. Then was a baby picture of me! Then an increasing series of photos of me through elementary, middle and high schools, after, then of me now. A gallery of pictures of men flashed next, all of them with X marks over them with the exception of Connie, Wilford, and me. It went black. Now there was a picture of Earth, a zoom in of the Americas, then of Metropolis, then a section of the supercity, then a district, then an overhead of my Pony! Then my Pony flying in the sky traffic in real time! The words "THANK YOU!" flashed on the screen, then it disconnected.

I had been scared in my life before, really scared. I was feeling that level of panic, my mouth was dry, my body frozen. We heard a noise. My vehicle's proximity sensors were going off.

"What's that?" It was the first time I had heard Wilford scared.

I grabbed the wheel and pulled it with all my might to me. I knew what was happening. The second we veered to the right, a hovervan fell from the sky barely missing us. It's hoverengines were dead.

"Cruz, we need to switch places!"

"There's no time."

"Cruz, who do you think should be driving? A guy who spent most of his adult life in hovertaxis and having a wife drive him around or a guy who built his own hovercraft in his parent's garage and raced hovercars? Switch!"

He was already unbuckling his seatbelt. I kept my hand on the wheel, and I don't know how, but I managed to hop over as Wilford passed behind me. A foot was off the accelerator for only a moment, so the vehicle didn't stall out and plunge.

I was in the driver's seat. I hit a button, and the seat belt auto-buckled. I hit the nitro-accelerator, and we blasted out of there. My only concern was to get away from the public sky-lanes and somewhere that could shield us from satellite surveillance above.

We both saw two different lights in the distance. In a rainy, overcast sky they were like balls of exploding light—explosions. I was already illegally racing over pedestrians twelve feet off the ground and turned hard right into a building's parking bay. No satellite could see us now, and in moments no one would know which building we were in because all these parking bays were connected all throughout the city. I rolled down the window and out went my mobile. I kept racing as I pushed buttons on my dashboard: I severed my vehicle's communication lines; I ejected the vehicle's transponder, then its vehicle identification beacon. I engaged my camouflage cloak, and the Pony went from bright red to muted gray. Another button turned the clear windows to dark tint, another extended exterior parts of the car, and it went from its sleek coupe shape to a box-ish, un-aerodynamic clunker. I pulled into space and stopped. I turned off the engine, set down, and cracked all the windows to listen.

I heard Wilford give a loud sigh. "Cruz, looks like you've done this before."

"It's standard op for any kid whose been on the amateur—meaning illegal—hovercar racing scene. Besides, I like to be prepared. You do know that those explosions were your hovertrucks?"

"Yeah."

"I only saw two explosions, though."

"The third landed right away, and all its cargo was unloaded."

"Unloaded?"

"Unloaded to a team riding hoverbikes. I like to be prepared too."

"So, your It destroyed two-thirds of the items?"

"Maybe."

"Your men?"

"I'm sure most of them got away."

"Most?"

"Well, Cruz, there it is. I've done my part. No human could have done all that so fast. Hope you're convinced now."

"You baited a killer AI and now want to hand it over to me."

"That was the plan. We wanted proof. We have proof."

"No, we have a killer AI, and it knows exactly who's after it. It even has its own kill list, and I'm on it, thanks to you. It seemed to enjoy showing us that it crossed off a bunch of people already and four are left. I counted more than 12 people on that list. Who were the other three crossed off?"

"Other scientists from the Lab."

"Polygon wasn't on the screen. Wouldn't he be in danger?"

"He's gone."

"Gone?"

"Polygon doesn't exist anymore."

"What does that mean?"

"He also worked at the Lab but has been erasing his identity ever since. We don't have to worry about him."

"You're going to tell me more about this Lab, but later. Is Connie safe?"

"She is."

"How do you know? She hasn't been erasing her identity. She's the head of Metro CIC."

Wilford was quiet and not looking at me. "You're right."

"It knows about Tiki. His face was there. Should we bother about him?"

"We should. He does keep some kind of order in that cesspool."

"A good criminal, huh?"

"Saw all those women working for him? They weren't prostitutes. They were employees. The woman I was talking to was his number two in command. He's a killer all right, but sells contraband only, and stays out of the other stuff. You have a long career ahead of you, Cruz. You'll be working with a lot of criminals to close your cases, so you better start learning the good criminals from the bad, because they're all criminals. We need to save him."

"Is there more to the story I should know?"

"There's more to the story, but no you shouldn't know. We need to save him."

"I'm not going back to Mad City."

"Tiki doesn't live in Mad City. He only works there. I know where he lives."

"More secret identities, I imagine. Then there's us."

"Yeah."

"What would be your next move from here?"

"Get Tiki to safety," he said as I looked at him, shaking my head. "What? We'd be walking into a trap? I know that, Cruz, but we can't let the man get killed. We have to at least warn him."

"Where are all the items going?"

"I have a large storage unit in Woodstock Falls."

"Yes, your storage units again."

"I thought it best to have it closest to you."

"Did you have a plan for this kind of situation?"

"Warn everyone."

"We have to do a lot more than warn them. When this whole thing started you created a nice trail of bread crumbs for me to follow. I bet you did the same thing for Wil to prepare him for your return from the dead. You led me to your shoe shop and then waited for me to come. Your AI friend is leaving a nice trail of bread crumbs for you too, and here you go."

"We're smarter than it, Cruz."

"Are we? We're acting in a predicable way. All it has to do is wait for us and then kill us when we show up. So we're not smarter than it. If we want to be smarter, then we have to be unpredictable—that's smarter."

"We get everyone to safety."

"You do realize that I'm taking this situation far more seriously than you. No G., we remove the *food*."

"What does that mean?"

"The AI is going to jump ahead to use all the people we care about to set traps for us. So, we remove all of them from its game board. If there's no food in the place, the rat won't want to be there anymore. It'll go someplace else."

"You're the programmer."

"Your calls better include more than just Quix, Tiki and Connie. It better include your family, your shoe shop friend, and everyone else you know. Anyone it could use to set a trap for you, and that's what I'm going to do on my end."

"Sounds sensible."

"G., you don't seem too excited."

"Hacking into the Earth satellite system and relaying that directly to your individual vehicle's view screen isn't something easily done. Metro PD couldn't do that so fast. I don't think the Up-Top police could either, not so smoothly. What else can it do?"

"We'll find out, but I don't want you to start fainting on me," I said.

Wilford started to laugh. "I've never fainted in my life, youngster." He had his confidence back, which was what I'd wanted. I'd been shaken too, but we had work to do.

"We'll walk from here to public phones. You make your calls, and I'll make my calls."

"First, I'll find out if Quix and the others made it out."

"We also need to get our hands on more weapons."

"Yeah, that would be a smart thing to do."

"Let's go." We got out of the vehicle and I walked to my trunk, which popped open.

"Couldn't It take control of your vehicle or shut off your engines like it did with that hovervan?" he asked

"No, the only thing remote-control with my vehicle is the alarm siren. You need the key engaged."

I threw my fedora in the trunk and took off my slicker. "G., you're going to have to ditch your snazzy shoes."

"I doubt you have my size in your trunk, Mr. Small hands."

I ignored his commentary. "No, but I have snug frubber coverings that reach right up to your knees. Not the height of fashion, but I'm sure you'll survive."

"And you'll want my hat, too, I suppose."

"Hoodies for all, G."

When we changed, we locked up and headed to the open street.

CHAPTER 24

The Mick

The AI knew of me. I didn't like that. It knew Wilford well, whether G. wanted to admit it or not. It didn't know me yet, but was pouring every scrap of data to create a behavioral profile of me. That meant I couldn't be the one to get all my family and friends into protection—I had to have someone else do it for me.

Run-Time had three senior VPs under him that handled different aspects of his business. The Mick, the tall, stout blue-eyed Irishman, handled all confidential security and counter-espionage matters. I didn't want to speak directly with Run-Time, so I called him.

He arrived in a Let It Ride hoverlimo. He normally drove himself, but this time, there was a driver, a bodyguard in the passenger seat, and he was in the back. He opened the door for me to get in.

"I'm on my way to a meeting, Mr. Cruz."

"I won't be long." I handed him a list. "I want you to contract this out to someone other than yourself, trustworthy, but a contractor or firm neither you, Run-Time, or the company has ever worked with before. Don't use a normal line to call it out."

"Intriguing. Have you met Mr. Candy?"

"Run-Time told you. I may have, so I want you to get them all into protection. No need for panic. All we have to do is keep them away from harm should a wayward AI program want to reach out and hurt them or worse. It's easy enough to do in Earth's analog world."

"Lucky we're not Up-Top."

"Then it would be impossible. Gotta love Earth."

The Mick glanced at the names. "I'll have it taken care of, and since Mr. Run-Time does have more interaction with digital systems than the rest of us, I'll modify his routine and upcoming business dealings. When might you deal with Mr. Candy?"

"It's all that simple to you?"

"Mr. Cruz, I'm sure we are of the same mind on this. There's a human behind the machine."

"I'm actually positive of it, but as Run-Time pointed out, it could be a man, woman, one person, or a hundred. However, it does have the machine."

"Machines can think faster than humans."

"But not better."

"Not yet." He smiled.

"When it's handled, I'll let both of you know."

"Happy hunting then, Mr. Cruz. You always manage to find the most interesting cases."

"That's one way to describe them. Have fun at your meeting."

I got out of the hoverlimo. It ascended into the rainy sky and jetted away; I pushed my hands into my pockets and jogged off.

CHAPTER 25

Phishy

The Mick was good at what he did. He was either ex-military, ex-intelligence, or both. I already found out he was a practicing attorney. I knew my family and friends would be more than safe. He'd probably assign a full presidential-level detail to protect all of them, so at least that concern would be taken care of. There would be no "food" for the AI rat to get at in Cruz World.

That left Wilford. I wasn't worried about Connie. In her case, I felt she was in an undisclosed bunker and untouchable. But what about Wil, Mary, and whoever else was in Wilford G.'s World?

We were in one of those 24-hour fast food diners, which doubled as an on-the-go workplace. I rented my own mobile computer (with Wilford's cash), and we watched the archived news. There were plenty of civilian videos of the hovertrucks being blown out of the sky by an air armada of postal drones.

"What are you looking for?" Wilford asked me.

"I'm watching how they move."

"They weren't controlled by any human, Cruz."

"I see that." The postal drones were not moving as a unit. They all were moving separately but with a singular goal—blow the hovertrucks out of the sky.

I scanned for other news, and we found out the poor man who happened to be in the hovervan that almost fell on top of us survived the crash, though he was about the enter the worldwide ranks of cyborgs—at least he lived.

"What about Quix," I asked, "and your men?"

"I haven't heard anything, but that's good. If they were dead, that would be on the news."

"Okay, so they survived too."

"All your people safe to your satisfaction?"

"Yes. What about yours?"

"Wil, Mary, and the grandkids are safe. Polygon and the wives are all that's left."

"Why can't you reach them?"

"Polygon is never reachable by phone. You get to him by intermediaries. The wives, I'm not sure. I can't even reach Perl."

"This is absolutely unacceptable, G. What did you and Connie think would happen if you were right? You were preparing for the evil AI, but you weren't. This is a trap."

"I know that."

"What's your plan then?"

"Cruz, what's our plan? That's why you're here. I have thought this through. It knows me, but it doesn't know you. You're my wild card. It can't anticipate you."

"It almost anticipated the death of us in my Pony. Who do we save first?"

"I don't know where the ex-wives are."

"I know where they are. You don't worry about that."

He smiled. "You've had my ex-wives followed all this time. Good one, Cruz."

"Don't good man me, yet. We don't have them. Guns. We need lots of guns. We get the ex-wives first, then Polygon. You do know that this will be like going into Mad City, but without the bodyguards and air-support?"

"I know."

"I can't believe we're doing this."

"Your call, Cruz. If this is how you feel we should play it?"

"We have to do it this way because it's the most insane, dangerous, and suicidal way to do it. It's expecting intelligence from us, so we have to be stupid, very stupid."

For a 90-something, Wilford G. had stamina. I had a feeling that he could out-run me any day of the week. My vehicle was in "secret mode"—my wife's term—but I wasn't taking any chances. Just because I built it from scratch didn't mean I had any desire to rebuild it again from scratch after a hovertruck falling on it or a million postal drones crashing into it. I also had no desire to be shuttled around Metropolis by hovertaxi, maybe okay for a senior citizen, but not me.

"Most of the world actually enjoys traveling the city by hovertaxi, Cruz," Wilford said to me as we waited.

"Not when a killer AI is after us."

"You're right there. Who are we waiting for then?"

"My people."

When you spent most of your commuting time in hovercraft high above, traveling by foot on the streets of Metropolis was like exploring an alien planet. People looked the same in their dark slickers and colored shades, but if you looked closer, the faces, and listened, the accents, dialects and languages—everyone was different.

Wilford and I were waiting on a corner of an alley. The main street was a congested pedestrian zoo, but the alley was empty as if it was quarantined for the Ebola virus. My people flew in—four hovercars in a row. They hadn't even landed. "Cruz!" Phishy yelled from the passenger window of the first hovercar, hanging out.

"Thanks, Phishy, for announcing to the killer AI where I am," I said under my breath.

"Ah, your sidewalk johnny friend," Wilford G. remarked.

"Phishy is a slider not a sidewalk johnny."

Wilford patted me on the back. "There you go, Cruz. Keep up using the slang of the streets. There's hope for you yet, youngster."

Phishy and his crew landed, and he had already hopped out, wearing some yellow shirt with fishes under his slicker and vest. I had to stop him before he started.

"Phishy!" I held up a money roll in my hand. "Look what I have!"

I got his attention all right. He had that look he got whenever he going to get money.

"Yours if there's no dancing—"

It was too late. Phishy began spinning around, doing his chicken dance. He had his trademark dress. This was his trademark way of greeting me. Wilford G. got a kick out of it, so did Phishy's crew. He knew he was getting the money roll, which is why he ignored me. We let him amuse and tire himself. When he stopped, Wilford led the applause.

"Don't encourage him," I said to G.

"Cruz, I don't have any friends who greet me like that."

"He can be your friend then."

Phishy walked right up to me, smiling. "We're partners, Cruz."

"Partners?"

"Partners in Liquid Cool."

I looked at Wilford. "The man behind the Liquid Cool T-shirts."

Wilford lifted up his shirt to show Phishy. "All I wear."

"See, Cruz. I told you, you have fans everywhere."

"Which one is it, Phishy?"

"Oh." One had to keep Phishy focused. He ran to the clunker at the end. Wilford and I walked to it. "Here's what you asked for, Cruz. Even if Martians were shooting lasers at you, you'd be fine."

"Good." I threw Phishy the money roll.

Phishy snatched it with a look on his face I had seen before. It was like when I threw a piece of chicken to this feral cat as a kid. The cat pounced on that piece of meat as if it had never eaten before and had this look, accompanied by a low, guttural growl. The piece of chicken was in a death-lock in its mouth, and if anything came near it, even its mother, it would scratch its eyes out. Phishy's face looked like that.

But it wasn't over. When Phishy's psycho look passed, then I had to witness more craziness. He turned around and was fiddling with the zipper in his groin area of his pants.

"Phishy, I told you never do that again in my presence!" I yelled.

Of course, Wilford was a laughing mess, and Phishy's crew was having a good time too. Phishy turned around to face me. "Done!" he said.

This time, Wilford G. almost fainted, he was laughing so hard. Phishy's crew was laughing harder.

"Yes, G., fall down, pass out, expire. That would be great. This is what I have to deal with as a street detective. You have Quix and ex-military. I have Phishy and his pants and company."

"Who's Quix?" Phishy asked.

"Never mind." I raised my hand with a folded paper. "There's more, Phishy."

"More?" Phishy ran to me and took the paper. "What is it?"

"A mission I'm entrusting to you."

There was the Phishy twinkle in his eye. "Oh, you can count on me, Cruz."

"I know I can, Phishy, but you have to leave now. It's time sensitive. Read it in your hovercar."

"Oh, okay," he began to run away.

"Phishy—" He stopped. "After you give me the keys."

He began to laugh. "Oh, yeah."

"Oh yeah." One of his crew members threw him the keys, and he threw them to me.

I looked at his man. "Why didn't you just throw me the keys? I wouldn't have shot you."

Phishy hopped in his hovercar and was again hanging out.

"Is the trio still there?"

"Still there, Cruz. My guys have them under surveillance."

"Good. Take care of your new mission."

"I'll be ready, Cruz!"

"Yes, tell that killer AI that we haven't left yet. Thanks, Phishy. Take your crew and get going."

The crew of men weren't the typical sidewalk johnnies he hung around with. They were more like thugs-in-training but not too bright. I would have asked who they were, but then Phishy would lose focus and spend the next hour or two telling me. I needed him in the sky now.

The three hovercars rose into the sky, with Phishy still hanging out of the first, waving.

"G., let's go get those guns of yours."

CHAPTER 26

The Ex-Wives

Wilford's storage unit of guns didn't have the most sophisticated weapons I'd ever seen, but there were a lot of them. Nothing fancy, which was what we wanted. You got shot by these old guns, you stayed shot. Sometimes, older was better.

Before I got sucked into Wilford's AI conspiracy case, my case was a simple "what were the three ex-wives up to?" case. I had Phishy put our Sidewalk Johnny Brigade on it—my own network of the harmless street hustlers of Metropolis.

Perl lived in Old Harlem, Go-Go in Silicon Dunes, but Isis was the leader. I figured that's where the three of them would be plotting how they could find Wilford's secret storage units of money. There was one piece of information that the sidewalk johnnies on stake-out at Isis's Elysian Heights apartment tower told me that gave me pause: the three women hadn't left the apartment in a day and a half. Elysian Heights was where my wife grew up and her parents still lived—when they weren't terrorizing me at our place. It wasn't as upscale as Silicone Dunes, but it was where the wealthy lived. At least, if Wilford and I got into trouble, we could always crawl to my parents-in-law's place.

However, Metro street detectives didn't crawl. With the gray clunker loaner from Phishy, I could park anywhere. Wilford and I loaded up with enough weapons from the trunk to hold off an army. He also had taken note of what the sidewalk johnnies had said and was expecting the absolute worst—that the women might well be dead.

We were about to step into the building with our guns and rifles under our slickers. "No," I said.

"No. What do you mean 'no'?" Wilford asked.

"That's what people do. They walk through doors and use elevators."

It was something that might happen in a place like Free City, but not booshy Elysian Heights. I crashed the hoverclunker through the penthouse bay windows of Isis' apartment faster than the building's security could react. The massive exterior blast doors rose to protect the shattered-out window and the alarms screeched.

I sat in the driver's seat, with Wilford in the passenger seat. We sat quietly looking out. The hovercar was sitting in the living room. There sat the three women, frozen in motion, on a large couch against the wall. Perl was in the center, Isis on one side, Go-Go on the other. In each of their hands were cups of what must have been coffee. How interesting, I thought. If a clunky hovercar crashed through my living room balcony window, my wife and I would be doing a lot more than sitting quietly on the couch drinking coffee.

The lights of the apartment were also flashing. When I opened the door, it seemed like the life was turning on within the women. Their eyes now focused on us. They set their cups down on the glass table in front of them in perfect coordination. I wasn't about to wait to see what they're going to do.

I hopped out and threw it. "Catch!" What we saw next was the stuff of nightmares. Isis' arm extended six feet to catch the stun bomb. She held it away as she crushed it, shorting out something. It half-exploded, but it wasn't the full charge. She dropped it.

"My turn!" Wilford said, which he shouldn't have. Go-Go had "extendo-rama" "super powers" too and knocked him on his back. I knew from previous experience that human versus android means human loses, badly.

"Our turn." We recognized the voice, and I looked to the left. It was the real Isis. She shot Android Isis with some kind of plasma rifle blowing a hole in the chest. The real Perl and Go-Go appeared next to her and opened up a hail of laser fire riddling the other two androids. I saw Android Isis begin to stand back up.

"Enough of this nonsense." I pressed the button of the tiny device in my hand. My portable EMP shock device worked on killer robots; it would work on killer androids. The androids dropped to the floor, lifeless, but everything electronic in the blast wave was fried too. We were all standing in complete darkness.

"Ladies!" Wilford called out.

"We're okay, G." It was Perl's voice.

"We're fine, G.," Go-Go said.

"Everyone, out of the apartment," I said.

We all got to the main door in the darkness and gathered in the hallway, which was still operating. The circuits were shielded from the EMP blast.

"What happened?" Wilford asked, his eyes red. He really had thought the three of them were dead.

"My apartment has a secret vault," Isis said, "where I keep my larger valuables."

"Your paintings," Wilford said.

"My paintings. We hid in there when we curiously saw ourselves coming up in the elevator."

"When?" I asked.

"Yesterday," Perl answered.

"What time?" I asked.

"In the late afternoon sometime," Go-Go answered.

I looked at Wilford. "I bet right after you placed the official order at the Shadow Market. "

"What was that device?" Isis asked. "I didn't know they made portable EMP bombs."

"It was a custom-made job, for when I have to deal with killer robots."

"Give me a hand," I said to Wilford.

"With what?" he asked.

"I want to look at these androids."

"Isn't that dangerous?" Go-Go asked. "They might wake up."

"They don't wake up," Isis said. "Mr. Cruz, turned them off permanently. Or, so we hope."

The apartment was still without power, but we dragged the Isis android out.

"I'll try not to read anything into your choice of androids," Isis said to me.

"You shot it," I said, as I knelt down and inspected it.

"What are you looking for, Cruz," Wilford asked me.

"G., look at this detail. Isis, take a look at this thing. How accurate is it?"

She knelt on the other side of the body and stared at the face, touched the hair, looked up and down the body, then touched a breast.

"Hey, don't make my partner blush," Wilford said.

I gave him a look. "Well?" I asked Isis.

"I can't see any flaws."

I stood up. "Wilford, it—It can make android duplicates on the fly in less than 24 hours—exact duplicates."

"I'd say that's a problem."

"I need my tools." I walked back into the apartment to the hovercar clunker.

"Thanks for destroying my apartment," I heard Isis say.

"Cruz and I were the Cavalry. We were coming to the rescue," Wilford said.

I returned with a small black duffel bag and sat down near the head of the Isis Android.

"What are you doing?" Wilford asked.

"Mr. Cruz is going to see if the android is still receiving or sending signals," Perl said.

Wilford took a knee. "Can you find It if it is?"

"Most people don't know this, but manufacturers always put transponders in their machines, in case it gets lost or stolen. Mobile phones, mobile computers, hovercars. I'm sure our android friends too. So, yes, I could find It."

"Cruz!" Wilford jumped up and clapped. "Where's that Phishy friend of yours? Let's do some dancing! Cruz, is after you android-making, killer AI!"

"Don't be so happy yet, G.," I said somberly.

"Why?"

"We still have to go get Tiki. And you've convinced me the AI is real, but I'm not convinced we're smarter than it yet."

CHAPTER 27

Nobody

Wilford didn't have to lecture me about the need of the street detective to cast a wide net when it came to the kinds of people one would have to work with. I'd already hired gang members to act as my bodyguards the first time I went to Mad City. Also, most of my clients weren't exactly the upstanding citizen types.

Wilford G. was risking his life to save Tiki's because he owed him. Wilford didn't trust him, but he owed him. I wasn't sure how I felt about my formerly-posthumous mentor owing favors to criminals.

All of this was to prove the AI existed. We did. I understood it going after everyone on that list, except for Tiki. The criminal was one of an endless number of brokers. Why go after the criminal? There were a million others to take his place, maybe even his number 2. For me, it was proof of the human behind the machine. For me, it was a hint that this wasn't all about world domination as so many other criminals try to get me to believe. It typically came down to the same, simple age-old vices, chief of which was greed.

Our hoverclunker was easy for me to repair; Isis's apartment was another story, but where we sent them to keep out of harm's way, they would soon forget all about it. Wil Jr. put them all in police protection in a swanky safehouse, guarded by single male officers. I felt good that Wilford called his son again, and at least Wil seemed glad to get the call. Finally, we were headed out of Downtown Metro in the congested sky traffic, again headed to another district of Old Metro I had never been to.

"Next time you decide to use this hovercar as a projectile, give me more warning," Wilford said to me.

"It worked didn't it. If you were caught off-guard, it would have been surprised too."

"Cruz, I'm not linked to this AI."

"I think it knows how you think."

"Well, I can't say I necessarily disagree with you there. It was another one of the reasons I went underground."

"What were you doing, while you were underground?"

"Making sure it couldn't escape this time."

"Escape?"

"Escape to Up-Top. When we end it here, it's over."

"But it had access to Earth security satellites. That's Up-Top jurisdiction."

"Don't worry about that. Connie will make sure it can never do that again. She's probably trying to trace it as we speak."

"What was this Lotus Lab?"

"Is. It's still in operation. It's where the cyber-scientists get to play with their AI creations in controlled environments. It's a joint-program of governments around the world and the Council of Corporations."

"How much of my taxpayer dollars is being wasted?"

"Tons."

"I bet you didn't care about things like that before."

"I'm a business owner and diaper buyer now. I care now. Is this Lab something I should be concerned about?"

"No. Everything stays in there."

"But you said this AI was created in there."

"That was over 50 years ago, Cruz. Different era, different people and city leaders. They all believed it was dealt with. Only four people know otherwise. And only two can stop it."

I pulled out of the sky traffic and found an open parking lot to set down in, located in a nearby market square.

"Why did we stop?" Wilford asked.

I was thinking. "We're the only two that can stop your killer AI?"

"Yes."

"Polygon is gone?"

"He's out of it."

"Connie?"

"Connie is great, but she doesn't do well outside the office. It's you and me, Cruz, man. Against the machine."

"Where does Tiki live?"

"The Byzantine. Cruz, the two of us can do this alone. We bring bodyguards, it'll know. I know the place well. If anything is off, we'll walk. We won't even go into the building."

The Byzantine was an old, predominately Asian district that looked like it was designed to be a real a maze. All the buildings were white, rare in Metropolis, and there didn't seem to be any reason for street design—short, long, circular.

I set down the gray hovercar clunker in a wide-open lot and we walked. The plan was to stay in the crowds of people. As we neared Tiki's residential building, I saw the real reason that Wilford was so "brave"—across the street was also a police outpost. They used to be quite common in Metropolis—small, one-story police outposts manned by beat cops to foster neighborhood communication and be a very visible and permanent presence.

"We won't go in the building," Wilford said. "We'll have him come out." He showed me his hand—on it was a neural scrambler. He put his hand back in his pocket. "But before we do that, where's the little boy's room."

"G., you have to be kidding me."

"Cruz, the bladder is not what it used to be."

I followed him as he walked into a corner open restaurant. Different Asian languages were being spoken all around me. Wilford probably could speak all of them. There he was talking another language to a waitress, and she pointed him to the back. I was not about to let him go anywhere alone. The bad news was my phobia about public restrooms remained. My last incident, which I nicknamed Jabba the Butt, left me scarred for life, even though I was making such good progress. The good news was that it was one of those open bathrooms, at least for the urinals, and that's where Wilford went. You could see the backs of everyone, and I always felt it was constructed that way so that people could see that you indeed washed your hands.

"Ah, Mr. Cruz." I heard a voice, and I slowly turned.

Two kids were smiling, both wearing Liquid Cool T-shirts. These T-shirts were going to be the death of me. "Picture, please, sir?" the little boy asked.

"Sure, yes."

I took my picture with the boy and girl. They couldn't be happier, and they walked back to a table where everyone waved and gave me thumbs up. I turned my attention back to the restrooms, and there was Wilford washing his hands and came out, smiling.

"I'm ready to work," he declared.

Back we went toward the residential towers. Wilford pointed to one building. "He's on the seventh floor."

Wilford and I stepped back to look through the large windows. We didn't see anyone.

"Are you sure he's here?"

"He's here. If he wasn't, the curtains wouldn't be open. Go ring the bell. The name is, surprise, Tiki. He always goes to the window to peek to see who it is." Wilford pointed, and I saw the shop across the apartment tower gave a good reflective view of people in front of the tower.

"Sure," I said and walked to the main entrance to ring the bell.

I took out a new throwaway mobile phone from my pocket that I had Phishy get me and dialed on audio only.

"Cruz!" Phishy answered.

"Do it."

"What?"

"Do it now."

"Cruz, but you said—"

"Do it now, Phishy. Seriously, right now."

"Okay."

I hung up, walked up to the steps, reached for the doorbell, stopped, and turned around. Wilford looked at me confused. "What's wrong?" he yelled.

The bomb dropped.

EMP-bombs were prohibited on Earth and Up-Top, except for law enforcement, but as with most things, they could be bought on the black market. I had used a portable one twice, but I had never experienced a big one. The wave that erupted from the bomb that Phishy's hovercar dropped ten feet from me had an effective radius of 100 feet, and the accompanying heatwave knocked me off my feet. It didn't hurt, but it was a sensation I never felt before—almost tingling, slightly warm.

When I sat up. Nothing was moving—nothing. I jumped up, and Wilford was...off. Every man, woman, and child was off. It was a city of androids.

I ran as fast as I could back to the open restaurant. Everyone were androids, sprawled everywhere, including the cute children. I ran into the restrooms, despite my phobia. I looked everywhere.

"Wilford! Wilford!"

I stopped and listened. I thought I had heard something. I yelled his name again. There was a thud. I ran to the wall and put my ear to it. The speed that I ran out of the bathroom and around the restaurant must have been a record. Bodies were lying on the ground everywhere. I came around the back, threw open the door, and there I saw several men on the ground. I looked at one and he was staring up at me, bound, gagged, and in tears. I yanked off the gag on his mouth.

"Where's Wilford?"

"We have to run!"

"Where's Wilford?"

"There's no time!"

"Who are you?"

"I'm nobody!"

"I'm not leaving without Wilford!"

"There's no time! The city doesn't exist! It's made to kill us!"

CHAPTER 28

G.

Anger welled up inside of me. As I held the man, his eyes widened in fear, but not from me. I looked up and from the upper floors of all the buildings people were leaning out of windows and over balconies. I had a sick feeling in my gut as I stood. The man jumped up and bolted.

"No need to run," I said. "We could never get away in time."

We were in a city of androids, and they were all jumping from their specific floors that were outside the EMP blast radius at me. From the corner of my eye, I saw it. Phishy's hovercar was racing to me. I looked at the shower of androids falling to me—who would arrive first?

I pulled my gun and shot the man in his leg. He collapsed, and Phishy's hovercar swooped in and I jumped into the backseat as someone opened the door and pulled me in.

"Phishy, get that man!"

The hovercar lurched forward, but one android hit the top of the roof, then a second.

"Grab that man! Don't worry about them!" I yelled to the man in the back, who looked like he was clearly out of his depth from the panic on his face.

He reached out to grab the man I shot. I saw an arm reaching down from the roof and fired. I blew the arm off. Phishy was hanging out of his passenger seat too, and he saved the day again by grabbing Mr. Nobody. The driver reached over to help Phishy pull him in. I snatched the useless associate in the backseat with me back in, then pulled the door shut.

"Phishy, close the door!"

He did. I leaned forward to the driver and whispered in the driver's ear. "If you don't get out of this city in two seconds, we're all dead."

The driver let go of Mr. Nobody, grabbed the steering wheel, and pounded the accelerator with his feet, then he hit a switch. The hovercar rocketed off, and we saw two figures fall off the trunk. I had been in the hovercar racing scene; the hovercar had an advanced nitro-accelerator better than my Pony, which meant it was faster and more illegal. Androids continued to fall from the sky, but they weren't falling haphazardly; they were falling feet first, arms outstretched to grab onto the hovercar despite our speed. But we made it. We were already out of the city.

There was a flash.

The city was exploding, and there was nothing for us to do but pray as a wave of fire and heat came at us.

I regained consciousness and glanced around. The hovercar had crashed to the ground and was upside down. We were very lucky because we had been flying close to the ground. The driver was buckled into his seat, hanging upside down; the rest of us were lying around on the bottom.

"Phishy, are you alive?"

His head moved, but his eyes were still closed. "I think so."

"Where's your mobile?"

His eyes were still closed but he reached in his pocket for it then handed it to me.

I dialed as I looked at the screen. "Hello, I'd like to schedule a hovertaxi pick-up please." They were all looking at me.

The hovertaxi was speeding, and I knew we probably had little time. My only advantage was that It didn't know what I knew. I had already been to a city where the buildings were really giant robots—that was Silver City. Now, I could say I had been to a city built by robots crawling with robot-made androids designed to kill. How was I, as a simple Metropolis street detective getting caught up in these things?

We were in a deluxe hovertaxi. In the backseat was me, Phishy and Mr. Nobody. In the middle seat was Phishy's associate, who had been driving and two other associates. We had already arrived in Whiskey Way, which was one of those crime hot spots of the city. In my hand was a locator device. Phishy was, of course, noisy as always, watching it as closely as I was.

"Driver, go up another 100 feet on the left," I called out.

"Whatever you say, Mister," he said.

All the streets of Whiskey Way were dark, even with the neon signs.

"Stop here!" I yelled. The hovertaxi stopped and then slowly landed on the ground. It was like so much of the neighborhood—lots of business establishments, but few had visible names. I hopped out and walked around the hovertaxi. The driver took notice of the big gun in my left hand but seemed more interested in the money in my right hand. "Here you go. I added a tip for putting up with us."

"Thank you, sir." He took the money. "You be careful now."

I looked to see that everyone was with us, including Mr. Nobody. The hovertaxi lifted into the sky fast and was gone. I walked up to Mr. Nobody. "Who are you?"

The man no longer had his frightened of the world look. It was a hardened squint—a man who had seen danger before and was not scared of it at all.

"You are Tiki," I said.

"Why are we here?" he asked. "How do we find G-Man?"

"You want to find G-Man?"

"Of course!"

I looked at everyone. "I'm going in and understand that anyone I see, I'm going to shoot. You all can stay here and keep a look-out."

"I'm going in too," Mr. Nobody said.

"Why would I give you a gun?" I asked.

"They kidnapped me and tried to kill me!"

"For all we know, you were the bait!" I yelled.

"Bait! Did I look like I was willing bait! And you shot me in the leg! Yes, I am Tiki. I'm going in whether you give me a gun or not."

"Phishy, you and your men watch the front. We're going in."

"Okay, Cruz," Phishy said.

"No gun for you!" I snapped at Tiki. He smiled, but followed me into the establishment.

I noticed something across the street. I could see the glow of the tip of an e-cigarette. At least two people were standing there, about twenty feet away.

"Mr. Cruz, you don't have to worry about anyone here." It was the Phishy associate I dubbed as useless, because he couldn't grab a man from the ground into a floating hovercar. I always had to remind myself that the average person couldn't do what I did. Phishy was a hustler not a criminal, so that meant he hung around the same kind of people. I had to remember, just because a person could shoot a million advancing evil cyborgs in some virtual life simulation (or VL sim, since Wilford G. said I had to use more contractions) didn't mean they could shoot one in real life. "In this part of town, everyone stays out of each other's business," he said. He was absolutely right. The thing about Whiskey Way was that you almost never saw anyone on its streets. Lots of crime, but to the outsider, it looked like a ghost town. It was a place for the low-key criminal class, who didn't want to show off, didn't want attract attention, and didn't want anyone to know they existed.

We were at a warehouse of some kind, and I shot the lock off the main door. It probably had a silent alarm, but I didn't care. It was large and empty, but I followed the indicator as Tiki stayed close, limping behind me.

There was a small office, and we slowly entered. I looked down at the indicator and looked around the office. I was confused.

"The vault," Tiki said. He seemed to know what to look for and walked to one wall. I touched the wall and then we both felt around. I found the switch and the wall rose up to reveal a large vault door.

I was about to blast it, but Tiki raised his hand to stop me. "Don't do that. Unless you know where to shoot, you'll make it worse. It'll activate its countermeasures then we'll never get in."

I took out Phishy's mobile and began to dial.

"Who are you calling?"

"The best safe cracking operation on the planet."

"How much will they charge?"

"Hello, Metro Police."

Tiki threw up his hands in disgust.

The police arrived in force. I counted no less than twelve police cruisers on the scene. It was a busy night for Metro PD with a fake city blowing up. As usual, there were police officers who knew me on sight, and they allowed both Tiki and me to stay in the room as they prepared to breach the safe; Phishy showed up too.

The machine they used flash-froze the vault door to dust in seconds. Two officers entered and yelled out for the medics. They lifted out a body that was wrapped up like a mummy. Tiki and I stood there holding our breath as the police unwrapped the body; it was moving. They got most of the wrapping off his head; it was Wilford G. He was alive! Shaken, eyes red, but he was alive.

We were all at Metro General Hospital in Downtown. Everyone else waited in the hallway, while I got to talk to him privately. He had been checked over by medical staff, and he was fine. The police would arrive any time to take his formal statement. I sat on the chair next to his bed, and he had refused to change into a hospital gown, but had no objections to stripping down to his briefs. At least he was under the covers so I couldn't see his Liquid Cool T-shirt either. On the bed's tray table he had a large, half-empty glass of water.

"All that lecturing you gave me about having to work with the bad to do good. Tiki is your son."

"Why would you say that?"

"I noticed you didn't deny it."

"It's complicated."

"Complicated, huh?"

"Cruz, you've been a private detective for only three years. Come talk to me when you get to year 30. Life gets complicated, even if it didn't start out that way."

"G., if I get to year 30 and it's that complicated, then I'll retire and go raise bees in London Prime."

"Whatever, Cruz."

"You have one son who's a leader in law enforcement and another who's a leader in the crime world. What other surprises do you have walking around?"

"It's not like that. He's my step-son. I was married to Tiki's mother. Perl is actually my second ex-wife. But I was only married to Tiki's mother for a month. I never counted it. We were kids, then she died."

"Wilford G., you're a walking soap opera. I knew there was more to you wanting to rescue Tiki, the crime lord."

"He's not a crime lord."

"I'm sorry. He's a good criminal."

"What did you tell the police about this?"

"What do you think? I told them everything. Killer AI, androids, Mr. Candy, everything. Did you and Connie really think this was the kind of thing to keep to ourselves? Why wouldn't you tell the police?"

"Cruz, I'm not a doofus."

"Doofus."

"What?"

"You even talk like me."

"I talk like you? No, youngster. If you're using old geezer terms like doofus, then you're talking like me."

"Something of this magnitude you're keeping to yourself."

"We did tell the police, Cruz! Connie's ex worked with law enforcement. No one believed us."

"Even though you said Connie's ex worked for a group that stopped something similar before?"

"Yes, even with that. They didn't believe us; they didn't want to believe us. It was politics. They didn't want to acknowledge anything that would remind people that The Crash, or something like it, could ever happen again."

"Well, the killer AI is finished. It can exist all it wants. It can't do a thing anymore. Everybody knows now, even Up-Top. I'm going to give an official statement that's going to paint this whole situation in the worst, scariest light possible."

"Yeah, I've seen you on TV. You're very good at the media stuff. You can bring down an entire criminal empire by simply giving an interview."

"Why not? If I can end a case with words, rather than dodging killer androids raining from the sky, why wouldn't I do that instead?"

"How did you find me, Cruz?" Wilford's voice had changed. It was almost a whisper.

"I never believed for a second that it would let us walk in there and back out. It was more than a trap. I told you. It was you. It was leaving you your trail of bread crumbs for us to follow, then exterminate us. I was certain of it."

"Then why didn't you stop."

"I was watching you. I wanted to know why you didn't stop. Now I know. Your son, step-son. Parents always do the dumbest things to save their children. It's one of the principles of the universe.

"It profiled you, G. It profiled me. Then it created the perfect lure and trap. That city it created?"

"Yeah?"

"That was created years ago. The people would have been created years ago too. It was its contingency plan for you, Connie, Tiki, and anyone else. Tiki gave me the whole story on how he got captured. It was a business meeting. 'Oh, let's try a new meeting place.' 'Let's meet in the Byzantine,' his business client told him. Even the most paranoid criminal doesn't count on an entire city being a trap—a trap of androids. There aren't supposed to be any androids on Earth; they're illegal, let alone a city of them.

"Then you had to go to the bathroom."

"What?"

"I been around you long enough, G. I know when you usually go to the bathroom, not to be too personal. There we were, going to Tiki's place, then you had an uncontrollable urge to go to the bathroom."

"How could they make me do that?"

"G., it's a psyops trick. I bet every neon sign in that city was flashing a subliminal message to you that you needed to go to the bathroom, maybe even audio suggestion too—sounds of running water or flushing urinals, sounds only you could hear. Then me—the germophobe who's terrified of the public restroom. I knew that's when they were going to snatch you. We go to the restroom, and then I suddenly get distracted by a couple of kids who want a picture with me. I didn't expect to see you when I turned around, but when I did, I knew it wasn't you."

"You figured all that out."

"That's what I do, G. Lucky for you, I implanted a homing device on you."

"That's how you did it. What if they found it?"

"They didn't, and I planted more than one on you just in case."

"I could have been killed this time."

"But they didn't. Why didn't they? They needed you alive for something. What was it going to do, I wonder?"

"I know." From his expression, I knew that he had done his own figuring out of things. He did know.

"How does one create an entire neighborhood in the city and no one notice?" I asked. "I should talk. How does a group of freaks like the Night People exist and no one do anything about it? I knew about them when I first started as a detective, and I forgot. Forget or purposely forget."

"Cruz, we can't be expected to do the right thing every single time. We're human."

"I should have done something then."

"It's taken care of now."

"The smartest thing you did was bring me in on this, then I brought in my cast of crazy friends. We introduced an anomaly into the equation. Programs don't like anomalies because we're unpredictable. It can't 'delete' the unpredictable."

"No, it can't."

"Since the killer AI is something we don't have to worry about for a while, we can shift to my interest in the case—that human behind the program. You said you know who that person is."

"I do."

"I'm going to hope he or she isn't more Wilford G. offspring running around."

"No need to be offensive. He's the great-grandson of the cyberpunk anarchists responsible for The Crash, very wealthy and annoying. I told you the I.T. departments of Metropolis are the source of the evil. It's because of him. It's not the law but has become de-facto law because of mandatory liability and confidentiality breach insurance. Every I.T. department, of every government agency, of every megacorp, multinational department has to be certified, knowing and complying with the latest and strictest cyber-security protocols and measures. Who do you suppose does that platinum-level credentialing? Earth governments and the Council of Corporations don't agree on much, but they agree on this. His firm is the sole official certifying and credentialing body for all the information tech departments of the city of Metropolis. His firm trains and re-trains all the I.T. techs in Metropolis—only his. How do you suppose such a thing could happen, Cruz? I've been warning the city about this man for 50 years."

PART FIVE

He's the Bad Guy

CHAPTER 29

Dot and Jr.

Two police officers had arrived to take Wilford G.'s official statement. I was in the hallway with Phishy and his crew. Tiki was sitting in a hoverchair; his leg had been worked on by a doctor. It took that doctor all of 10 seconds to repair his wound, but Tiki was still giving me the evil eye. I walked over to him.

"I thought you were one of the androids," he said to me.

"Did you now. What would you have done if you had known it was me?"

"I was explaining why I was scared. You had no right to shoot me!"

"I didn't know who you were, and you wouldn't tell me, then you were running away, so I shot you."

"You're lucky you saved me, or I'd get even."

"Getting even is what criminals know."

"I'm not a criminal. I'm a businessman."

"Whatever you say. So, what are you going to do to help your stepfather?"

Tiki's expression was a combination of surprise and disgust.

"He didn't have to tell me. I figured it out. What are you prepared to do against these maniacs?"

"Tell me who they are and I'll take care of it."

"Now you're talking my kind of language. This whole business isn't over by a long shot. Once I know who the bad guy is, I'll make sure you know who the bad guy is. I'm sure you have the same philosophy as me. If a guy tries to kill you once, don't give them an opportunity to ever do it again."

"Same philosophy."

"I got a job for you then. Phishy, come over here because I have a job for you too."

Phishy ran over with his men. "What do you got for me, Cruz?"

"Phishy, you were there. How does someone construct an entire neighborhood, buildings that tall, crawling with androids more life-like than we've ever seen in our lives, and no one knows about it. What does the street say about that? That's your job, Phishy. How did androids take over an entire neighborhood?"

"That's scary, Mr. Cruz," one of Phishy's associates said.

"Yes, it is. Find out for me and report back. And be careful."

He smiled. "I'm always careful, Cruz." He was already running with his men to the elevators.

I could see the police wrapping up with Wilford in his hospital room.

"Tiki, I have a much more devious task for you. Put the word out on the streets that someone has access to a killer AI to take over people's turfs, people's operations, legitimate and not. Even using it to kill people with accidents and create robots and androids to take a more direct approach. All those items you sold to G., use all the best lies; say things like 'the rumor on the street is,' 'I heard so-and-so say' so people believe it and feel threatened."

"If done right, maybe even rightly scared." Tiki was on my wavelength.

"I'm thinking everybody should know how to kill killer AIs and their android soldiers. What do you think?"

Tiki gave me a very devious smile. "I think so, too."

"You think you can handle that?"

"Consider it handled."

"The police are finished with your stepfather. I'll find out who the bad guy really is."

I noticed coming down the hall from the elevators was Quix, with a whole new crew with him. Quix looked pissed. Good!

The police officers left, and I thanked them as I walked in and closed the glass door behind me.

"What did you tell the police?"

He was grinning. "I told the cops what I could."

"Quix is here. He has a new crew."

"Good. We have our bodyguards back."

"We'll need them until this whole thing is wrapped up." I was back sitting in my chair near his bed.

"Where did all that psyops analysis bit come from? About the subliminal suggestions and bathrooms?"

"I'm taking profiling classes."

"Profiling. Like a Fed? A Fed profiler?"

"Yes, G. I'm going to be like a Fed profiler."

"The boy's in college!"

"I don't believe in college. I believe in learning. Connie pulled some strings to get me into the course."

"Well, look at you. I never heard a Metro street detective who's also a fed profiler. You got that Up-Top weaponry. Connie told me you're memorizing the faces of all the criminals in Metropolis, and she didn't think you were crazy. Cruz, you're going to be quite dangerous soon."

I laughed. "Glad the mentor approves of the mentee. What was Connie going to tell me at the office about this evil counterpart? Is he the bad guy?"

"You don't forget a thing. Evil counterpart. Even without her ex, and I can't remember how she first came to suspect it, she learned there was someone out there like her—but on the criminal side. She called him the Professor. Later when we put it all together her nickname was right on the money. He is a professor."

"A teacher?"

"Teacher of the Decade for the supercity of Metropolis. Founder and CEO of I.T., teaching and certifying the heads of every I.T. department and division in Metropolis—for 50 years."

"Why would they allow him, with his background, in such a role?"

"Why Cruz? Because you can't discriminate against a person because their great grandfather was one of the criminal psycho anarchists who hacked, then destroyed the Net, and brought down the world. That's illegal. It's against civilization and all the principles we stand for."

"What's the real reason they ignored you for 50 years?"

"I don't know."

"What's your theory?"

"He was blackmailing the right people."

"Are we talking about Mr. Candy again? Is this I.T.S. Founder Mr. Candy?"

"How would we prove it?"

"Do you believe he is?"

"Some years I did; others I didn't. What never changed was that the AI was there, waiting, and he was the one behind it."

"Are we after one human or two?"

"One. But the AI was here before Venn was here."

"Venn?"

"Mr. Venn, the Founder and CEO of I.T.S."

"I know that guy."

"Of course, you do. You've probably seen him on TV or maybe even in person."

"He's the bad guy?"

"Yes."

"When are we going to see him?"

"What? Is that how you play things, Cruz? You go right up to the bad guy and tell them you're on to them."

"Yes, then it's a sure thing they'll do something stupid."

"Yeah, like shooting you."

"G., they already tried to have an entire city blow us up, sent postal drones after us, dropped hovervans on top of us, and sent killer androids after us. You're worried about getting shot? We stroll in and look him in the eye, and I'll say, 'You're the bad guy and we're taking you down.'"

"Sure he won't laugh at us?"

"He won't laugh. He'll smirk, but only in our presence. Then, when he's alone, he'll go into a psychotic fit, yelling to himself, how did I not kill these guys? How are they not scared of me? How do they know I'm the bad guy? Things like that. Then he'll do something stupid, and we'll get him."

"Your reasoning makes sense, Cruz, except for one thing. I've been after him for 50 years. I've done exactly what you're saying, and he laughed at me."

"But now there's two of us, and he isn't getting any younger. He can't be patient anymore because there's something he wants to do, or we're closing in on something he doesn't want us to know. Let's rattle him and find out."

"Yes, but not today. Don't you have a family to see?"

"Oh." I had completely forgot about Dot and Cruz Jr.

"Senility already, Cruz. You're supposed to be the youngster."

I stood from my chair. "I've been working the case."

"Okay, okay. You don't have to convince me. I was there. Just remember, I have three ex-wives."

"Four."

"Need I say more?"

I was so glad I had driven the Pony to what I would always refer to as the killer town. To quote a common line, if I had to do all over again I would, but I wouldn't do it a second time. If my prized possession had been blown to bits, I wouldn't have built a new Pony. I'd have to buy a hovercar. The time and precision it took to build a classic hovervehicle was time I no longer had with a business and a family. But it was good to be flying through the sky in it. Wilford was in the passenger seat. Quix and crew were in three hovercars, following.

The Mick had a full security detail at the Concrete Mama, also known as home. A chunk of a granite apartment tower in Rabbit City that could take a planetary shockwave from a nuclear blast or a direct hit of an asteroid crash. My apartment there was my legacy housing willed to me from my maternal grandparents. When I got married, we switched my 100-story domicile for a larger one on the 150th floor—the previous occupants, an elderly couple, welcomed a smaller, easier to manage place.

I was able to take my room number with me—number 9732. Quix came up with us in the elevators and waited in the hallway with The Mick's security—men in suits. Inside I went and immediately saw a living room full of people around the TV—Dot, my parents, and her parents (also known as the Hell Spawn). I just heard laughing and little feet, and there was Cruz. Jr. running to me. He lifted his arms to be picked up.

With Cruz, Jr. in hand, I began to introduce Wilford G. to everyone, but I was getting distracted. Wilford was having a conversation with my son, and not in English.

"What are doing?" I said to him. "Stop talking to my son when I'm introducing you to people."

"Your son is going to be a fine linguist."

"How do you know that?"

Wilford then started speaking Chinese with my wife and the Hell Spawn, and then Spanish with my parents.

"Oh, good grief, I'm leaving," I said, and they all started to laugh, even Cruz. Jr.

I always had to remember that as a top Metropolis fashionista at the Eye Candy, my wife had access to as much intel as Phishy did from the streets. Wives and girlfriends loved to gossip while they got their hair, face, and nails done.

"I thought you weren't talking to him," Dot said.

"Wil is talking to him again, so I can."

We'd left Wilford in the living room with the parents, watching TV. The man was speaking Spanish and Chinese like a pro. He was even making jokes, that they laughed at.

Dot had Cruz. Jr. sitting on her lap, and we were all at the kitchen table.

"How's the security?"

"Cruz, bodyguards everywhere I go?"

"It wasn't necessarily for you. I had to make sure there was no possibility that anyone could get to you. What do you know about—Mr. Candy?"

She smiled. "Why do you think I'd know anything about the criminal world?"

I took out my small notebook from my jacket and got ready to write. "Do tell."

"Well," she began, "he's been collecting favors for ages."

"What kind of favors?"

"Blackmail favors."

"How do we know he's a he or even one person alone?"

"The people who know about him are always very positive about it."

"As if they owe Mr. Candy a favor?"

"Yes."

"Are they scared of him?"

"Terrified."

"That he'll hurt them."

"Not violence. Exposure. He has the kind of info on them that will ruin them."

"Yes, the rich and powerful fear that more than violence."

"Not just them. Lots of people."

"Lots of people? Like who?"

"Silver and black people."

I looked up. "Police?"

"And red and black."

"Firemen?"

"Everyone."

"What are you saying?"

"I'm saying he has collected favors from lots of people, not just rich—government, politicians, business, police, fire, Feds—"

"Feds?"

"Yep."

"How do you know all this?"

She smiled. "Cruz, I listen. Most of my job is listening."

"Is this Mr. Candy—dangerous? With all these favors, is he dangerous?"

"Maybe. If he's collecting all these favors, who knows what he could make people do."

"Police and Feds?"

"Yes."

"Even with the Police Watch?"

She nodded.

"Dot, I thought he was doing this to criminals only."

"Criminals? He's been collected favors from criminals too. Cruz, then you could have a problem."

"I'm seeing that now."

"Does he know you're investigating him?"

Clearly, I was not going to tell her about the exploding city. "He might."

"Cruz!"

"It's not me. It's Wilford G.'s case."

"Wilford G.!" she called out.

"What did I do this time?" he called.

Then the rapid-fire Chinese began. I took Cruz Jr. from her. "Cruzie, time to leave. Let's play with your toys."

CHAPTER 30

PJ

I had been off-base. I thought this was confined mostly to the criminal world. Based on my conversation with Run-Time, I thought it also included the shady corporate world. But based on my wife's intel, I was beginning to think that maybe this whole thing was much, much bigger than we had originally thought.

He thought it was probably low-level corruption, but my wife mentioned Feds. That was not low-level corruption; that would be de-facto high level. Blackmail a Fed with what? And blackmail a Fed to do what?

PJ also lived in the Concrete Mama on the 20th floor, but she had been spending most of her time at the office. She came up, and I met with her in my home office. Again, Wilford G. was annoying me, now speaking French with her.

"G., go away. I want to speak to my secretary in peace, and I don't want to hear any French."

They laughed. "Oh, Cruz," he said. "You have bullet holes near your front door." PJ started laughing.

"G., go away."

"I'm going."

PJ stepped into my home office and closed the door. I sat down at my desk; she sat down in the side chair.

"You didn't tell him about the shoot-out in your place with the killer robot."

"It was a misunderstanding with a friendly robot."

"Android," she corrected.

After what I had experienced, my definition of android had dramatically changed. "The humanoid robot."

"What happened?" she asked.

"I called you in here for a job." I handed her a list.

"I'm about to tell you something confidential."

She inched forward. "What?"

"I need you to make the Liquid Cool offices android-proof, and I need you to build us some android-killing weapons."

"What are you talking about, Cruz?"

"Call Phishy and ask him."

"Stupid man? Why would I call him?"

"Humans can't make life-like androids, but what about robots?"

"What? Killer androids?" She looked at the list.

"Neural scramblers are devices that fit over your hand. They emit very strong E.M. fields that can disrupt machinery. You pass it over an android's face or go to shake their hand, and you'll instantly know it's an android."

"What? They can fool people?"

"We need more portable EMP devices. Get Bugs to give us more, much more, so we can fend off any killer robots or killer androids in the future."

"What about me? My arms."

"Oh, that's right."

"*Hello*, I have cool, buff bionic arms, with my own personal modifications, but they won't be cool anymore with this."

"Okay, only I can use them then, but get them. Wait—what modifications?"

"Never you mind."

"PJ, you remember what happened when the police caught that cyborg client of ours with illegal cyborg modifications."

"Yes, Bionic Betty. I remember her. She punched my arms out. That's why I got my modifications, and I'm not going to get flash-frozen by cops either. What about the scanning arches over the doors? That will catch them."

"Yeah, that should, but I want the list. Here's one you could use too. The ROS controllers—robot operating system controllers. Fire one of those at them, clamps on, and you can control them like a puppet, or at least keep them from moving to you."

"Have you used these yet?"

"Just the EMP device and the EMP bomb."

"Bomb? When did you use the bomb? How come I wasn't invited?"

"Invited? PJ, we were almost killed. Don't tell Dot. All of this is confidential."

"Will you be using an EMP bomb again?"

"No, PJ."

"I want to see."

"Here's my favorite one. The nano-tech weapon."

"What?"

"Fire the nano-stream at them and tiny robots take down the big robot."

"Cruz, that's extremely dangerous. What if they get into the office security monitors, the security arch, the coffee maker, the fridge, they could destroy your whole office."

I obviously hadn't thought this through carefully. "Maybe you're right."

"What if they got into the elevator, or...the Pony?"

"Okay. No nano-stream weapon."

"Some things are illegal for a good reason, boss."

"No nano-stream weapon."

"Like nuclear bombs."

"That was not on the list."

"How am I supposed to get these? Beside the EMP devices."

I placed a key on the desk. "We already have them, and they are in a storage unit. I'll leave it to you to get what we need to the office and leave the nano-weapons there."

"I feel very uncomfortable as a cyborg with this task, boss, very uncomfortable."

CHAPTER 31

Quix

In my last major cast, I lamented over the fact that I was supposed to be a simple street detective but had been thrust in a role that had more to do with an intergalactic secret agent than anything else. I did manage to have some fun with it, even enlisting Dot and Cruz. Jr. in a small (and safe) role. This time I was like a military commander. Once again, I was holding my meeting in my home office, but this time, Wilford G. and his man, Quix, joined me at my desk.

"Quix, I was thinking that we should analyze exactly how we beat this thing, because it will be ready for that next time, if there's a next time," I said.

"It learns and adapts," G. said.

"Yes, so we must too. It failed last time, so it will do it differently if there's another chance."

"Do you believe it's not going to try again?" he asked me.

"I prepare for the worst, but our job is to make sure it doesn't get to that point again. Even though we got you back, you got snatched. Even though we escaped, a fake city we were lured to was blown up around us. And your man Quix here escaped but had his vehicles blown up by postal drones. In some people's books that would be called a win, because we survived. I'm not one of those people. We didn't win. We survived."

"Sometimes, Mr. Cruz, that's all that's required to call it a win."

"Quix, I appreciate that, but we were never in real control of the situation. We simply reacted."

G started to chuckle, and Quix was smiling.

"Did I say something funny?" I asked.

"Cruz, you're young and you're new. That's not how this biz works. It's not a hovercar race where you can study every inch of the course and plan accordingly. You rarely if ever know what the whole course is until you get there. The detective biz is the business of reacting—reacting to the lie, the scam, the chase, someone trying to shoot you, something not turning out the way you expected, someone turning up dead who was not supposed to. Life can't be planned."

"Mr. Cruz, if I can add," Quix said. "I've been on many operations. You can plan a military op for years, and all those plans can go out the window in ten seconds when it's real and something shows that no one anticipated."

"We still need the plan."

"Quix already analyzed the situation with his new team," Wilford said.

Quix pulled out a tablet from his jacket. "My team's weakness was that we didn't have adequate defensive capabilities for our hovertruck transports. Pluses and minuses—we did have adequate escape procedures in place, but for personnel only. We saved the people, not the cargo. Strength—we did have in place a contingency to lose everything, so we did remove a third of the cargo for a secret ground transport. That we saved.

"G-Man's weakness is obvious. He should never have gone to Byzantine to save Tiki. He should have let it go. However, plus is that we categorically proved the existence of the AI and its capabilities.

"Mr. Cruz is the anomaly. Without him, the mission probably would have been over. The fact that the AI quickly incorporated his aversion to public restrooms into its trap shows it has already identified him and is making use of his psychological and behavioral profile. However, he remains ultimately unpredictable. I suspect that three years of cases is not enough data for it to create a foolproof profile. That is our greatest strength."

Wilford nodded. "It knows me. It can guess you because you're military-trained, but not our man, Cruz."

"Yes," Quix replied.

"We use what it knows of your weaknesses against it and make me even more unpredictable than before," I said.

"Which you're already doing," G said. "You putting your people to work."

"Yes. When do we go meet the bad guy?"

Wilford laughed. "He's not what you expect."

"I don't expect anything. I want to meet him."

"He's slippery."

"I've dealt with plenty of slippery before."

"Okay, let's meet him."

"Quix," I began, "I'm having my secretary use that gear to create our own anti-android weapons. You should do the same."

"We already have, Mr. Cruz." He clenched his fists and nozzles popped out of the thick wristbands he wore.

"What are those?" I asked.

"We're calling it the 'nano-mizer.'"

My mouth hung open. "A nano-mizer?"

Wilford began to chuckle. "The killer android wouldn't know whether to run or pee its pants."

CHAPTER 32

Phishy

Wilford stayed in our guest bedroom, and Dot was off to work with her parents who would be minding Cruz Jr. My parents had left the night before. Wilford and I were about ready to go when Phishy called in with his report.

I took his call and forwarded it to the vid-phone in my home office. I sat at my desk, with Wilford standing over me.

"Phishy, there has to be an original legacy holder."

"I know, Cruz. We're looking. It's been passed from one company to another for ages. We've gone back thirty years and are still working."

"What you're telling me is that Byzantine has been like that for at least the last 30 years."

"I talked with a few sidewalk johnnies who used to live near there, and they said Byzantine was always like that. There was no construction out of the ordinary."

"When did they live near there?"

"One guy about 15 years ago, but the main guy left when he was kid. He's 60 now, so 50 years, maybe."

"The fake city has been there 50 years?"

"Seems like it."

"Phishy, get your people to search the records from 50 years ago then. There has to be an original legacy holder. A live person who was the original person who sold it to a company."

"Okay, we'll keep searching."

I hung up the vid-phone.

"This is the kind of thing organized crime does to hide ownership," Wilford said. "An endless string of dummy companies passing ownership."

"This may be factoid for your side."

"That the AI came before the man."

"Yeah, or maybe there was always a man behind the AI, but they also passed control of it to someone else."

"Which would bolster your theory. The original cyberpunk hacker, the great grandfather, passed that control on to his son, and it made its way to the great grandson."

"Wilford, we need to find out if this guy is anarchist crazy, which you and Connie believe, or a common, low-life crook, which is my position. We determine that and we can do a proper profile on him to catch him."

"Cruz, he tried to kill us. Our course of action is already determined. You said so yourself: kill him before he gets to try again."

"Then why haven't you done so in the last 50 years? You've suspected, but don't have the hard proof yet. Let's get our hard proof."

My mobile rang again. I didn't bother to forward it.

"Yes, Phishy."

"Cruz, we started just skipping back centuries, and we're at 300 years back and still no individual owner. We'll keep at it."

"Thanks, Phishy." I hung up again. "Wilford, is it even remotely possible that this fake city could have existed for centuries?"

Wilford stood there thinking, but not saying immediately. I looked at my mobile again. This time, it was a text from him, and I said it out loud.

"Back 500 years and still going." I looked up from the display. "I'm going to tell him to stop searching. We're going about this the wrong way. Maybe it's always been owned by some company, and it just took over somewhere along the way. These cyberpunk anarchists behind The Crash—did they have an official group name?"

"Yeah. They called themselves the Cyberteurs, and their AI destroyer program was called Daemon."

"Cute."

"You don't have to have your people research them. Connie already did that years ago. She has a complete file on all of them. I didn't say anything because I was hoping they'd find something new."

"I want to look at Connie's file then."

"I have it, but let's get on the road."

"Yes, the bad guy."

CHAPTER 33

Venn

Wilford G shouldn't have told me his last name. Venn already sounded like a bad guy's name. Venn Diagram made him sound like a cartoon clown. G told me not to let it fool me. Then for the rest of the drive, I was treated to Wilford's history of names course. How, in the past, people named their children after chapters and people in the Bible, Japanese anime, superheroes and heroines, computer languages and programs. How people wanted to be "of the future"—names ending in numbers, named after sci-fi authors, sci-fi movie characters, or variations of some tech device or scientific concept. I had to remember that Venn was from Wilford's generation so his parents would have though Venn Diagram was a "cool" name. I thought it was stupid, but took Wilford's point: don't underestimate him.

"What's down here?" I asked, surveying the area from the fast lane. Again, we were in Old Metro, which meant I had no clue as to the neighborhoods.

"We're going to New Morocco."

"What? There's a New Morocco in Metropolis?"

"There's a new everything in Metropolis. That's how districts were named back in my parent's day. Like Old Harlem. It was actually New Harlem when Perl and I moved in there."

"After 90 years in this supercity—all the things you must have seen change, come and go."

"You'll get to experience it too, Cruz. You'll be as amazed with this city as I am and will do whatever you can to protect it, despite its many flaws."

Wilford G. was at it again—speaking to people in a language other than English. I never met someone who could speak so many languages. We had set down in another open parking lot. I was learning that Old Metro had plenty of open parking lots, but not many enclosed parking bays. But people didn't seem to mind at all, with their slickers and umbrellas as they strolled the streets.

"What language this time?" I asked when he returned from talking to the two guys at a market.

"Arabic. I had to verify the club's location. It's one of those exclusive, members-only with its own secret entrance and all that."

He led me through the streets, and it was definitely an Arabic district. I had been to enough restaurants to know the smells of authentic Middle Eastern food. Quix wasn't with us, but we had a solid five-man bodyguard team. Even with them, I walked with one hand in my jacket on my omega-gun, and Wilford always had his hands in his slicker's pockets, so who knew what he was packing today.

"Here," G. said to me, and we walked up to a simple closed wooden door in the middle of wall of a huge establishment. He opened it and disappeared inside; we followed. Inside was a multi-level restaurant but arranged in a unique way.

All the tables on all levels were arranged in a semi-circle overlooking a stage with a hover-viewscreen. Two men were at a large chess table, but they were blindfolded and sitting with their backs to each other.

"Is this another betting place?" I asked G.

He nodded.

"Knight to queen's bishop 3," one man's voice said over the overhead speakers.

"Are they playing—"

"It's blind speed chess, Cruz. I see him."

That's what I wanted to hear. I stepped to him and who he was pointing to. The man was wearing a white suit seated at a table, staring out with red tinted shades. He wore a black skullcap, but it wasn't a casual one, more military-issue. It was something I'd know, but not the average person. However, more than all that was his little companion. The man had on his lap in his hands a white fur cat with a silver necklace. A grown man stroking a kitty cat in his lap. I glanced at Wilford G.

"Take him seriously," G. warned me. I looked back at the great Venn, and it was a great internal struggle not to laugh.

I saw a huge giant of a man stand. Him, I took seriously. He was dressed in a black suit with another black skullcap, mustache and beard, looking right at us. I began to walk to them, but noticed Wilford wasn't walking with me.

"Venn and I have said everything there is to say to each other. There's nothing new or interesting left. This is your show."

Wilford waited where he stood. Our bodyguards split up, two remained with him, the others followed me. The giant stepped in front of Venn's table.

"Auto," Venn said. "Don't be rude. Let our new guest at least get to say hello, first."

"Hello," I said.

"Mr. Cruz, have a seat in Auto's chair. He's going to stand to keep your bodyguards company."

I pulled the chair closer to his table as I sat. Auto walked past me to stand *very* close to the bodyguards.

"Nice kitty," I said.

Venn looked into the eyes of his cat. "He said hello. My cat says hello again."

"Again?"

"You've met before. Why is Wilford being shy? Did he say that we've said everything possible there is to say over all these decades of him chasing me? He says that to all his unfortunate accomplices."

I sat there realizing Venn at least knew how to push a person's buttons. I was not going to play his game, though I had no doubt he'd pull me into his game, regardless.

"Wilford has had many accomplices over the years in his quest to 'get me.' They always ending up moving on or dying. Can you believe Wilford is 95, and he has the energy of a 20-year-old?"

"G. tells me you're a bad boy," I said.

"I'm sure he's told you a lot more than that. I'm the mastermind behind a secret plot to destroy all of Metropolis. Do you know Wilford is regarded as a joke within the city's power circles? If it weren't for his police son running the Metro Police Union, they wouldn't even allow him on the premises to sneak in to see that ex-girlfriend of his in the CIC basement."

"Mr. Venn, you seem very quick to belittle G., but at least he isn't the descendant of a sick, anarchist hacker cult that killed a lot of innocent people because they were too bored with life to live it like normal people. Rather than do good to make up for them, again something a normal person would do, you want to replay what they did and double it."

"Is that what you believe?" Venn leaned forward, almost snarling. He wasn't wearing his red shades, and his cat stood on the table as if it were going to jump on my face. "It's all lies, Mr. Cruz. What do you really know about The Crash? What if I were to tell you that the Crash was a government cyber-war game? That the government did it to see if they could? When it went horribly wrong, they found convenient scapegoats in my great-grandfather and all the hackers they could find."

"Venn, let me save you the time. I know your great-grandfather and company did the Crash all by themselves. They did it. They crashed the government and all of digital society on Earth. Please, give me some credit for knowing the true history. In my case, I'm a direct descendant of people who lost everything because of the Crash. Put your red shades on and stop with the play acting. G. told me you'd do this too."

Venn laughed. His red shades were back on and his cat back in his arms on his lap. "Some of his previous accomplices were quite the novices. They were so easily manipulated I probably could have talked them into jumping off a 200-story tower."

"I'm sure you could have. Good for you, Venn. You have super powers."

"I do have super powers, Mr. Cruz. I can even draw you a diagram." He started to laugh.

I was back to my original impression of him. How could Wilford G. not have been able to close the case on this bozo after 50 years?

"In my great grandparent's day was the age of the cyberpunks. Hacking the megacorps, hacking the government, Big Academia, Big Media, a wild open wilderness where the cyberpunks ruled. They didn't go after organized crime because they didn't have anything interesting enough to steal. Stealing from the bad was no fun. You stole from the righteous and the innocent. They did the Crash because everyone said it couldn't be done. Reminds one of the invincible, unsinkable British RMS Titanic, until it sunk. Digital tech is invincible, until it's not. They didn't hack the Net and breach systems to steal identities, bank accounts, credit card files, money as if they broke through a giant wall. They said there was no wall at all and passed through as if it never existed.

"They're called cyber-anarchists today, but that's not what they were. They wanted to show humanity how pathetic and helpless it really was and how useless all their tech toys were. If a world can be brought done by a bunch of kids, Mr. Cruz, or even one person, then maybe it doesn't deserve to exist after all. Is it not a fair question?"

"That's no argument. They crashed the world because they, the self-appointed arbiters of humankind, said it to be so. My grandma has a word that sums it all better than any: whatever."

Venn laughed. "Your grandmother is right. It can all be summed up with one word or another."

"Earth abandoned digital tech to return to advanced analog. Up-Top went to a new digital tech—floating digital, alternating digital, rolling digital, they always have a new phrase for it. And all the Cyberteurs were killed, or 'disappeared.' Even if you're related to them, they do seem to be a strange group to emulate."

"Emulate? Is that what Wilford thinks I'm doing? I emulate no one. I forge my own path."

"What path is that, Venn?"

"No theories as of yet? I'm sure the decision to meet me was yours. You must have some working theory."

"I'm starting to believe it really doesn't matter. Doing evil for revenge against the world, because you hate human beings and want cats to take over, simple blackmail for profit and power. What does it matter? You're a crazy maniac. Are you glad I came to see you?"

"I am."

"Good. We each got to see the other."

"What comes next?"

"That's the fun part. See who's smarter than who."

"Wilford's been at it for 50 years."

I stood up. "Venn, I'm not Wilford."

"No, you're not."

"You have a good time petting your kitty and watching blindfolded men play kid games. I'll let you get back to your rewarding life."

"Thank you," I heard him say. I did not like hearing him say those two words, and I liked less the faux-robotic tone he used.

My bodyguards followed me back to Wilford and the others.

"Well?" G. asked.

"Ask me when we're out of here." I was already leading the way out of the establishment. One of the bodyguards put a hand on my shoulder, and he moved in front of me with two of his colleagues.

We got to the main entrance, and when he pushed the door open, I knew we were in trouble. Wilford pulled me to the side. The red and blue lights were blinding. People from inside walked out too, out of curiosity. Wilford and I slipped into the crowd and followed.

There were seven police cruisers hovering in the air and over two dozen officers arresting our five bodyguards. As they were handcuffed, other officers patted them down and starting finding all the illegal weapons on their bodies. One hovercruiser set down, and they were pushed in.

I looked at Wilford. I knew it was a bad omen when Quix wasn't with us. Now we were without any security. As the crowds spilled out of the establishment and the police cruisers flew away, Wilford and I quickly walked away.

"We can't go back to the Pony," I said.

"Okay."

"Call a taxi for you and get back to the Concrete Mama. That will be our most secure place to go. I'll get someone out here for my vehicle and call a taxi too."

"Okay."

"Go!"

He ran to one side of the street, and I went to the other side. His hovertaxi arrived fairly quickly. I finished my call with a Let It Ride dispatcher to send one of my regular mobile security guys to my vehicle immediately then dialed my own hovertaxi. Wilford's waited until mine arrived. Only when I got in did his fly off.

"Rabbit City," I said.

There were times in life when time itself froze. The man staring back at me from the rearview mirror, in the driver's seat, this time with blue shades, was Venn. The doors were already locked, and the hovertaxi was ascending straight up in the air—we had to be at least 20 feet up already.

"There was a poetry to it all, Mr. Cruz. Back then, the individual was free to dive into the Net for him or herself, explore freely, see what they wanted, take what they wanted. But you're right. The Cyberteurs and the Crash destroyed it all. There's no real hacking nowadays—it's all done by governments, megacorporations, and organized crime. The true individual has been completely cut out of the loop. All the best cyberpunks—the term back then for the ultimate hackers—were all captured or killed. What does the term mean today? Nothing. A punk who plays on the Net. That's not what they were, not my great-grandfather, or the others. They were the gods of new knowledge.

"I did say something true at the beginning, Mr. Cruz. The government didn't destroy that knowledge. They should have, but they didn't. They wanted to use it again. They wanted to use it against Up-Top. Up-Top knew Earth had the AI. That's where the distrust between the two began centuries ago.

"Did Wilford tell you about the Lotus Lab and the loving cooperation between Earth's governments and megacorporations in creating the Lab to test their AI tech. That's a lie. They've said so many, continue to do so.

They needed a controlled environment so the AI could create its own world, regardless of what that might be, free from human interference, who tended to want to pull the plug on that evolving future life form. They wanted to understand the AI and how it did the things it did, how it thought, how it created the new languages it did to communicate with other programs, how it solved problems the way it did. All lies.

"They created it to play with only one AI. My great-grandfather's AI. They controlled it and made it stronger. Lotus Lab was the prison, and my father let it free. Then they used Lotus Lab to create another AI to track and destroy it. How do you think the ex-husband of Wilford's girlfriend and his associates were so certain about its existence and their fear regarding it? They were there when it was released. They were the ones tasked to search and destroy it."

"What do you need the AI for?" I asked.

"I'm sorry, Mr. Cruz, but I'm not going to tell you. I could. It would be cathartic in a way, live up to your cartoon criminal perception of me, but I'm not going to tell you. I'm going to send the body of Polygon to Wilford, and I'm going to personally deal with this situation. Oh, I was so rude back there at the table. I didn't tell you what my cat's name was. She met you at Byzantine, but you didn't see her. Her name is Daemon."

I was startled by the loud, sudden noise as Venn ejected out of the hovertaxi. I was about to lean back and try to kick out the passenger door, when something traveling at incredible speeds rushed in a circle around me, ripping up the metal interior like it was paper. I grabbed it, but I was too late.

I yelled out as the cat crashed through the front passenger seat and crushed my hand around my omega-gun in its mouth. It wasn't going to let it go. Its reflective eyes watched me, but I made sure not to look at my right hand. I might have passed out. It exerted more pressure, and the pain was at a level that was truly beyond what any human could take.

With my body trembling, I casually reached into a pocket with my left hand. It seemed unconcerned with what I was about to reveal. I slapped my hand against the side of his head. The device on my hand clicked. The eyes of the android cat widened and locked. I heard a click in its body.

Slowly, I grabbed the top of its mouth and yanked up. I began to cry as I pulled my crushed hand with my gun out. I let the cat fall, flicked my left arm, and blew out the lock of the door with my pop-gun, and kicked it out. We were more than 50 feet in the air, but I leaned over and let my body fall out.

As I fell, watching my approach to the normal sky traffic below come up fast, I heard the explosion. There was nothing for me to do but hope and pray the debris of the exploding hovertaxi didn't fall on and possibly kill me.

CHAPTER 34

Wilford G

I was in an underground clinic in, of all places, Mad City. Since it was the last place on earth I would go, that's exactly where I went. The medic was an absolute scum-dog—droopy dark eyes, pockmarked skin, needle-marked arms, dirty white scrubs, but beggars can't be choosy.

"You should replace it with a metal one," he said as he continued to stitch.

"How many times do I have to tell you I'm not getting a bionic hand?"

"Your hand is gone. You won't be able to squeeze anything with any strength."

I ignored him. He kept working, and his mobile phone on the desk was flashing. He picked it up with the other hand and looked at the message. "He's here."

"Send him back. You can wait outside," I said.

He got up and walked out. I left my hand on the work tray table. I didn't even want to look at it. I did glance at the crumbled metal mess that was my omega-gun. My primary weapon was history.

Wilford G. walked to me and sat in the medic's chair. The room was dark and barren. The one light on the table illuminated both of our faces. He looked at my hand and sighed.

"What happened to Quix?" I asked.

"He suddenly got orders recalling him into service."

"I thought he was out for good."

"He thought so too. He tried to fight it, got a lawyer, but military officers came and picked him up. Shipped him out of the States while we were still talking to Venn."

"Are the men okay?"

"They made bail, but understandably, we won't be seeing them again."

"Did we hear back from Tiki?"

"We also won't be seeing him again for a long while. It was a good plan you two had, but someone beat you to it. Only they fingered Tiki as the one behind it all and said he was the one trying to kill off the competition with machines. His entire operation went underground."

I looked as much of a defeated, beaten-up, sad-sack as Wilford. We sat quietly in our chairs for a while. There was the sound of dripping water in the corner of the room.

"How did you get away?" he asked me.

"They have this collapsible hand glider that folds up and you wear under your slicker. They don't make jetpacks small enough yet and it's metal. Venn was my taxi driver."

"What?"

"It was him. That cat of his was an android cat. A killer android. I've never seen anything like it."

"Is that the right term—android cat?"

"Can't say robot cat because it looked identical to a real cat, until it attacked. It ran around me like a whirlwind, destroying the hovertaxi. That probably was its plan to rip apart the vehicle and let me fall to my death, but it had to attack me when I reached for my gun. I would never have been able to hit it; it was moving so fast, so it must have thought it was one of our killer-android weapons, maybe even the nano-mizer. You can see what became of that move."

"You really need to have your hand fixed properly."

"I plan to."

"Cyborg detective?"

"No way. Looks like I'm going to do what most Earthers frown upon."

"Cloned hand?"

"Yep. If I can't have my original hand, I'm at least going to have the next best thing, and that isn't a bionic one. I actually want to be able to use a nano-mizer in the future and not have to worry."

The medic popped into the room. "Do you want me to finish it?"

I looked at his silhouette at the open door. "Make that call for me. Have them send a hovertaxi."

"Okay." He closed the door.

"Thankfully for me, they have Up-Top doctors here on Earth."

"I don't imagine it would be cheap."

"It's not, but it'll be taken care of."

"Polygon is dead."

"Yes, he told me."

"He told you?"

"He said he'd send his body to you, and he'd personally deal with me."

"He had the body dumped on the steps of the Concrete Mama. Only I knew who it was."

"Did I ever meet him?"

"Yeah, today. Mr. Auto."

"What? That was Polygon?" Polygon was a small man and Auto was huge. That was advanced disguise-craft I'd have to learn some day.

"He was supposed to be my ultimate move to get Venn."

"Venn's primary bodyguard was Auto?" I was stunned. "How long ago?"

"Over twenty-five years ago, he got in and started moving into Venn's inner circle. He was the final plan. If we failed and didn't make it, Connie would call him and then he'd find the moment, any moment, to walk up to Venn and blow his brains out."

After what I'd been through, I had no doubt at all that Venn was all the evil that Wilford said him to be. I had dealt with many criminals before, but this was the first time I felt so out-of-my-depth. Maybe it was the fact that I had been thrown into a case that existed before my father was even born, and the bad guy was still alive, kicking, and outsmarting the good guys. If they had been failing all this time, what was I going to do?

"Cruz, I'm sorry about all this. I really am."

"We can't touch him, G. This is one situation where the fish is just too dangerous for us."

"Yeah."

"He knew we'd go to him, knew I would. Had everything ready for us, waiting. He knows my profile too. We can't get him this way. He's like a bull in a china shop, and we're the china. We can't have him anywhere near the shop."

"You said you wanted to meet the bad guy, confront him because then he'll do something stupid. Doesn't seem like Venn does stupid."

"No, he doesn't."

"No." Wilford sighed again. "That's it then?"

"No."

"No?"

"G., he tried to kill me, not you. Why do you suppose that is?"

"I don't know."

"It means he no longer considers you any kind of threat at all, but he thought I was plenty of one, and I just got here."

"He thinks you can hurt him somehow."

"He thinks we can stop him somehow. We're going to do things differently now. We'll do things in reverse."

"How so?"

"I get to play the dead detective." Wilford gave me a look. "He thinks I'm dead, and we're going to do everything there is to do for him to believe I'm dead."

"But an explosion needs a body."

"It's already there, G."

"My Mad City medic already took care of it."

Wilford was smiling. "Cruz! Good man."

"We'll have all my people put on a show for him. After a while, he'll believe it and move on."

"Then how do we get him."

"'Sometimes, as a detective, when you get stuck or you feel in your gut that you're on the wrong, the only way to get right again is go right back to the beginning and start again. Often, it's a waste of time, but will at least put you back on the right track. Sometimes, you'll miss that piece of evidence or clue that you overlooked somehow, but now, it screams out like a flashing police siren. Either way, you're on your way to closing the case.' *How to be a Great Detective with 100 Rules* by Wilford G."

He began to laugh. "Cruz, you amaze me. Back to the beginning when? When I resurfaced?"

"You said you started the case 50 years ago with Connie's ex-husband hacker. Then that's the beginning. Also—"

"What?"

"I think we may have drawn some wrong conclusions. We thought Mr. Candy was either Venn or the AI, but I don't think so. Venn named his cat, Daemon. Daemon is the AI. Mr. Candy is something else altogether. Two detectives, two cases, two bad guys. We need to figure out how the two cases fit. I think when we're able to figure that out, we'll know how to take down Venn."

Wilford glanced at my hand on the tray table again. "I wished we could have figured this out without all the damage."

"Actually, that may end up being a blessing to us as well."

"How?"

"I think Venn's androids have been upgraded. If you turn them off, like with an EMP device, or use any of our other toys, a manual switch is triggered. Then it blows up."

Wilford's face was angry. "How did you stop it then?"

"I used my own toy. Something I used in the past from my hovercar restoring days. It's a device that puts all mechanical systems in a sleep-mode; everything pauses."

"What made you bring that with you? Because it saved your life."

"I wanted Quix's nano-mizer, but decided to whip up a new toy myself in my workshop. I was making more modifications to the Pony to prepare for our next encounter."

"Lucky then."

"Yeah, I'm alive because of blind luck."

"That'll work."

"But we'll need a lot more than luck to close this case. Steady, simple investigating will do the trick. Let's go make me dead."

PART SIX

Who's Mr. Candy?

CHAPTER 35

Prima Donna

I loathed hospitals, in general, but here I was in a Mad City "medical establishment" geared around the fine skill of reconstructive surgery. They were really "chop it off, replace it with bionics" doctors. We couldn't call anyone we knew associated with the Up-Top medical community. If I were Venn, I'd assume I was dead, but I would still put out feelers on the street to make sure—or have the AI Daemon do it. The first thing they'd do is inquiry into anyone—on the planet—asking for right hand surgery services. We had to keep everything in house.

My Mad City medic did his part; my new "doctor" would do hers. The matriarchal founder and owner of Eye Candy—my wife's boss, Prima Donna. The anesthesia she used knocked me out for a full hour. That was plenty of time for her to rebuild my hand. When I first awoke lying on the hoverbed, I was in that in-between waking state for a while. She was moving around collecting her operating equipment.

"How is a salon owner also a surgeon?" I asked.

She walked up to the side of the bed. "I started out in plastic surgery, Cruz, but took it further. I've done more reconstructive surgeries than I can count. When I started in the business, it wasn't uncommon for clients to ask for a face lift and repair a gunshot wound all in the same session. Eye Candy doesn't discriminate—as long as you can pay, and criminals need to look good too. We keep our clients happy. You're not the first."

My eyes wanted to close, but I wanted to get up.

"Cruz, you need to rest. No running around yet. Rest. Keep your right arm in a sling and leave it alone."

"For how long?"

"Why ask me? You're not going to listen. When you can move it."

"How bad was it?"

"Cruz, it was nothing. It was crushed, but everything was still there. I replaced all of it. It's good that you saw that other doctor first. He kept it all fresh and preserved. The main thing is the nerves. Got to keep those fresh."

"How did you do an operation like this so fast?"

"Me? Cruz, people don't do operations like this by hand anymore. That's what robots are for. Reattach the nerves, repair blood capillaries and vessels, replace all the crushed bone, stitch it all up. The robot does all the work. I take all the credit."

"I thought you were a founding member of an anti-robot union."

"The robot isn't taking my job. I'm still getting paid. It's allowing me to do my job without getting my manicured hands dirty."

My wife, Dot, and Prima had formed an anti-robot union for hair stylists, manicurists, pedicurists, skin techs, nutri-techs, tattoo artists, fashion consultants, and fashion stylists. "Them robots not stealing our jobs," one of their members often said. But fortunately for me, in this case, they weren't fanatical about the issue.

"Thanks, Prima."

"You're welcome. But don't let it happen again. And please, let it heal. If you have to shoot a gun, use the left hand instead for as long as you can."

"I will."
"When are you going to see your wife and kid?"
"I'm dead."
"You will be dead if you don't find time to see them."
"I'll have G. sneak me away."
"You better. Okay, get some sleep."
"Yeah. Thanks, Prima."
I was already drifting away as I felt her pat my shoulder.

CHAPTER 36

Phishy

To any observer, it would have looked as if something was very wrong in the Liquid Cool world. Rumors of his wife passing out in the middle of Eye Candy and going out on an immediate and permanent leave. The boss of Eye Candy, Prima Donna, going out on leave. The CEO of Let It Ride Enterprises suddenly canceling all business appointments and abruptly leaving Metropolis. Rumors of security details at both the Rabbit City apartment tower and Liquid Cool office being pulled. The Liquid Cool office closed; Punch Judy, the office manager, unavailable. Behind the scenes, we left a phone trail of contacts to quite a few funeral services firms in the city. It all looked more than genuine.

Wilford arrived in a hovercar loaner in Free City. The old Jarvis Laws created Legacy Housing. Once a mortgage was paid off, it could be passed on to family and descendants forever, but it also created Free City—those unlucky not to have a legacy. Rich, poor and in-between had legacies; the unlucky had Free City—government created housing, which meant it was the dumps. It was also going to be our base of operations. I had always thought, like everyone else, Free City was only residential housing, but in my NeuroDancer case, I learned it also had a commercial storage and business office section. We rented a warehouse office for ourselves.

Wilford G. was always wearing a black fedora now and even kept his two-tone loafers. We no longer had our ex-military bodyguards, but we replaced that with two beefy sidewalk johnnies. I personally knew them and they were actually legends in the amateur fight club scene—and they could shoot. Thanks to Phishy, most of the sidewalk johnnies around wore fedoras. I was supposed to be unique with my tan fedora, and Phishy had them all copying me—at least their hats weren't tan. I rode shotgun. Since I was "dead", my trademark tan fedora and slicker were in storage. I was dressed like any other sidewalk johnny in dark clothes and had a fake mustache and goatee.

Our Free City temporary headquarters had sidewalk johnnies hanging around the front entrance, the back alleyway, and inside was a group that played cards all day. We didn't need commandos, just a constant presence to watch over the place from all angles.

I had drilled it into all of them not to acknowledge me in any way, and for the most part, they followed those instructions, though a few smiled when they saw me walk in the main entrance with Wilford. In the center of the warehouse was our stand-alone office—four walls and a flat roof.

"You two get some rest," Wilford said to our two sidewalk johnny bodyguards.

They nodded and walked over to a section of the warehouse that had several cots for people to relax and take a nap. This was one of those low-tech operations that could last for a long time. Hot coffee was always percolating, any kind of alcohol you wanted was in a makeshift bar, and there was always the smell of food in the air from the open kitchen. People who hung around all the time were always eating and drinking. This was where we had been working for days.

We had to keep as low a profile as possible, but had lots of work to do. Our new office was small, but he had his desk and I had mine. I spent all my time going over all Wilford's old case notes. Over the years, over the decades, he called it everything from "Killer AI," "Venn Case," "The Cyberteur case," "Venn the Slippery Bastard", to "Venn Equals Candy Man?" The case was the same but the names kept changing. I wanted to read everything on the Lotus Lab and everyone from it that Wilford and Connie had come into contact with or investigated. Wilford spent his time going over everything that had to do with the modern-day world of Venn. He was far too clever to leave any clues for us, or anyone else, to follow, but being a detective was about following the steps anyway, verifying, and re-verifying. There were many a bad guy who was sitting in prison, captured, because they were driving their hovercar, weren't paying attention and were speeding in a school zone, got pulled over, and the traffic officer saw something "suspicious" in the vehicle—like a bag of guns or something, with one thing leading to another. Smart criminals made dumb mistakes all the time.

"You really believe Venn has upgraded his androids to become walking bombs if we use an EMP on them?"

"I'm positive of it. I didn't blow up the hovertaxi. The android detonated, but if it wanted to do that, it would have right after Venn flew away. It was going to kill me one way, but thought I was going to use an EMP, so it was programmed to stop me, then detonate."

"But you had your own toy it didn't count on. But I thought a machine couldn't do anything after an EMP attack."

"It's easy to rig. All power goes off, and a trigger manually engages. My Pony has something like it. It's not new tech. Criminals used to use EMP devices to try to get into vaults, back when you were a youngster." Wilford laughed. "Now it's standard practice for all vaults and—storage units."

He smiled. "Venn has his upgraded androids, but he shouldn't have any androids. There shouldn't be androids. You said you met one in your last case."

"Yeah, from Up-Top."

"What does that mean? Is Up-Top crawling with androids indistinguishable from humans. When I was younger than a youngster, there was the fear of the replicants. Please don't tell me they've created them for real—the machine kind."

"That could be our next case to solve."

He grinned. "Yeah, but we have to survive this one first. Where's your sidewalk johnny friend?"

"He'll be here. When, I don't know, but he'll be here."

It was the first time I had ever seen Phishy not wearing his trademark fish shirts.

"Why are you in disguise, Phishy?" I asked. He didn't even do his chicken-dance when some of the johnnies led him in to the office.

"In case, I am being followed," he said. Phishy really wanted to do his best.

I smiled. "You're right, Phishy. Good call."

Phishy was smiling again. In his hands were two big cases, and he walked to my desk to set them down. "I have it all for you."

Wilford was eager to see what my "sidewalk johnny friend", as he called him, and licensed gun dealer had for us. I moved closer to my desk. Outside the door, some of the other sidewalk johnnies were gathering around.

"Make sure to keep an eye out for anyone!" Wilford yelled out to them.

"We got it covered it, G-Man," someone answered back.

Phishy opened both cases, and Wilford was already reaching for a weapon—it was some portable cannon.

"I got big hands," he said to me. He tried to make me laugh, and he did.

Phishy handed me a piece wrapped in a cloth. "What's this?" I asked. When I unwrapped it, I thought I was seeing things. "My omega-gun! You couldn't have fixed the other one. It was destroyed."

"I had two of them."

"Two? You had two all this time."

"Yeah. In case you needed a replacement."

I aimed it, smiling. I shook Phishy's hand. Phishy was very happy that he came through for me again.

"Can we pick what we want?" Wilford asked.

"Oh yeah."

Wilford took what I called the hand-cannon and then a normal gun. For me, all I needed was the omega-gun.

"We need to remember that, on this case, our problem isn't the humans," I said. Wilford nodded.

"More androids?" Phishy asked, concerned.

"More androids—possibly," I said. I didn't want Phishy panicking.

"You really think we can't use any of our android-killer weapons?" G. asked me. "None of them?"

"We can use them, if you want to have his androids also turn into moving bombs."

"Bombs?" Phishy said.

"G., we have to assume Venn has already built in all kinds of counter-measures to our android-killer weapons. Neural scramblers, ROS controllers, EMP devices—we can't use any of them."

"Yeah," Wilford realized. "He didn't stop Tiki from flooding the market with them. He took over the operation."

"My point exactly."

"But he doesn't know about your android pause weapon."

"Android pause weapon?" Phishy asked.

"It pauses them but doesn't stop them. It was still able to countdown to explosion."

"Explosion?" Phishy asked.

"What about the nano-mizers?"

"Nano-mizer?" Phishy asked.

The mere mention of those words turned me into a kid. "Nano-mizer? What about them? Didn't Quix take them?"

"Quix left them behind."

I smiled. "We can't use them, but—"

"You want to keep them anyway."

"Yes, but I have something far better," I said. "Maybe we'll be able to use the nano-mizer." I looked at Phishy and shook his hand again. "Thanks, Phishy. G. and I have what we need now. We'll get in touch later."

Phishy nodded and packed up his cases. Of course, he knew most of the sidewalk johnnies in our warehouse headquarters so, though he was supposed to be walking to the door, stopped to talk to everyone. I knew he'd be there for hours.

"G., you run the case, and I'll do my stuff in the background. You lead, I follow."

"Yeah, you're dead. Let's go."

I had no idea where he was going, but he was working the case. I didn't have to tell him what to do.

We gave our two sidewalk johnny bodyguards time get some coffee—they had gotten up from their nap when Phishy arrived—and then all four of us left the warehouse to walk to G.'s hovercar.

"You still think Connie and I are wrong. That Venn isn't Mr. Candy."

"G., the man in that hovertaxi was a person filled with hate and revenge. He wasn't going to blow me up. That was my doing. He was going to have his pet android rip me to shreds. How did Polygon die? Was it quick?"

"It was very far from quick."

"Tortured?"

"Tortured and killed as slowly as possible."

"Does that sound like the profile of a blackmailer? Someone running around Metropolis peeking through windows. You've dealt with far more blackmailers than I have."

"I have and plenty of them were filled with hate and revenge, especially the wealthy ones."

"It doesn't fit for me."

"It could be about the money."

"Venn has money."

"You can never have too much money, Cruz."

"I think we are dealing with two different people here. Why are you so sure, though? Did he tell you he was Mr. Candy?"

"He did. A long time ago. He taunted me with it and said that's why I would never get anyone in the city to listen to me about him."

"We're missing something."

"Maybe Candy works for Venn."

"That would make more sense, but there's more."

"Who's Mr. Candy? Sounds like we have real investigating to do."

"But we have on dry shoes and got our guns."

"Yes, a Metro street detective is naked without his gun. We're on the case, Cruz!"

We all piled into his hovercar parked a block away, guarded by another group of johnnies.

CHAPTER 37

Exe

When I realized we were in Elysian Heights, I glanced at Wilford in the driver's seat—surely, we couldn't be going to see my parents-in-laws, also known as the Hell Spawn. We set down at a familiar residential tower.

My first case as a real detective was actually two separate cases that ended up being connected from the start—the Lutty Girl Kidnapping Case and the Police Watch Conspiracy Case. The first case put me on the map in the public eye, but the full scope of the second case was buried from the public, and rightfully so. The Police Watch was the government agency in charge of the entire body-cam system for all of Metro P.D. street officers. The head of the division was a woman named Exe (pronounced ex-ee), but she, like her board colleagues, had retired—not by choice. This was her place.

I had been here before in my Blade Gunner case, so I was prepared for the shock of seeing green plants in the lobby along with a tree that seemed to go straight up to the top of the building that was over 200 stories tall. The last time I was there, the doorman said it was all synthetic, but looking at it again, I wasn't sure I believed it. For the average Metropolis citizen, real plants struck fear deep into their hearts. Plants were the natural paradise of insects, isopods, and who knew what other infestations. This apartment tower was built in a time when the supercity wanted to create a green paradise. All they did was create a nightmare for the people, and everywhere, those plants and trees were taken away as fast as they had been planted.

"They're not real," Wilford G. said to me as we walked to the elevators. "So, no fainting."

"I've been here before. Did you date every women in Metropolis, G.? I'm starting to wonder how you had any time to do any private detection work at all."

Our two sidewalk johnnies laughed.

"You can wait down here in the lobby with your tree, youngster, if you want."

We came out of the elevators and there was Exe standing at the door when we came down the hallway. She was a Black woman with her hair pulled back in a ponytail, wearing a casual brown pants suit with a sheer white and gold scarf around her neck. Wilford had dialed her on his mobile when we were landing his hovercar. I was in an awkward position of pretending not to be me, so I couldn't even say hello to her. She had been instrumental in helping solve my first big case, but I couldn't even say hello. She was normally a very gregarious woman, quick with the vigorous handshakes, but she simply looked at all of us. I didn't believe for a moment she didn't know who I really was, though she played along perfectly.

"Hello, G-Man."

"Exe."

"Are your friends staying out or coming in?"

"My apprentice stays with me; the other two will sit inside near the door."

"Sit near the door. As long as you didn't bring any trouble to my front door."

"Never Exe."

She let us in. Near the door were a few chairs. It was a design common to older buildings: a hallway for chairs or to take off your shoes and leave them against the wall. We followed her to the living room, which I also remembered. She motioned for Wilford and me to sit at a table in the corner, as she walked into her kitchen. The water was boiling.

"Your apprentice? G-Man are you now in the teaching business?"

"You didn't seem all too surprised to get my call."

"Why would I? I knew you weren't dead. I figured you wanted a vacation from your ex-wives and girlfriends."

He chuckled. "I didn't think of that."

She returned to the table with a tray of cups of tea and sat herself. She gave us each a cup and a spoon.

"You were supposed to be dead, and here you are. I'm hearing rumors about this other Metro private detective who got himself killed on the job."

"Really?" G. said as he sipped his cup of tea.

"Seems like I'm coming across a lot of dead people walking around." Exe didn't look at me as she sipped her tea. "Maybe I should get an apprentice or intern, but you have to be working to do that."

"Exe, if you're not working, it's because you don't want to."

"My turn for a vacation."

"I'm sure you have a ton of offers already."

"I do. Metropolis, other countries, even Up-Top."

"Take one of them. I'm sure one of them is head of some big division. Don't run part of something next time; run the whole thing."

She smiled. "The one I'm looking at is the one closest to my grandchildren."

"Sounds like your job awaits."

"Why are you here, G-Man?"

"You couldn't talk freely before, but you don't work for Metro anymore."

"I'm going to say the exact same thing as before. I'm actually surprised. You come back from the dead, but you're no wiser."

"I never did understand why I was so roundly dismissed about Venn."

"Are you serious?" She stopped sipping her tea and set it down on the table. "Maybe because you had no proof for your allegations. Maybe Mr. Venn is an upstanding citizen, liked by all, and people felt you were persecuting him for the sins of his ancestors."

"If it was about him, then okay, but the allegation was more than a serious one."

"G-Man, the Crash AI. That's what you claimed. Do you know how crazy that made you sound? You had people in the room who had family directly affected by the Crash."

"Yes, I'm one of them too."

"I told you this back then, and I'm telling you now. Even if there was a version of the Crash AI out there, so what? It couldn't and can't do anything."

"And the accidents?"

"The accidents you claimed weren't accidents. Did you ever show us any proof? All this based on one man."

"He wasn't simply a man. He worked the Lotus Lab."

"Yes, worked, past tense."

"Why did he leave?"

"I can't say because it's classified, but I can say not to read anything into it or draw any sinister conclusions. Confidentiality for any type of separation is standard practice for all government and corporate employees, and you know that. I say he lied to his ex-wife, and he lied to you."

"My hunches said otherwise."

"Hunches can be wrong. People can be wrong. It happens all the time. Fifty years. I never understood why you never let it go. It's a sick vendetta with you. Don't you see that?"

"You know why I never let it go. Venn confessed to my face what he was plotting. He would destroy the city and the people who killed his great-grandfather."

"He denies ever saying any such thing, or that he even met you when you said you did. All we ever needed was proof. If you had that, I'd take him in myself, but you never had it."

"I realize something right now. You really started to disbelieve me when I linked him to Mr. Candy."

"Mr. Candy. You did a lot more than that. You linked him to every manner of foul crime in the city you could find."

"I admit it. I stretched the truth to get him. I wanted to throw as much suspicion at him, so someone would nail him."

"We knew that."

"Where is the Lotus Lab."

"G-Man, that's classified. I don't know, and if I did know, I wouldn't and couldn't tell you. The Crash AI is gone. It was gone before we were born. If it survived and someone found it on a disk and even released it on the Net, it couldn't hurt a fly or anyone else. This isn't digital Earth anymore. This is post-digital Earth, the new age of analog— decentralized and operations and systems reside in physical hubs, not the Net anymore. The Crash could never happen again. You're afraid of a cyber-attack scenario that can't happen. There's no big, bad AI coming to get us."

Exe was always convincing, and as I sat listening, I believed everything she said. If I hadn't experienced what I had, if I hadn't been in that hovertaxi with Venn and his killer cat, I would have started distrusting Wilford then and there, but Venn did, personally, try to kill me. Exe didn't know that, and we had no proof of it, other than our testimony to give.

"Who's Mr. Candy?" Wilford asked her.

Wilford had adopted my premise that Venn and Mr. Candy were two separate people. He may not have been convinced of it yet, but his questioning was covering all bases. It happened; police and prosecutors were convinced they had their man (or woman) in custody, prison, or the morgue only to learn that the real criminal perpetrator was still running around. Sometimes, there was no one running around, but for whatever reason, you began to question your original conclusions.

"There never was a Mr. Candy, G-Man, only a string of criminals calling themselves by that name. The last major one was brought down a few years back—around the time of your 'death,' I believe."

"Why do you say major?"

"Based on the size of his black book, he was a very prolific blackmailer."

"There were others?"

"Dozens."

"Can I talk to them?"

"Why? What does this have to do with your Venn vendetta?"

"I'm finished with that. You've convinced me. I'm interested only in Mr. Candy now—another case."

"You're interested in Venn, same case. I know you, and I'm not giving you any list. I'm retired."

"Who can give me the names?"

"I have no idea, but you're a detective. You can find out for yourself."

Wilford stood up. "Thanks, Exe, as always. It was good to see you again."

"But that isn't your last question or why you really came. What's your last question, G-Man." Wilford smiled. "Don't smile. I know how you operate. You're about to leave then you spring your big question."

"You know me better than myself. Yeah, I have a question. Are you sure you want me to ask? I don't want you to get mad at me."

"What is it?"

"Have you ever been blackmailed by Mr. Candy?"

"G-Man, you can show yourself out and take your apprentice with you."

CHAPTER 38

Connie

No one spoke until we were back in the hovercar and on our way back to Free City. "Did you get what you needed?" I asked from my passenger seat.

"I did."

"I do the same thing—spring my last, real question on people at the end too."

"All the best questioners do. Get all the small stuff out of the way first, so when you get to the real question, and possibly get shut down or thrown out, you'll have at least gotten some information."

"What's next?"

"I have an important call to make, and you'll be on the research all day."

"Me?"

"We need people with their own mobile computers to do research, and we need people on the phone. We need a lot of them, fill that warehouse. It's how the Feds do it when they're building the long case against an organized crime crew, only we won't have the cubicles and nice, comfy-butt chairs. Line them up on the floor to work. We'll hide you in the office and no talking. I don't want your image or voice accidentally captured by anyone."

"You're having them go through everything."

"Everything from the beginning. I don't expect them to find anything at all, but it will be a fresh group of eyes, and who knows, we might get lucky."

I was happy to see Wilford work. It was my chance to see a veteran Metro detective at work. I needed to keep my mouth closed and eyes and ears open. How many people alive had the chance to have their posthumous mentors come back from the grave and sit right next to them for them to learn something?

"Is Exe being blackmailed?" I asked.

"She is or someone close to her is. She's not waiting to make a decision for a new job, and she'll never do the retirement thing. She's hiding."

Wilford had it all taken care of. My new office-away-from-the-office was a long hovervan parked outside. It allowed me to work unseen and, if I wanted, look outside tinted windows to see who was coming and going from our warehouse. It looked like he'd put some kind of announcement on the college Net because kids were arriving all the time. One of the sidewalk johnnies did a mobile video for me, and it was just as Wilford wanted: people everywhere on the floor, in chairs, on cots typing and searching on their mobile computers or talking on their mobiles.

A man with a small, but thick, black metal briefcase had been standing outside the main entrance for a while, near a group of sidewalk johnnies, but not acknowledging them in any way. Wilford appeared, and the man followed him to my hovervan. They stepped inside, and Wilford pointed to a center table for him to set up. I knew what the case was—a secure mobile phone system. The only question was, who was Wilford calling?

When the man was finished opening the case, configuring and then activating it, he got up to leave. Wilford thanked him and the man was gone. Wilford sat in the chair and pushed a button. As it dialed, the viewscreen lifted up and opened larger.

It was Compstat Connie. She was trying to look around Wilford's face.

"He's right here," Wilford said. "We made it." I moved closer to the screen so she could see me.

"But not Poly."

"Polygon was a good man."

"Yes, he was. You're not supposed to contact me, G."

"It was important. Lotus Lab."

"Yes."

"Is Lotus Lab Byzantine?"

I looked at him, surprised.

"With all that has happened, I think so too."

"Think so or know so?"

"Its location was always classified."

I got Wilford's attention, pointing to my mouth.

"You have a computer, type your question," he told me.

I typed it and showed him, but he ignored it.

"They tested an AI in a city."

"I went through all the city plans through the years and you can't tell now, but Byzantine is an island. That's why they chose it. We call it a killer AI, but it's an AI program. It was built to test AI programs, not contain a killer one. That's our assessment, not theirs."

"That's how he was able to create a district to kill us, create all those androids. The city was always there."

"Yes, that's why there were no indications on the satellite records. It was always there. The only question is, who's in charge of the Lab now—Venn or the City?"

"Connie, how can that be possible?"

"We'll never know the answer to that question. No one is going to confirm the existence of the Lab. It's classified. And if we can't even find that out, then we can't find out who's really in charge of it."

"I had quite a few people pass by there. You'd never know that most of the district blew up. It's all rebuilt, people going about their business, as if nothing ever happened. Nothing in the news anymore. But are the people real?"

"We have to assume they're not."

"I'm having the team look over all the reports, including the accidents. Maybe we missed something."

"We didn't, but that's fine."

"We have to get the proof somewhere, Connie."

"G., we accepted a long time ago that we'd never get the proof, but we'd act as if we had."

"Yes, but that approach isn't really working out in our favor. There's only two of us left."

"Three," she corrected.

"But Mr. Venn is still walking around with his cat. Our mutual friend asked if there's only one Lotus Lab.

"Yes, of course. Up-Top has something similar but it's a space station. But the question reminds me of a conversation we had many years ago. The prospect of a back-up Lotus Lab, should the original one become compromised or destroyed."

"Where do you think that would exist if they had it?"

"That's easy. The Hinterlands. Far outside of Metropolis but defensible. I think that's where Lotus Lab was before the Crash. After that, they wanted it closer because, at the time, they didn't feel they could defend it."

"From who?"

"Up-Top. There was a fear that they would seize it to use against Earth."

"Because Up-Top felt Daemon was really created as a weapon against them."

"Yes. But why do you want to know this, G.? How does this help us?"

"We need to know all the assets Venn has. We both believe he's about to make his move. He's built the power he needs to destroy Metropolis. We never were sure how he would do it, but knowing he has Byzantine and maybe one other place gives us some important clues. Hinterlands, you say?"

"Yes."

"How are you doing?"

"As well as a person can, living in a bunker," Connie answered.

"You'll be fine. How close are you?"

"I'm almost done. But I'll shift some resources into looking into the Hinterlands."

"Good. One last favor. I need our man, Wize. I don't want to reach out to him directly. I don't want to risk it."

"I'll contact him."

"Thanks."

"We need a breakthrough, G. Neither one of us is getting any younger, and you're right. I also feel, any day now, he'll unleash his doomsday plan."

"Well, we have our mutual friend on the case too. He seems to have something up his sleeve that he's working on. All three of us should have something new for Mr. Venn."

"Hopefully, it's in time and enough."

"Connie, we're the good guys. It will be."

CHAPTER 39

Wize

I had no idea where we were this time. With Wilford it was either my Metropolis or his Old Metropolis. We piled into his hovercar for our next job, and our two sidewalk johnnies were also trying to figure it out when we finally landed.

We got out and walked across the open parking lot in the rain. I stared at the people in the crowds to see what kind of neighborhood we were in. There was lots of laughing, people standing around smoking, joking and drinking bottles of alcohol, men and women, so it had to be some bar, club, or party part of the city.

"You should start a travel agency, G.," I said. "Give tours to the uncharted regions of Metropolis."

"Watch where you're going." I had seen the man walking erratically toward us with an empty bottle in his hand. "Lots of dips out here."

"Dip?" I asked.

"I told you about this already, Cruz. Dip. D.I.P. Drunk in public."

I laughed as he led us into a no-name establishment.

I bet myself before we entered as to what we'd see, and I was right. Another betting parlor—poker, black jack, and roulette. It was a real casino inside. Wilford walked up to one of the roving waitresses.

"I'm looking for Wize."

"Wize Guy?" she said.

"Yeah."

She pointed to a corner.

As we walked, I noticed a very fat guy stand from his card game that four other guys were seated around. He made eye contact with Wilford and started walking to an open doorway to another section of the establishment. We reached him and followed him into a dining area. People were at round tables and on stools at the bars, booths lined the wall, and in the center of it all were a million viewscreens with the featured poker games of the day.

Wize strolled to a booth at the furthest end of the room and slid in. Wilford gestured to us, and we all slid in, opposite Wize, and then he came in last. Wize tapped the table, and then a privacy screen closed around us, but it wasn't over. The entire booth started to move toward the wall.

The johnnies and I watched as the wall opened and out the booth went into another open room. It looked like the one we came from, but the lights were dimmer, and there were more waitresses and waiters working the floor.

"Slide out, gentlemen," Wilford said, "but you two will have a meal on me with Wize Guy. The youngster and I have work to do."

We came out, then the two sidewalk johnnies sat back in. Wilford led me to the nearest open table across from them. I looked back and a waitress was already taking Wize's food order. He had a digital menu in his hand and so did the sidewalk johnnies.

I looked at Wilford. "We're playing secret agent."

"There are lots of places like this around Metropolis."

"All catering to the criminal class."

"That's the profession you chose, youngster."

Another waitress walked to the table, but she sat down with us. "G-man," she said.

"Wize," he answered. Wize Gal? I thought to myself.

"Who's he?"

"My associate, but I'm not here about him."

"What then?"

"I need you to get me to someone who's been blackmailed by Mr. Candy."

She laughed. "Why would you think I could do that? Mr. Candy is a name used by lots of different people, men and women."

"Yeah, like Wize."

"My father only did that one time."

"It's important."

"Why would you think I could find someone like that? The great blackmailers are never caught. They find marks that would rather die than have their secrets revealed. They would never talk to you. No offense, G-Man, leaving aside that your son is the head of the police union, a private detective is just another kind of cop."

"Wize, I don't care about their secrets, and I'm not interested in them reporting it to the cops. I want to talk to them, know what they know, find their blackmailer, and put an end to said blackmailer."

She smirked. "G-Man, that's very vigilante Santa Claus of you."

"I think you'll be able to find someone for me."

"You never answered me. Why would you think I'd be able to help you with this? This is very out in left field compared to the other jobs you've had me do."

"It's not important. I need brains and discretion on this one. This isn't amateur time. Whoever you find, make it clear to them that no one will find about their secrets; there will be no police, prosecutors, courts, or any of that. I want Mr. Candy, and I don't want any outsiders interfering."

"This will not be the normal rate."

"Wize, I don't care about that either. Call me when you have something, but I can't wait long."

She stood from the table, thinking. "I'll get in touch soon."

"Good. I'll be ready. Don't use my name on any systems. Don't even say his name on any systems. Top secret all around."

She said nothing as she walked away, and Wilford stood from the table too. "Let's join the others, get some food, and get out of here."

"Do you really believe she'll be able to find a victim?"

"All we need is one."

"What if it's not the real Mr. Candy?"

"Then we'll look for victims until we find the right one."

I stood from the table. "Haven't you tried this before?"

"Not this way. This is new, and the person doing the tracing has never done anything like this before. Youngster, if I tell you the secrets of all my magic tricks then you won't think I'm amazing anymore. I know things. That's all you need to know. When you work this city for as long as I have, you'll know things too."

CHAPTER 40

Bite-Size

At the warehouse, Wilford had a team researching Venn's companies and any business or government agency in business with it or had ever done business with it. Another team looked at all of Venn's friends. It was activity that might flag Venn, but if we hadn't been still looking, Venn would've viewed that as very suspicious, rather than expected.

G. also had a team of tech geeks go over all of the I.T. protocols established by Venn's company used by other government agencies and megacorps in Metropolis. All the specs were classified, but Wilford had them work on the following problem: How could someone "crash" the analog tech of Metropolis today with a rogue AI? The kids were all jabbering about inherent bypasses and back-doors and all kinds of technical-ese, which meant they were the right guys and gals for the project. Technically, what the team was doing was extremely illegal—trying to figure out a way to bring down the infrastructure of Metropolis, but Wilford had that covered by making sure he had a lawyer in the warehouse too. The lawyer drew up papers and had them all sign it that the project was a "simulation" whose ultimate aim was to stop such a thing if possible.

I could understand Wilford's desire to protect everyone, after what happened to Quix and his team, thanks to Venn. He ran everything as if Venn had direct access to every surveillance and listening device and satellite in the supercity. There were a lot of people working at our new warehouse headquarters. We were ready this time, but every time we saw a stray hovercar coast nearby, I knew he was as nervous as I was.

I first met Bite-Size in my NeuroDancer case; Phishy introduced us. He was a roly-poly of a kid with spectacles, and he smoked. He ran the Netsite Movie-Town Madness and knew more about movies than anybody. I didn't think I'd ever work with him on a case again, since I planned to stay as far away from the movie industry as possible, because I felt it had an overabundance of crazy maniacs. But I had been impressed with him, and his name was one of the first that popped in my mind when I was thinking about who I could hire to run my own secret project.

I told him not to, but he showed up in a Liquid Cool T-shirt. What was worse was that the hovercar he arrived in was driven by his parents! I watched from my hovervan as he wandered into the crowd of sidewalk johnnies outside. He waved to the parents as they flew away. I could already hear the laughter. My great contractor was a little kid being shuttled around by his parents.

He was led inside, so I waited. Wilford would give him the debrief not to say my name out loud. One of the sidewalk johnnies waved to me from the main entrance. I wasn't looking forward to this part.

I got out of the hovervan and immediately, it started. The sidewalk johnnies at the main entrance were laughing. I came in and all the people on the ground, chairs, and cots were laughing. In the center office,

Wilford was red; he had been laughing. Bite-Size stood there with arms folded—not laughing.

"Bite-Size!" I yelled. "How could you? You're old enough to drive. Why did you have your parents drive you?"

"I don't drive."

"What's wrong with hovertaxis?"

"Why am I going to pay for a hovertaxi when they can drive me? They were going the same way."

All this did was start the laughter again, with Wilford leading it.

"Is this your secret operator?" Wilford asked. "A toddler? When's Cruz, Jr. getting here?"

"If I'm going to be laughed at, I can go home," Bite-Size said with a huff.

"They're laughing at me!"

Bite-Size raised his hand in the air. That got my attention, and everyone else's. We heard commotion outside and then the door opened. Ten kids marched in, walking to him—they were all identical in every way. They stopped and turned to face out.

"Ladies and gentlemen," Bite-Size began. He put his cigarette in the corner of his mouth. "Which of these individuals are real? Which are them are evil killer androids ready to rip your guts from your belly? I know what you're going to say! Just shoot them, but that's too slow. Robots will always be able to move faster than a human, unless you're one of the few 90% cyborgs. No! You need—my Turing Glasses! You need the ability to know human from android at a glance. Look at them! Who's who?"

Bite-Size pulled a gun from his jacket and aimed at them. Of course, we were not able to tell who was who. The real kids were ducking.

"Bite-Size!" I yelled. "Put that gun away, and the safety's on."

Wilford walked to Bite-Size's demonstration group and looked at him. "Turing device?"

"Yes," Bite-Size said. He held out a pair of shades.

"How does it work?"

"I can show you."

"Where did these androids come from?"

"The movie studios, of course. People have no idea that the entire stunt performer industry is practically gone. No one says anything for political reasons—the whole robots taking people's jobs thing. I borrowed them. Not the actors, though. They're quintuplets I had to hire, which I expect a certain person to reimburse me fully with a bonus."

"Okay, Bite-Size," I said.

Wilford looked at the shades. "You made this?"

"Cruz designed it. He gave me the specs. I had some guys I know create them. I told them it was for a movie."

Wilford looked at me. No one was laughing now.

CHAPTER 41

Wize Gal

Wilford was at the wheel of the hovercar, me in the passenger seat, and our two sidewalk johnnies in back. The sky traffic was bad, and the weather was worse.

"How would you even know how to go about creating such a thing?" he asked me.

"Back when I was thinking of my next move in life, I had been fooling around with some programming design work. Even in the illegal hovercar racing world, there are lots of rules around the specs for vehicles, but it's the illegal world so people are always trying to break them. People always coming up ways to beat the sensors and inspectors. What if you could simply look at the vehicle and tell whether it was up to code?"

"AI glasses," Wilford said.

"Yep. You could wear them for the duration of the race, so if a hovercar suddenly had the power to do something it shouldn't be able to do, you could see that too. I modified it for people. People move a certain way, breathing, eye blinks, thousands of variables you wouldn't think of. Could a machine mimic all of those variables? Maybe, but I don't think so. We tangled with three of them, so I was able to add those variables in too. We have lots cyborgs around, so they may have bones made out of alloy or even be able to stretch an arm across the room because of illegal modification, but humans have brains. Venn's androids don't have brains or anything that even pretends to be brains. Their brain is their entire body. We called it a Turing device to be cute."

"The Turing test. The test used by AI scientists to determine a machine's ability to exhibit intelligent behavior indistinguishable from that of a human being. Amazing. The life of a modern-day Metro street detective requires you to know a lot about a lot of different things. So, if you hadn't become a detective, you'd still have been famous."

"I don't know about that, but I'd be making money and be busy."

"And androids are just a machine."

"Just machines."

"Wize called."

"Wize Guy or Wize Gal?"

Wilford laughed. "Wize Gal."

"Is she really a waitress?"

"No, she does that to help out her folks. Wize Guy owns the place. She's actually a paralegal, as good as a full attorney, but has no desire to be one. I've worked with her for years. She found someone."

"Someone for us to talk to?"

"A live person, but she wanted to speak with me first."

"Why?"

"Wize sometimes pretends to be my late mother like you. She's probably going to counsel us."

"She can say what she wants, but I'll be wearing my Turing glasses all the time."

There was no betting parlor, restaurant, or club this time. Wize Gal was waiting in an alley, and Wilford descended nicely to hover just a foot from the ground. She walked around to his side as he lowered his driver's side window.

"Wize."

"G-Man."

"It's not like you to want to meet me in person when giving me some info."

"G-Man, I'll be straight with you. You've been good to me over the years. Got me started. Helped me when I needed help. You were always looking after me like a daughter. That's why I'm doing this. Drop this."

"I can't and you know that."

"Ever heard of The Confidential?"

"I haven't heard that term in—"

"Yeah, before my grandma was born, something like that. It's real."

"Who would even use that term today?"

"Who else but crime bosses who want to get it for themselves. Mr. Candy's black book of names is the new Confidential. The person you're going to speak to is on it. You'll get everything you want and more. But, at a price. You start lifting up strange rocks and don't come crying to me when you're covered with roaches and worms."

"I'll be okay, Wize."

"No, you won't. That's what I'm trying to tell you. *Everyone* is in The Confidential."

"What does that mean?"

"You'll see. Mr. Candy, the real one, hasn't been protected because he has such terrible dirt on people that they're too scared to get out from the blackmail. He's not blackmailing them. That's how it starts, but then he makes them partners. That's how he's been untouchable."

"Partners?"

"Mr. Candy is leader; everyone else are the accomplices. They're going to come after you, G-Man. They're going to try to kill you."

"I've been dead before," Wilford said.

She smiled. "I tried. I don't know how you knew I'd be able to find this person, and you'll probably never tell me, but I tried to warn you. That's all I could do. I tried." She flipped a disk into the hovercar and walked away.

PART SEVEN

The Confidential

CHAPTER 42

Sly

We were back at the Free City warehouse headquarters. Wilford G. told our two sidewalk johnny body guards to head inside while we remained in the hovercar.

"Exe," I said to him. "I have a friend who knows her well. Maybe I can get him to speak with her. Say it's only to help, if she wants it. Only an offer."

"Sure, do it. Is it your Run-Time friend?"

"Yeah."

"Sure, do it."

"What was this Confidential?" I asked.

"The Confidential was a...list of all the cops, politicians, judges, attorneys on the take in Metropolis."

"On the take?"

"I hope you've heard that term before."

"I know what 'on the take' means, G. How could that happen? Corruption on such a scale? The megacorps would've taken over."

"It's true. I was there. And there was no Council of Corporations back then, and the megacorps weren't like today. "

"How would something like that even remotely be possible nowadays?"

"Let's talk to our insider and find out."

"Who is he?"

"His name's Sly. I know who he is. Let's go in, review his criminal file, and prep."

"Criminal?"

"Yes. If it has to do with a new Confidential, then everyone involved is a criminal, even the legitimate ones."

Nothing. All our teams came up with a big nothing. They did their best to find something we could use on Venn—through his friends, companies, even enemies, but nothing. When Wilford first told me that IT was the source of all evil in Metropolis I laughed, thinking he meant normal information technology departments and division, but it was Venn's cyber-security credential firm for the supercity—I.T., Infinite Technologies. The tech teams found nothing there we could use either. Again, it wasn't surprising, but I couldn't help but to be disappointed.

The direct path to Venn was a dead-end. We now had The Confidential, which could be an indirect path to him, or it could lead nowhere. However, it could also lead us into whole new worlds of danger.

"You think too much," G. said to me as we sat in the center office. All the kids were gone from the inside of the warehouse. We were back to the normal contingent of sidewalk johnnies out front, out back, and inside at a card table.

"I'm trying to anticipate his next moves."

"That's easy. If he believes we're a threat again, he'll come for us to make sure we don't have to pretend to be dead anymore."

"Connie's doing whatever you have her doing. I have the new toys I've brought to the table."

"And the nano-mizers."

I smiled. "Can't forget them."

"Let's see if this new Confidential thing will lead us to Mr. Candy and then Venn."

"Let's hope, because we have nothing yet to go straight at Venn again."

"We have Sly, though. We'll review his criminal files, meet him, and question him. We'll do that next, after we prep to do a killer interview, then see what we have. Here's our chance, youngster. I've heard all these great things about your natural skills to interrogate bad guys and clients alike. I had that rep for 60 years. It'll be two against one. Us against this Sly. At the very least, I'd think you'd be eager to be a part of that."

"Of course, I am."

"Then save the gloominess for later. I've been running down leads about Mr. Candy for decades, but this is the best one ever. We need to know what we have. Study up. Do your profiling thing. When we're ready, he's going into the box with the two of us, and he's not coming out until we have everything."

"Box."

"What about it?"

"You're using another term that I use."

"Whatever, youngster."

Wilford didn't make the call himself, but he told one of our sidewalk johnnies who to call. We had our interrogation site. None of us were taking any chances at all. This was big, and we wanted to make sure wherever we were going to interview Sly, that it was nothing less than a fortress. He had to feel safe and we had to be safe. Where did we go? Downtown Metro with Metro PD at the end of one street and City Hall at the end of the other.

I didn't how Wilford got access to the old empty government offices, but he did. Sidewalk johnnies had everything covered—parking bay, elevators, hallway. It was a nice set-up. There were lots of empty interview rooms, so I assumed it was used from time to time when such extra space was needed by law enforcement. He already had the kitchen well-stocked. He picked out the room we'd use and had the johnnies clean it thoroughly.

"Were you ever a Fed?" I asked. We were both in the kitchen getting coffee.

Wilford smiled. "People always ask you if you were ever a cop."

"Well, I was in a way. I was a police intern."

"That was when you were a kid in high school."

"That would be enough for some people."

"I was a Fed."

"You were?"

"Yes, but I didn't play nice with the higher-ups, so we both agreed that I should do something else."

I began to laugh. "You are just like me. Police brass hate me down to their DNA."

Wilford and I studied everything there was to know about the man called Sly. He was a sleazy crook who liked the high-cons—taking rich people's money with scams, rather than the gun. He had a couple blackmailing convictions, all pled down, and he was getting better at his craft. The arrests were getting fewer, and the convictions had become non-existent. For someone like him, it was all the biographical information that was key. As an interviewer, you never knew what weakness you'd be able to exploit to get them to trust you, or at least talk to you. We didn't know if he was going to be hostile to us or friendly. Wilford thought the man was familiar somehow. That was no surprise to me, him being a detective in Metropolis for 70 years.

Sly arrived. He came alone, which did surprise me a bit. A johnny took his black full-length slicker, and he had a nice slim, black suit underneath. He had the white shirt, black tie, white pocket hankie look. They led him down the hall to us. We decided not to play any kind of "good cop-bad cop" routine—too juvenile. We didn't want there to be any games. I wouldn't be wearing my trademark tan fedora, but I wouldn't be wearing my fake mustache-goatee disguise. We would just be three guys having a conversation over drinks. We greeted him with handshakes, and we led him into the interview room.

There was a simple mahogany table with chairs. Wilford didn't want the chairs too comfortable; he said people, after a few hours, would want to sleep, not talk. We needed Sly to talk. There was no telling how long we'd be in the room. Would it be hours? Or would it be five minutes, after we learned he didn't have a thing worth anything? Sly sat on one side, his back to the wall. We sat across from him with our backs to the door.

It was Wilford's show. He'd lead the whole interview. I'd jump in with the occasional assist. We'd never worked together in this capacity before, and I had expected Wilford, at some point in the days before, to go through all the questions we'd cover. Wilford never did that. It was an instinctual trust between two guys who knew what they needed to do and what information they needed to get. We would be three guys having a conversation over drinks, only two of us were the pros.

"How did you find out about this Confidential?" G. asked.

"It existed before."

"Yeah, I know," Wilford said. "I was there."

"I'm sure you were. Were you one of its participants?"

"No, but a lot of street detectives like me were in high demand during the scandal. With so many people tainted, it was only the testimonies of people like me that juries would listen to."

"I bet you snitched on a whole lot of guys."

"I never snitched on anyone, but I helped put a lot of killers, rapists, and psychos away."

"Well, my father was one of the participants. Gunned down by cops who turned out to be part of the Confidential themselves."

"You're that kid I gave the hoverbike to."

Sly stared at him with a smile. "You remembered. I'm bigger; you're older."

"You asked for me."

"I guess doing a good deed in your life can pay off after all."

"What can I get you to drink?" I asked. I stood from the table.

"I don't know," Sly replied.

"Coffee, alcohol, kid's juice, milk."

He laughed. "Booze would be good. Something strong."

I left the room for a moment. We had every possible drink and beverage someone could ask for. I came back in the room, kicked the door close with my foot. Silk coffee for me, saké for Wilford, and vodka for Sly.

He took the glass, sipped it, and smiled. "That's a drink. East countries know how to make drinks. Never cared for any of the Asian stuff."

"We know each other, Sly," Wilford said.

"We do."

"What happened? I helped your mother out, before she took you and moved on."

"She didn't like charity and was too proud to admit she needed help. I got caught up in the wrong crowds, and one thing led to another. I always remember that bike you gave me. It was the last gift anyone ever gave me in life."

Wilford sipped his drink. He didn't speak, even though Sly looked at him, wanting him to ask something. The silence lasted several minutes until Sly began again.

"You two probably thought you'd have to beat the information out of me."

"Not at all," G. said. "It's your meeting. We were told you wanted to talk."

"You never see his face—Mr. Candy. He calls, you meet, but he wears a mask. It's funny, but he wears those clear plastic masks that you can see the face but can't actually tell a person's face. He wears a pink tie. That's who you're supposed to look for. It's also some small, out-of-the-way dark, dank restaurant that's empty. There was a bartender when I first met him, but the bartender stayed behind the counter and wiped glasses the entire time. No one ever came in besides me."

"What part of the city?"

"Nil Point. The center of the city's garbage and waste management, which fits. I always felt he picked the place so if you got out of line, they wouldn't have far to go to dump your body."

"How does the racket work?"

"Straight blackmail. Pictures. Video. Audio. He has it all. There's nothing to deny. He's very polite about it all, but there's nothing to say. He never said, 'Pay me money or I'll release this.' He never did that. He threw it down on the table in front of you and sat there. He made you ask, 'How much do you want?'

"But it's not about the money. It's almost like he asks for the money just to ask. And we pay it. There's no doubt, because he knows exactly how much you can afford. Enough to make it hurt but not break you. But it's not about the money. Mr. Candy doesn't care about money. He collects favors. That's what the racket is. That's why the real Mr. Candy has never been caught. It's all about the favors. He gets you to do a favor and then he's got you for life. He makes you an accomplice. The favors never end. Sometimes, you won't hear from him for months. Other times, he'll have you doing work for him for days on end. You never know, and you can never say no."

"Sly, why are you coming forward?"

"I did the last job, but I won't do anymore. Wize told me what you said. That you could make it end. When I learned it was you who said it, I knew she was telling me the truth. I want it over."

I realized that Wilford G. was, indeed, the master. He didn't just spontaneously remember that he knew Sly. He knew him and knew that Wize Gal knew him. In all those days of pouring over his old case notes, he did see something. He saw it and put it in motion like the master of the biz that he was.

"Is this punishment?" I asked.

"Punishment?" Sly asked.

"For trying to take the Confidential over."

Sly laughed and was nodding to himself. "Yeah."

"How do we find Mr. Candy then, Sly?" G. asked.

"I don't know, but I've had years to think about it. He came at me when I tried to do my own. His favors involve forcing you to blackmail others, hurt others, threaten people. I have four names. You get to those four people and get all their names. Before you know it, you may have the whole Confidential, and when you can piece it all together, you'll have the identify of Mr. Candy. I'm certain of it."

"Sly," I asked softly. "What will you do if he releases your blackmail file?"

"They can't get out." Sly eyes were tearing up.

"Then we'll have to move fast, won't we?" Wilford asked.

"You start, you can't stop. You have to be able to get information fast and move to the next person faster. I wouldn't be surprised if he started killing everyone off himself."

"Do you have any theories on who he might be?" G. asked.

"No idea. I tried to identify him, secretly. Never got anywhere. Then he gave me a job I almost died on, so I took that to mean that I better not do it again."

"We'd have to put you in protective custody," G. said to him as he got his tablet from his jacket.

"You can do that, but if he comes for me, I don't think you'll be able to stop him."

"You might be surprised at what we can do," I said.

"If you say so."

Wilford gave him the tablet. "Who are the names you're going to give me?"

"One D.A., one CEO, one cop, one court bailiff."

"Write it down."

He looked at us then began to type. "You'll never get this chance again in your lifetimes. I'd think long and hard about this. It won't be pretty."

"I want Mr. Candy," G. said to him, taking the tablet back. "I've been after him for 50 years."

"I want him dead. That's the only way I get free. Or he kills all of us, and I'll get free that way too. I remembered that you liked betting too. Those are the only two plays here. He's dead or we're dead. I hope you know that."

"We know," I said.

CHAPTER 43

Exe

When I contacted Run-Time days earlier about Wilford G.'s and my visit to Exe and that she might be in trouble, he was more than happy to help. He was, after all, the person who introduced me to her. I hadn't heard anything from him, but Run-Time always followed-up, so it meant he had no news yet. His call was perfect timing and gave me an idea on the spot; Run-Time loved the idea and he set up the meeting.

Wilford had re-assembled the "boiler-room"—his nickname for the army of kid researchers he had assembled before at our temporary warehouse headquarters. When we began, as Sly had said, we'd have to move quickly and diligently. We'd have to move as quickly as a rogue AI ourselves because we had to get to as many people as we could before Mr. Candy, or Venn, had time to react. The researchers would be in place to try to tie anyone we identified back to Venn somehow. But to get to all the names from Sly and beyond, we'd need to do that in a way that Venn couldn't anticipate or stop.

G. and I returned to Elysian Heights. Our same two sidewalk johnny bodyguards in the back, same place we had parked before; the only thing different (I kept my tan fedora and slicker in storage for a bit longer) was that I didn't have my facial "disguise."

"Your idea better be good," Wilford G. said to me.

"It's good. You'll see."

We didn't see her face on the vid-screen when we buzzed her, but we got on the elevators anyway.

"Hopefully, we're not going to be greeted by any more psycho androids," G. said.

There was Exe at the door—she was not smiling as she watched us approach. This time, her attire was all black. "Walking dead man number one and two. Cruz, if it weren't for Run-Time, this meeting wouldn't be happening."

"I got it," I said.

"Got it? What do you got?"

"You haven't invited us in yet."

"Should I?"

"Yes, you should."

"He says the idea is good," Wilford chimed in.

Like before, she let us in and led us down the small hallway to the living room. We sat in her same chairs at the table, but no water was boiling and no tea was offered.

"The Confidential," I said.

"What?" She looked at G.

"It was—"

"Cruz, I know what it was. Remember, G-man and I were here, and you weren't born yet."

"It's been resurrected. Politicians, police, judges, more. I'm certain your name is on the list, but don't throw us out yet. We have an inside man. He said part of the racket is not only the original blackmail extortion but to get them to do other illegal activities so they are pulled in deeper. It includes blackmailing others. So, each blackmail victim has the names of other blackmail victims, so you find one, then you could conceivably unravel all of it. But! This can't be an operation where we work over the course of days, weeks, and months. We'd have to get it done in days—hours."

"Cruz, why are you telling me this?" Exe asked.

"Because you'd lead the effort. Everyone knows you got a raw deal with the Police Watch scandal. You were forced out, even though you had nothing to do with it. You would run it."

"Run what?"

"What was the name of the special task force that wrapped up the Confidential the last time in Metropolis?"

"That was decades and decades ago, Cruz."

"The Metropolis Four Corners Anti-Corruption City Commission," Wilford answered. He looked at Exe. She stared back.

"You're both crazy."

"You could do it."

"You said my name is in this Confidential file."

"The perfect cover story," I said. "You were so outraged by the brashness of the blackmailers you wondered how far it went. An informant came to your attention, and you realized it went far beyond anyone could have imagined. You impanel this new commission to arrest everyone involved until victims and perpetrators could be sorted out."

She sat back in her chair. "You're crazy, Cruz."

"Why not, Exe," Wilford said. "You can call the Mayor right now. Would he prefer you to run it or an outsider? An outsider who'd use the whole thing against him."

"Exe," I said. "It has to be like a hurricane. You'd have to put together your entire team of prosecutors and investigators, line up all your arresting officers, have all the warrants issued—all in a day."

"Impossible," she said.

"Then arrest the first three, get their names, then go arrest all of them. It's not just to figure out victim from perpetrator, but to get everyone into protective custody. Once Mr. Candy finds out what's going on, people will start disappearing or getting killed all over the place."

"You both believe that?"

"Yes," G replied.

"Yes," I said.

"What about me?"

"You won't be the only person involved who'll want the details of their extortion sealed. You'll make sure yours doesn't get out, you'll make sure theirs doesn't. Isn't that how it was done the last time, before I was born."

"Exe," Wilford said in a pleading tone. "Do it. You do this you get out from under your problems, and you'll really be able to pick any job you want here on Earth or Up-Top."

"I don't know if it can be done."

"It can be. It'll just mean than none of us will get any sleep for 36 hours or longer. We'll never be able to stop, just keep going as the dominoes fall."

"Mr. Candy? Or is it Venn again?" she asked.

"G. always felt Venn and Mr. Candy was the same person. I believe Mr. Candy works for Venn. My theory is Mr. Candy tried to blackmail him and Venn turned the tables on him, made Candy his lackey for his plot. It's much easier to destroy a city when you own all the people who run it."

"Terrorism, Cruz. That's what you're both suggesting."

"Exe, if that's the word you need to throw around to get everyone to sign on the dotted line to give you the power for this new commission, then feel free. When we move, we don't stop until we end it."

"How big?" she asked. "How big do you think this is? This is not old Metropolis when corruption was rampant. This is modern Metropolis."

"We don't know what we have, Exe. We only have the first domino and know the identity of the next three. You're right. We may have a whole lot of nothing. But you're the only one in the room who would know. If Mr. Candy has something as serious as he has on you on people in City Hall, Metro PD, the Feds, the Courts, what might such a criminal be able to make people do?"

Exe pulled her black scarf from her neck and dropped it on the table. She was distressed. She didn't have to say a word. We had convinced her.

CHAPTER 44

Chief Hub

I had been to Chief of Metropolis Police Hub's office before, but this time, I wasn't alone—Exe was in the front and Wilford was at my side. We were led into the large office by an officer, but no Chief. He came right in—six-feet tall, muscles, dark hair, thick mustache, and dark green eyes.

"Hi Exe," he said.

"Good to see you, Chief."

He got to his desk, turned, saw me, and his joyful mood was gone. Then he glanced at Wilford and his eyes narrowed.

"Have a seat, everyone." He was standing, trying to figure out who G. was. "Wilford G.?" He looked up, surprise on his face.

"Hi Chief."

"Aren't you supposed to be dead?"

"Just a rumor on the street."

"Rumor on the street? I'm pretty sure Wil Jr. attended something that resembled a real funeral with his family."

"Junior is outside."

"Junior is outside. Well, that's good to know, G-Man. I wouldn't want him to find out his old man is actually alive, get mad, and then shoot you right here in my station."

Wilford thought it was funny. The Chief turned his gaze to me and started shaking his head.

"Why are you doing that?" I asked. "I didn't do anything."

"You didn't do anything. Trouble follows you like the Four Horsemen of the Apocalypse."

"I solve my cases," I said.

"Exe, what do you need, so I can get these two out of my office?"

"Chief, I can sympathize with you, believe me. I dated the older one once, and the younger one wants to be him. I'm going to heading a new anti-corruption task force."

"Anti-corruption task force?" The Chief sat down. "Anytime a government official walks into my office, active or retired, with words like anti-corruption, I hear the words 'how do we railroad some cops.'"

"Chief, let me finish. I have already been to see the Mayor."

"And he signed off on it?"

"He has, but—"

"Exe."

"The commission has a temporary charter, Chief, and I'm here for your help."

"My help?" the Chief asked.

"I need you to assign a staff of officers to me."

"For what?"

"To arrest a lot of people, a lot—some victims, some will eventually be booked, but all need to be in police protective custody."

"The charter is for what? What case? What organized crime crew?"

"The Confidential."

The Chief looked at us. "You can't be serious. That's a myth."

"It wasn't a myth in the past."

"Yes, Exe, I know. My father and grandfather worked the original Confidential case. That's ancient history. It doesn't exist. Do you know how many Mr. Candys or Candy Men we have locked up in prison right now or have died in prison?"

"I know it exists."

"How?"

"I can't tell you."

The Chief stood from his chair. "How many officers?"

"Three days. As many as you can spare. We may need to take a lot of people into custody."

"The Mayor approved this?" Exe reached into her sleeve pocket and pulled out a disk. The Chief placed it on his computer's reader, and the papers appeared on his screen. He wasn't happy. "I can't spare all the officers that you need. We do have current criminals to deal with."

"Then give your police union chief the authority to deputize the officers we need from the civilian population."

"When is this happening?" he asked her.

"Immediately, this minute."

CHAPTER 45

Venn

Sly was the first one taken in. His four names were an up-and-coming assistant district attorney, the CEO of a Silver City robot manufacturing megacorp, a police officer who worked primarily outer districts of Metropolis, and a court bailiff of Metro Municipal. Sly's four names gave us more names. The interrogations took hours, but it was the CEO who gave us not one name but 10. The media tried to figure out what was going on—someone tipped them off, but people kept being brought into Metro PD from all around the city. It wasn't until we brought in a judge—the 125th named on the Confidential that bad things started happening.

Exe had her new commission offices right in the Mayor's building, though the Mayor was nowhere to be seen. He was on "city business." Wilford and I waited in the commission lobby when Exe came out from the main double glass doors to the executive offices.

"Everything okay?" G. asked her. We couldn't hide that we were worried. We heard that an ambulance responded to a judge's suicide. There was a rumor that a CEO either jumped from his 300-story office tower—or was pushed.

"We're okay," she said. "We put all Metro employees and staff on lock-down. Everyone's guarded by police, and no one goes home until they're cleared. There won't be any more suicides or accidents."

"Good move, Exe," G. said.

"Do we know anything yet?" I asked.

"Mr. Candy has been a very busy blackmailer. I don't know when it will all end, all these names. It's a lot of people to have in your Rolodex who will do any favor for you that you ask. But if you're asking if anyone has identified the identity of Mr. Candy, all we have is the same description of a man in a plastic mask. If you were hoping for some link to Mr. Venn, there's nothing."

"I'm sorry," Exe said. "But we have a long way to go to unravel this whole thing. There is, however, something that we have found interesting." We both perked up. "How did this all go on for so long, involving so many people, people at these levels, without anyone coming forward? Someone would have come forward to stop Mr. Candy. Someone would have tried to turn the tables on him. It was money. Everyone who stayed quiet, after a while were able to get "candy"—the term they had for it. Mr. Candy would allow them to share in the blackmail profits of "real criminals." They were told that millions of criminals had to pay him a "protection tax" and they, the blackmail victim, would have a secret account where money would be deposited, not for them, but for them to give to anyone they wanted. After they had paid their blackmail money to the end."

"What is real?" G. asked.

"We have five people that we can confirm did get their 'candy,' but not everyone got that offer. It's interesting to me because it almost suggests two different blackmailers working together—only a theory. Again, Mr. Candy's identity is still unknown and no link to Mr. Venn. However, there's a lot more people to interview. Hope that's helpful in some way."

"Thanks, Exe," G. said, and I nodded.

"Thanks," I said, and she returned to her office.

"Venn doesn't know we don't have anything," G. said.

"I know what you're thinking, but let's play it the other way."

We both marched out of the offices.

We made a pit stop at our warehouse headquarters, switched bodyguard teams, and got back into our normal "uniforms." Wilford was driving fast back to New Morocco. We landed, and three big sidewalk johnnies followed us. I was back in my tan fedora and slicker. Wilford G. had a black fedora and his trademark two-tone shoes. This was Venn's territory, and the last time we were here, things didn't go well, but we were feeling invincible.

We marched through the district to the same simple wooden door in the middle of wall of a huge establishment. This time, I led the way into the multi-level restaurant. We spotted him on the second level this time. The last time I saw Venn in his white suit, red-tinted shades, black skullcap, and stroking his white fur cat with a silver necklace on his lap, I almost laughed. I would never underestimate the maniac again. He didn't have his big bodyguard Auto (he killed him) but three bigger ones around him instead.

We were back for another blind chess match, but he'd noticed us from the second we entered the establishment. I quickly walked to Venn's table as one of his bodyguards approached me to stop my advance. I didn't hesitate. I shot him in his knee; he fell to the ground, then I shot Venn's cat with my omega-gun. The robotic cat was blown out of his hands, and Venn jumped up from his chair.

I kept my arm extended with my omega-gun, alternating between pointing it at the other two bodyguards and Venn.

"Sit down, Venn," I commanded.

The chess match was over. The two competitors and the referee-timer had run out of there before the first bodyguard hit the ground. People were screaming and running for the exits all around us.

Venn sat back in his chair.

"Gentlemen, please lie down on the ground with your arms interlaced behind your head," G. said, aiming his big gun at them. Venn's two bodyguards didn't hesitate to comply.

"Hey, Venn. Look. My new hand." I punched him, knocking him back in the chair. I stepped over a bodyguard and reached for Venn. "Get up!" Venn, with a bloody nose, slowly got up. I lifted the chair back up and pushed him down in it.

He wanted to say something but didn't. He stared at me, trembling with rage.

I leaned down to him. "Venn, we wanted to come here and personally tell you that you're better than us. I'm being very honest with you right now. You are. G. and I have 150 years between us of life on Earth, but you're still better than us. We can't get to your killer AI, affectionately named Daemon. We can't identify Mr. Candy. We can't tie the Confidential to you. We got nothing. We'll never have anything and we've tried. We gone through your friends, associates, employees, companies, enemies, and we still have nothing. You're better than us, Venn.

"But that's okay, Venn. We can't get you, but you'll never be able to launch your plot—never. You probably killed the real Mr. Candy a long time ago. I wouldn't put it past you, but it doesn't matter. It doesn't matter if he's one of your bodyguards on the ground or one of the waitresses that ran out of here. Also, your killer AI is done. You'll never be able to activate any of your Confidential blackmail victims, ever. Sometimes, a detective has to be content with not getting the bad guy. I am, Venn. I am content with the fact that you'll never, ever fulfill your psycho criminal destiny.

"Don't cry. You can build another kitty for your crotch to pet. You have a nice life, Venn."

I led the way, with G. following. We kept our eyes on them from the mirrored walls. The bodyguards looked up but stayed on the floor. Venn was a quivering mass of flesh—he was overcome with such rage, I expected him to spontaneously explode.

All G. and I had to do was wait.

PART EIGHT

A.I. Robot Vampire Zombie Apocalypse

CHAPTER 46

City Hall

Venn genuinely thought I was dead, and me showing up in his establishment and doing what I did was enough to push him over the edge. The last time, I wanted to confront him to make him do something stupid. He almost blew me up after his robot kitty tried to eat my hand, after it first tried to claw the hovertaxi apart and send me falling 50 feet to my death. This time, I confronted him and successfully made him psychotic. It was the only way we could win; he had to make a mistake. However, that meant we had no idea how he'd come at us. All we knew was that it would be soon. We also, still, didn't know how he planned to destroy Metropolis.

Exe had her hands full with the Commission. Chief Hub was personally leading the protective police custody operations, knowing the Confidential was real. We needed to do one final thing that would push Venn from the rational psychotic zone to the irrational dimension.

"You're that Cruz character," the man said, staring at me on our vid-call view screen. It was Metropolis City Council Leader Hugo.

"I am, sir."

Wilford and I were back at our warehouse headquarters in our center office.

"What did the Mayor say?"

"He's unreachable."

"The coward. Why am I not surprised? When the scandal is over though, he'll rematerialize right in front of the cameras."

"Yes sir."

We heard voices around him. He obviously had other council members on his video-phone screen. We couldn't see them, but they were watching the call too.

"I'm not going to get the city council to do any such thing," he said. "We'd have to get the Council of Corporations to agree, which they won't."

"Sir, you don't have to do it for real. All you have to do is make the public announcement."

"Mr. Cruz, you want the city of Metropolis to knowingly lie about a private citizen."

"Yes, sir."

"Why?"

"To prove once and for all he's plotting to destroy Metropolis."

"G-Man, are you still on this Venn vendetta of yours?"

"I am, sir," Wilford answered.

"Why are you convinced of it, Mr. Cruz?" Councilman Hugo asked me.

"Because he told me, sir. Moments before he ejected himself out of a hovertaxi 50 feet in the sky and tried to kill me. You've been able to dismiss G.'s claim—that Venn confessed to him, but he did the same thing to me, and tried to kill me with an exploding robot."

"Exploding robot?"

"Yes, sir."

"My colleagues are asking, how on Earth do you destroy Metropolis? We're the largest super-city in world, over 50 million people. How?"

"Sir, G. and I were in an entire district filled with people that weren't people at all. Men, women, children even, all androids, all indistinguishable from any human you'd meet on the street, in the hallway, in any public meeting. Androids are robots, and robots are faster and stronger than any human. Androids all illegal worldwide, but there they were, thousands and thousands of them. Androids made by robots. Who knows how many they've made, or are making." I could tell a scary story.

The City Council President was visibly disturbed. "What do you want me to do?"

"Have Metro City make the public statement. Have the Council of Corporations make the public statement. Bribe them with the offer that every member caught up in the Confidential scandal will not be exposed, and depending on the involvement, likely won't be charged."

"Yes, they'll go for that. Okay, Mr. Cruz. You'll have the statements within the hour. I'm only doing this because of Exe. You could have burned her, the Police Watch program, and the City, but you didn't. She said you two uncovered this Confidential thing. Bad business, this is. We can't have the public lose confidence in its government and institutions. Okay, let's get on with this."

Mr. Hugo did what he said he was going to do. Besides the Mayor, he was the only other person in authority who could make such a thing happen. He would have cleared it with the Mayor, but he could have done it without him, as long as he had the agreement of the full council. The Metropolis City Communications office announced it was severing all ties with Infinite Technologies because of possible implication in a high-level, ongoing corruption investigation. The Council of Corporations put out an endorsement statement ten minutes later.

With that, Venn's business empire was over. If he were rational, he'd have an army of lawyers haul City Hall into court, but no such thing happened. He was coming.

CHAPTER 47

The Kill Crew

This wasn't new—waiting for a bad guy to show up. G. and I were in the center office of the warehouse. Most didn't want to leave, but we sent most of the sidewalk johnnies home. We had a smaller crew left, but they knew how to handle guns and, more importantly, knew surveillance. We had remote cameras in hovercars around the area keeping watch from the ground and air; the johnnies watched the monitors.

G. had all his weapons spread out on his desk. My desk had one laser rifle only; everything else was in two cases on the floor nearby. We had lots more, but in our minds, we were trying to anticipate how Venn would come at us. I, for one, had a very active imagination and could come up with a lot of ways Venn could wipe us out. However, both of us felt it would have to do with androids or robots of some kind. That's what he liked. He had invested a lot in them, and that was what I was betting on. However, G. reminded us that we didn't exactly have a foolproof defense against them, especially if Venn did as I suspected he had done—turn them all into walking bombs.

There were a few sidewalk johnnies inside. They weren't at a card table but seated outside the center office, smoking, and waiting, like us. One of them got up and knocked on the door. He came in.

"Phishy sent a message," he said.

We looked up. "What did he say?" G. asked.

"He said that people are running out of the Byzantine."

"What does that mean?" I asked.

"I don't know. I tried to call him, but the line is dead. I mean, no signal at all."

I got up from my chair. "No signals. What about the other guys?"

"None of us can get a call, and none of can get on the Net either."

I glanced at him. "Take the other guys and go."

"What?" he asked.

"Go. Now."

"What about you?"

"Don't worry about us. You need to go now," I repeated.

He had a look of fear, and he went back out. We heard him talking and we heard the others get up from their chairs too.

One of them popped his head in. "G-Man, Cruz, if we can get a signal further out, we'll send help." He left with the others.

"He won't be able to get a signal further out," G. said quietly.

"We've been dumb all this time, G. We assumed he would try to do the Crash like his great-grandfather did, when the way he planned to do it was staring us in the face all the time. The AI is not on the Net. It's in the androids. He's going to have them attack the city and literally rip it apart."

I ran to my mobile computer and tried to turn it on. There was nothing. "G, how long do you think it would take for the Byzantine androids to get here on foot?"

"We don't have much time at all. You think he's sending them here first, not the City?"

"Here first, then there. We're on the way."

G. started grabbing guns from his desk. I grabbed my two cases.

"We need to leave to warn everyone. I wish you had that red Pony of yours. Now's when we need it."

"We'll do the best we can."

"Out the back?" G. asked.

I shook my head. "Out the top."

He smiled.

"Follow me. We'll move fast and stay low."

"No, Cruz, we need to split up."

"No," I insisted.

We stood in the center office, both of us wearing jetpacks. I had my briefcases strapped to my vest. There was no time to argue.

"Cruz, get to the City and warn people. I'll head toward Byzantine and see where they are and meet you there. You have the same idea as I have. They're moving as a pack, same as when it controlled the postal drones. We need to do both. No time to argue, youngster. Go!"

He activated his jetpack and flew up. I heard him shot-gun the ceiling, and he flew out the hole. I activated mine and flew out the same hole. I saw the light from his pack heading north. I turned and flew forward to Downtown Metro. Thankfully, there was no rain, but the sky was overcast, and there was plenty of traffic. I had only recently become used to jetpacks. PJ forced me to sign up for classes, and now I was glad she had.

I flew as fast as I could above pedestrians. What I was doing was illegal, but I didn't expect anyone to call the police on me, though it was what I was praying for. I had a strange sensation as if someone had touched my leg, but how could that be possible if I was 10 feet in the air well above pedestrians and well below the slow lane of sky traffic? I felt a presence.

I instinctively fired my omega-gun and blew the jumping android in the head. It crashed to the ground, and I heard screams of pedestrians below. I could see them now, several of them running on the ground behind me. The androids could run as fast as a hovercar flew.

I shot a second and a third one "dead." The others scattered. They would either hide until they could jump at me again or—

I saw the blasts and went straight for the windows of an office mega-tower. I crashed through, and while I was rolling on the floor to a stop, I shot out the lights in the office. It was not an empty office. There were three people sitting around a small TV eating pizza. They were scared out of their wits and bolted out of the office.

The first android appeared at the window with gun in hand, and I was ready. I blew its head off. I had to remember that these were robots disguised as people who could see in the dark. I got up and jumped out of the office—it also meant they might have infrared. I heard bullets and lasers shower the office.

The hallway wasn't big enough to activate my jetpack, and running with two suitcases strapped to me meant running away was impossible. I opened the case and tossed one into the office. I heard one of them run to it and catch it in its hand. There was a flash, and it collapsed to the ground. I heard more footsteps running and crashing. They had jumped out the window. I had no choice.

I flew away just as the android exploded. I tried to stop, but shot down the hallway and slammed into the wall. I went into another office and ran to the phone. There was no signal.

I was about to step back out in the hallway when I saw a shadow. A man ran in screaming. "You killed my friend!" He was crying.

They were good—too good. I flicked my left wrist and blew the android back out the door and dove for the floor. It exploded.

This had to end. I had to get to Downtown Metro, and I would never get there this way.

I heard so many feet running down the hall that I could feel my heart drop into my stomach. I activated my jetpack and crashed through the window.

CHAPTER 48

The Cavalry

ilford G's *How to be a Great Detective with 100 Rules* clearly stated the street detective should never be afraid to get help when needed. It wasn't a sign of weakness, only a sign of sanity.

I lay on my stomach motionless on the ground, as the androids approached. They looked like real people in every way, dressed as anyone would be dressed on a typical Metropolis rainy day, except for one thing—their eyes were lit up like hovercar headlights. To real people around, especially little kids, I could see people gathering and staring, asking how they could get their own "glowing zombie eyes." People had already spontaneously made up a name for it. For me, the half dozen androids, slowly stepping to me, with their headlight eyes was far from amusing. They were here to kill, but what they were really doing was keeping me from Downtown Metro. The AI didn't know why I had stopped and was lying on the ground. The AI was saying that my actions didn't match my profile of being a germophobe because I was lying on the nasty ground. It was saying that I wasn't trying to escape, when obviously, I knew I was in mortal danger. I noticed that all the eye lights were focused on my hands. The AI assumed I wanted them to get close enough to use another "android killer" toy on them. I knew how fast these machines could move, and I wasn't interested in having another hand crushed like a wet muffin. They were watching my hands; I flicked my wrist.

There was a flashing sound, and the androids froze. The AI didn't know about my "pausing" device yet. I got up and ran into the crowd. "Everyone, these robots, androids, may be explosive."

People were already running away. I was satisfied that people were far enough away, aimed and fired with the new setting. My omega-gunshot one explosive round and blew all six of the androids apart. They couldn't blow up if I blew them up first.

From the corner of my eye, I saw lights coming. I already knew what they were even before them came around the corner. The androids were moving at better than 50 miles an hour. As I reached to open one of the cases, I heard a familiar voice.

"Mr. Cruz." It was Quix. I turned and saw him running to me with about two dozen men.

"Quix, you're back."

"Get out of here, Mr. Cruz. We'll take care of them. All you have to do is look for the first cop responding to the sound of explosions."

"G. sent you to back me up?"

"He sent me to make a special delivery. Here." He gave me a small case. "You know what it is."

The androids were coming fast. I wanted to talk more but had my own mission. "What about, G.?" I managed to ask. He ignored me.

As I ran, I could hear Quix and his men open fire on the androids. His team was also using explosive rounds. It was over in two seconds, and by the time I glanced back, Quix and his men were gone. I heard running in the distance, and there wasn't a glowing set of android eyes anywhere.

Quix knew Metro PD protocol like I did. I saw a police hover cruiser coasting in the air. All police vehicles had audio scanners—an explosion of any kind would bring them.

I ran to it, waving my arms frantically. It saw me, and its spotlight blinded me.

"Mr. Cruz." I heard when it touched down and the first officer exited.

"I need to get to Downtown Metro now!"

"Why?"

"Are your comms working?"

"They are."

"Call the Chief, but we have to get in the air. I'll explain on the way. We have to go."

He reluctantly opened the door to the backseat. "What is that?" I heard the officer in the driver's seat ask. I turned, and it was a man running faster than any human. I aimed and fired. Unexpectedly firing a weapon near two Metro officers could immediately get you shot, but when they saw the "human" blown in half by my explosive round, they pointed their weapons at it, not me.

"What was that?" the driving officer asked again.

"That, officer, is an illegal killer android. Do you think we should get in the air now before the rest of his thousand brothers and sisters get here?"

The officers looked at me. "Brothers and sisters?"

"Officers, we have to go!"

I didn't wait for them. I jumped into the back of their cruiser. The police officers got in, and within moments, their standard five-seater hovercraft was thirty-feet in the air above all the normal congested sky traffic.

"Call the Chief," I said. "We have to warn them."

"What's going on, Cruz?" the driver asked. It was lucky for me that most of Metro PD knew me by sight, and the street cops, at least, liked me.

"Call the Chief and I'll explain. We're fighting the machines."

"Fighting the machines?" the officer in the passenger seat said.

"Wasn't that a machine pretending to be a man that I blasted?"

"Dispatch, I need a priority patch-through to Police One Command," the driver said into his mouth-comm. "This is a priority red, over."

"Unit 4-3-9-3 understood. Patching through, over," a voice answered over the vehicle's audio.

"Unit 4-3-9-3 this is Police One Command go ahead, over."

"We have a civilian in the vehicle who needs to speak with Victory," the driver said. "It's the private detective, Cruz, over."

"Victory is unavailable, Unit 4-3-9-3. Return to Police One immediately. Confirmed priority red. Hostile army is approaching City One, over."

The passenger officer activated the sirens, and the cruiser blasted away like a jet.

"Hostile army?" the driver asked. "Cruz, what's going on?"

"I told you. Killer androids. Do you have a line I can use to call out?" I asked. I felt a huge weight off my shoulders. Someone else had warned them. Maybe it was G., maybe it was another cruiser noticing a crowd of humans running down the street at 60 miles an hour with headlight eyes.

The officer in the passenger seat reached back with a black mobile phone. I took it. Metro PD and other emergency divisions of the city had mobile phones on a different network than the public.

"PJ!" I was so happy to see her face on the tiny screen.

"Boss! We've been trying to reach you, but we couldn't call out on the phones."

"PJ, get in your hovercar, get your crew, and find me at City One."

"We'll be there."

Downtown Metropolis was the nerve center of the supercity, the center of its power with City One—the office of the Mayor and City Hall—and Police One—Metro PD and all the supporting intelligence and emergency department. Why did I think I needed to save the supercity? As we flew over, I saw lines of police troops on the ground and heavy police cruisers in the air firing a barrage of lasers. At the receiving end of that brutal damage was a litter of metal and small craters everywhere. I didn't know if it was from police mortar rounds or the androids inadvertently detonating.

Our cruiser landed behind the perimeter. I thanked the officers and jumped out. I stopped and looked around. Every officer in military gear and civilian in a suit were wearing strange goggles. I saw Connie.

"Connie!" I ran to her.

"There you are," she said. "At least I know you're not a killer android."

"What? Your goggles can see that?"

She smiled. "Sorry, Cruz. G, told me about your invention."

"No patent for me then?"

"Sorry, but no."

I looked up. A Metro PD Destroyer hung above us—it was an aircraft carrier-sized hovercraft armed with missiles, lasers, and so many other world-annihilating-potential weapons that one couldn't help the warm feeling of comfort that came over you. You felt like a little kid bundled up by Mom in a couch, drinking some nice, warm cocoa. It didn't matter how many killer androids were on the way. They were no more than spitballs bouncing off a standing heavy hovertank. The people of Metropolis were saved from the AI Android Zombie Apocalypse!

PART NINE

Swan Song

CHAPTER 49

AI Robot Zombie Vampires

"Hello, Cruz."

I snapped out of my "moment." "Yes? Oh, I was saying no patent for me then for my new invention." I adjusted the pair of Turing shades I'd been wearing since I jetpacked out of the warehouse after G. Their shades had an orange tint; mine were clear.

She laughed. "The City has had visual android-detecting tech before you were born. We've always had them because of Up-Top. We make the best cyborgs. They make the best androids. That's why androids are banned on Earth, but it doesn't stop Up-Top from making them. Didn't ever think we'd have to pull them out of storage for androids made by an Earther."

"Did any of them get through?"

"No. This would be classified as a riot suppression action, and the police are very good at it. This time, they were authorized to use live rounds, and they're enjoying every minute of it. There was another army of androids coming from outside the city, from the Hinterlands, but they've all been stopped."

"EMP bombs?"

"Yes. These here are the only ones left, but there are patrols out looking for more."

"Connie, are you an android?"

"What?"

"Connie, this was too easy."

"This wasn't easy. And it's fembot."

"What?"

"If I were an android, I'd be a fembot, not an android."

"Yes, it is, Connie. Wouldn't it be fem-droid?" I digressed.

"Fembot. And this wasn't easy at all. I was the one who had forces deployed for the androids from the Hinterlands."

"Venn has stayed ahead of you, G., your ex, and all his friends all these years, and this is it? This is the end to his great, grand plot."

"We haven't gotten him yet."

"That's not the plot either. There's Venn and there's the AI he controls. That's what we all believe. These androids are the AI, not Venn. Is the AI really allowing itself to be killed, or does it just want us to think so?"

"What? What are you saying?"

"Connie, I don't see you carrying a gun."

"Why do I need a gun?"

"Connie, get a gun and let's go inside."

She had no problem getting one of the officers to lend her a laser rifle. I led her back into the City One building.

"Cruz, where are we going?"

I waved and said hello to officers as we went. All the hallways were filled with security, every hallway, on every level.

"Where are we going?" she asked me again as we entered one of the hallway capsules.

My finger paused over the button. "Are we going up or down?"

"Where are we going, Cruz?"

"To the Metro Main Frame."

I could see her thinking as she reached to the buttons and pushed a button. We were going up. "It's not possible. You can't get into Mainframe."

"Venn wouldn't want to get into it, Connie. He'd want to destroy it."

"How?"

"When we get off on the floor, we'll see for ourselves."

"What does that mean? There's no way to get past security, and we can detect his androids."

"Can you?"

"We can."

"Feeling pretty secure with your goggles there."

"I am."

"Who maintains the vault where they were kept?"

"You know who, Cruz. We've meet Mr. Hertz many times, and I think he even has an interest in fast hovercars like you."

"Mr. Hertz's name is in the Confidential. Every hour Exe's Commission has been secretly releasing names for G and me to review. When I saw Mr. Hertz's name on the list, I said I know him, and then I said, why the hell would Mr. Candy be interested in him? He's in the basement and maintains old vaults that hold items with no value whatsoever."

Connie looked down at her laser rifle in her hand.

"Is the safety on?" I asked.

"I know how to use a gun, Cruz." She flicked off the safety.

"It's a—rifle," I added.

"Shut up."

Metropolis, like all the supercities of Earth, had main computers to house all kinds of critical data and systems. They never were all on one mainframe but rather dozens, hundreds or thousands of them. However, if you said the Mainframe, you meant the one that networked all of them to act as one. Without it, none of the others could talk to each other. I learned the classified factoid in my Blade Gunner case when I was figuring out what his gang's real scheme was all about.

We stopped on one of the middle floors, but no number flashed. It was strange because, as the elevator capsule door opened, there was not a sound, but as soon as we stepped out, there were a dozen conversations. The entire hallway was a sea of police on guard wearing those special goggles.

A few of them stopped us. "This is a restricted floor," one of them said.

"Ma'am, I'm going to need to hold that rifle," another officer said and took the weapon from her.

"Officer, this is Compstat Connie," I said. "The Chief wants her to inspect the floor."

"We have no such orders from the Chief, sir. You're going to have to go back down."

"Can we call the Chief from here?" Connie asked.

"No, but if you want us to go down with you, we can."

"No, it's fine. We know you're doing your jobs, officers," Connie said. "We'll come back after the crisis is over."

"That would be best. Thank you, ma'am."

We got back in the elevator, and one of the officers handed Connie her rifle, and he reached and hit the lobby button. The door closed and down we went. I pressed the "Hold" button, and the elevator capsule came to a stop.

"Initiate it," I said.

"Are you sure?" Connie asked me. "You have to be sure."

"I'm positive," I said. "They're all androids."

We stood there listening to instructions in our ear-buds. Then the Chief told us that is was "All Clear" to return to the floor. Connie pressed the floor number button.

When the door opened, it was a haze of icy dust. In the hallway were walking robots, hovering ones, and sweeper bots running along the floor. What was left of the sea of android police was a sea of debris being swept and vacuumed up by maintenance bots. There were protocols for everything when it came to maintenance, including one to blast incinerate an entire floor with liquid nitrogen and clean up the mess. (I never did ask why the City would have such a protocol, and I didn't want to know.)

We reached the closed entrance at the end of the hallway. Connie tapped the wall, and a video screen appeared to show us inside. We both were confused at what we were seeing.

"What's he doing?" I asked.

We kept leaning closer to the display on the wall. There stood the external tower access to the Mainframe. On the side, with his entire head pushed through the housing, was a man. He stood motionless, leaning in, arms at his side. I tapped the screen to zoom in.

"I know," Connie said. "His entire head is the connector."

"The AI android zombie is also an AI android zombie vampire," I said. "We need to do something. Open up."

"Cruz, we have to wait for police back-up."

"This is how Venn's crashing the Mainframe, Connie. The AI is in the androids. It's uploading itself."

Connie turned to look at the display again. "No, not uploading. Rewriting the code."

"I'll go in then." She looked at me. "Its head is buried in the computer."

"Who says it needs its head to see you?"

"I can stop it."

"Use any means necessary to stop it. I'll get to another control display and try to activate a power surge."

"Shoot or electrocute. That plan works for me."

"Oh no!" Connie yelled and reflectively fired her rifle, scaring the life out of me.

I turned to see a man lying on the ground.

"He came out of nowhere," Connie yelled and dropped the rifle to the ground, making me jump in the air.

"Don't do that, Connie! Rifles can go off like that and shoot someone!"

"Sorry!"

I leaned over to the man with my arm extended, and my gun ready to shoot.

"Please don't tell me I shot a real person."

"Relax, Connie. He's an android too. Where did he come from?"

We looked around the room. "Was he just standing here?"

"He was listening." I was staring at the screen. The man floated upward, ripping a path with his head to the top of the Mainframe tower. "It heard us."

"The androids are linked to each other," Connie said, as she typed in the access code and the door opened for me. I stopped. It was an empty room, except for a huge twenty-foot tower in the center that reminded me of the Neolith object of my last Alien Hunter case.

"I don't think it hovered up to the top of the tower thinking that would be enough to stop me from blasting it to pieces."

"It wants you to go in."

"Which is exactly why I won't. Can what we did in the hallway be done in that room?"

"Something like it. Wait here."

Connie walked away as I watched the screen. The android's body floated back down to the ground, and it pulled its head out of the computer housing. The head and face were surprisingly mostly intact, but with the sides, including ears, ripped apart with loose wires and fibers dangling out. It knew where the camera was and looked at it—looked at me.

"People of Metropolis. I wanted you to know that I, Venn Daemon, have won. I gave you Crash Alpha. You thought you destroyed me and my creators, but I was only waiting. I wanted you to build up again, bigger than before, so I could tear it down again and laugh. I will give you Crash Omega." The android smiled and lifted its arms in the air. Then its body disintegrated into droplets, rising to the ceiling. Its fabricated flesh was gone, then its alloy body liquefied. There was a flash and then the room was an electric light show; I had to turn my head away from the display. Connie probably rerouted more power into it than it would take to power all of Metropolis.

She joined me at the display, but not alone. Officers in black and white uniforms start to file into the room. The regular officers had laser rifles, and the science officers had scanning and monitoring devices in their hands.

"Did you see everything it said?"

"Yes."

"Did it get into the broadcasts?"

"No, we were the only ones who saw it," she said. "You were right. The room was filled with poisonous fumes. If we had opened it, we would have been overcome and probably died."

"Did you stop what it was doing? Do you know what it was doing?"

"Yes, and yes, Cruz. It's over, or this part is."

"What was it doing? How could it destroy Metropolis by getting into the Mainframe? The Mainframe talks to the others. The worst it could do is shut down automated services, power. That's not destruction."

"The Mainframe is also linked to our satellites."

"Satellites again. What could he do with surveillance satellites?"

"We have much more than surveillance satellites in space, Cruz."

I realized it. "Defense satellites."

"Heavy laser defense against meteors, but any site on the planet could be conceivably targeted."

"Complete city destruction and mass murder."

"His ultimate revenge. He fooled a lot of people."

"Venn's very clever," I said. "He might have gotten access to the back-ups too, and this was another ruse to get the City to upload that."

"Cruz, we have it handled. Venn's smart, but we have smart people too."

"I'm thinking of every possible scenario."

"I know."

"He must be a bit smart if he managed to escape you and G. for 50 years."

"But he didn't count on you."

"Thanks, Connie. Speaking of G. Where is he?"

"He went after him."

"Went after him?"

"He said he wouldn't allow Venn to escape again in all the chaos."

"Went after him where? New Morocco."

"Venn lives in the Byzantine, Cruz. That's what G found out. He's always lived there."

"Aren't the police there?"

"No, Cruz. Not yet. Half the forces were here to protect Downtown Metro; the other half went to destroy the roving androids outside the city coming in."

"But what about G.?"

"I don't know."

I ran out of there as fast as I could.

CHAPTER 50

The Rescue Crew

I was in panic as I ran out of the City One buildings. I had a small black case in my left hand, a big one in my right. Police were everywhere, on the ground and in the air. All I could think of was getting to Byzantine as fast as I could.

"Cruz!"

I had totally forgotten. Across the street were quite a few civilian hovercars, including a lot of reporters. PJ was hanging out the passenger window of one, and I ran to them as fast as I could.

They touched down, and I hopped into the back with two big men. "We need to get to the Byzantine as fast as possible."

"Boss, we can't go there," PJ said.

"Why?"

"That whole area I closed off," the driver answered with a French accent.

"That's where I need to go, so if you can't get me there, take me to a vehicle and I'll get in there myself."

"What's happening?" PJ asked. She could see I was distressed.

"G. is over there by himself against who knows how many of those androids."

"Androids?" the man sitting closest to me said. "The rumor is true."

PJ yelled something at the driver in French. He nodded and increased his speed as he flew toward sky traffic.

"Don't worry about anything, Mr. Cruz," he said. "We'll get you into Byzantine."

We flew for more than forty minutes. The area was cordoned off by police, but we blew past a checkpoint. I looked out the rear window, and the police manning it were not interested at all in giving chase.

"That's not like them," I said.

"They'd never catch us," the driver said. "But the reason is that." He pointed. "They're not going into that without heavy backup."

Ahead of us we could see what looked like a full-scale war within the city—lasers, tracer rounds, and explosions.

"You're sure, Mr. Cruz?" the driver asked. "Because I'm sure this isn't normal, even for Metropolis."

"We need to get down to the ground and find out who's shooting at who. That will tell me how to find G."

He set the hovercar down about a half mile from the shooting. It was all centered in Byzantine, and I had no idea why the police hadn't arrived on scene to stop it. Metro PD doesn't create perimeters around active shootings; they invaded and killed all the shooters if they didn't stop. I looked and PJ had a laser rifle in each arm.

"PJ, stop that nonsense. You can't shoot a different weapon in each hand, even with bionic arms. This isn't the movies. You don't have two heads and four eyes. You use two hands to shoot one weapon, so you don't shoot something or someone you're not supposed to."

"But we did that all the time when I was a gang member."

"And how did that work out for you?"

"Okay, Cruz, I'll give one away. You're always a party pooper, poopin' the party."

I opened the small case and strapped on the special weapons.

"What are those?" she asked, stepping back. "Remember, keep those anti-cyborg weapons away from me. They make me very uncomfortable."

I opened the large case and took out a huge pulse rifle.

PJ was smiling. "What is that?"

"This is so, when I speak to the killer androids, they'll be able to understand me clearly and in all languages."

They laughed.

I offered to lead the way but one of the men insisted he would. After about fifteen minutes of traveling, we saw a group of men ahead, and he yelled at them. They yelled something back, and there I was listening to people speak languages other than English around me again. It was annoying.

"Who are they?" I yelled.

"Do you know Tiki?" he asked.

"Yes! Where is he?"

We joined the men at a hovervan doubling as a barricade. We followed them down an alley away from the heavy shooting. When we turned the corner, I realized it wasn't going to be a short jog. I was getting increasingly irritable, but there was nothing for me to do but keep quiet and keep going.

We reached them. Tiki was back in his fat ninja attire. He didn't have his hoverthrone, but he did have his silly silver scepter. All around him were armed men in ninja suits—ninja masks, business suits, laser swords.

"We meet again, Cruz," he said.

"Are you running this?" I asked.

"We're the muscle. G.'s running it."

"Where's G.?"

"Moving in to get Venn."

"Moving in?"

"Don't worry yourself. He has Quix and his team with him, and they're in a hovertank that not even the androids can destroy."

"Hovertank? How did they get a hovertank?"

"G. has more resources that anybody in this city."

"What's the plan?"

"Keep the androids busy by killing every last one of them. We're making sure none of them get out."

"I need to get to him."

"Impossible. We're keeping them in, but they're keeping us out."

"Why won't the police move in?"

"If it weren't for us, they'd have broken out and been swarming the city. They show up to protect Downtown Metro, but leave the rest of the city to fend for itself," one of the men yelled.

"Stop it. When the Animal Farm Crime Syndicate was running wild, didn't the police protect the city? Didn't they put them down? They left Downtown Metro to fend for itself. How do I get to G.?"

He gestured to me, and I followed him to one of his men wearing headphones, who opened up a mobile communication center in a briefcase. Tiki typed one set of numbers then another. The video screen lit up. We saw the face of a man looking back. He said something in another language, then Quix's face appeared.

"Quix." I stepped forward. "Where's G.?"

He disappeared then the Man himself appeared. "Cruz, you made it," G. said with a big smile. "I knew you would."

"How do I get to you?"

"You help Tiki clean up the machines."

"G, we started this to get Venn. Let's end it."

"You're right—"

"What happened?" G. asked.

"We lost the signal," Quix replied, just as the signal returned.

"I'll come to you," I said.

"No, Cruz."

The signal cut out.

"Get the signal back!" G. yelled.

Quix worked the machine but shook his head. "Nothing."

"What do you mean? Were they hit?"

"I don't know."

"I don't want him coming to us. Could they find us?"

"G-Man, all they have to do is follow where the robots are shooting the most rounds."

G. was not pleased. "I don't want Cruz coming here."

There was a metal knock on the hovertank. Quix and his men jumped up as one of them flipped on one of the exterior camera displays. It was Cruz with some of Tiki's ninjas.

"It figures Cruz would know the exact entrance to a modern military hovertank of the Americas," G. said.

There was another mortar round explosion.

"Let him in?" one of the men asked

"We have to now. We can't let him get blown up outside."

The men and G put on the anti-android goggles. The first man ran to the bank of the tank, slid the door panel to the right to peek out the door viewer, was satisfied and opened the door.

He yelled as a sword blade thrust threw his chest. Cruz and the ninjas rushed in firing weapons. Quix and the men opened fired themselves.

Tiki decided to lead me in. We had several of his ninjas, PJ and her crew. As we ran in, shooting laser rifles and pulse mortars, I couldn't help asking myself: "How the hell am I in this situation? I'm a detective, not an urban commando." We were literally running through an active war zone.

An android, with no synthetic human skin covering, jumped from some debris to attack. PJ punched its head off with one blow, then with another sent the rest of the body into the air away from us. The android wasn't alone. I got to see for myself the modifications (illegal) to her bionic arms. She had some kind of strobe lights added to them. The flashing was disorientating to me, but for the robots, it was blinding. They didn't know what to do as PJ punched and pummeled her way through them.

The men looked at her, smiling. Not one of us had to fire a round. But then more came. We shot and bombed our way forward, when Tiki raised his hand and pointed. I looked and noticed the hovertank. Quix was waiting for us at a semi-open rear door.

We ran to it, and Tiki and I both froze at the same time. On the ground was—me. The android copy was riddled with bullets. I looked up at Quix, and he had a saddened face.

"No!" I dropped my heavy rifle to the ground and ran in.

Immediately near the front door was one dead man, and then a second. I ran to the front where there was one very badly wounded, bloodied man, and then G.

"Hey youngster," he whispered.

I leaned over him. They had him on the ground and had tried to dress his chest wounds as best as possible.

"G., you have to make it. That was the deal. We get Venn together."

"You'll get him for me."

"No, but you're supposed to be my mentor. Where will I get my inspiration? Your book only has 100 rules. I need the rest from you."

He smiled. "Cruz, you don't need me to be inspired. Bad people don't need incentives to be bad. They find excuses to do what they were always going to do anyway. Good people are no different. I was a P.I. for 70 years. No one was inspired by me until you. But you were always going to be a great P.I., with or without me. The city had me for a while, I pass the torch onto you. That's how life is, Cruz. In real life, someone always dies. No one can stop that. I was never going to live another 20 years anyway. 95 years is more than enough in Metropolis. You're the man, now."

In G.'s shoulder was one of those adrenaline pens. G. was literally pumped with stimulants to stay alive, but it was a street remedy that wouldn't last long. The ambulance had to get here in time.

"I already made the arrangements. Since I was dead and came back, that messed up some legal stuff, so I'll have my attorney make it all official and public with your office."

"My office? You're my secret benefactor?"

"It was Connie who called me back then and asked if there was anything I could do to help this kid who was starting out as a private detective. She said G., 'I know you got a spare office somewhere.' So, I gave you the one I had in Buzz Town. Looks like I bet on the right one again."

My eyes were already tearing up. Now, I was crying.

"You're the man now, Cruz. Go get Venn. Quix will tell you where. I'll hold on until you bring him in—alive or dead; it'll be justice either way."

My emotions went from sorrow to anger. "Then you hold, G. I'll be back."

CHAPTER 51

Venn Daemon

When I left the hovertank, there was only one thing I wanted off my mind. But as I began to speak to Quix, he stopped me and told me that G. already had him make the call. Wil Jr. was holding on the mobile.

That gave me some comfort. Wilford G. and son would get to have their last conversation. I stepped outside, and PJ had a mobile call waiting for me too. We all took shelter as the bombs fell. In fact, Quix and his team flew their hovertank out of range. Byzantine was showered with EMP bombs. They couldn't use a mega-bomb, or that would have rendered surrounding districts without power.

Electromagnetic pulse technology wasn't new, and neither was the science of making EMP-resistant machines. Maybe Venn had androids that could shield their internal functions from conventional EMP attacks. As I walked to his mega-tower, I was prepared to do battle with more than just Venn.

I told Metro PD not to enter until I called them. If I didn't make it, they'd know that too. I don't know who it was in the police brass, whether it was the Chief or not, but my request was sanctioned.

A castle. In the center of Byzantine was a castle of steel alloy and glass. Who knew, when it became Venn's secret home, I was going to do battle in a castle. However, no swords for me—medieval knight or Japanese samurai; I had my heavy rifle in hand, and "other" weapons under my slicker and on my body.

I entered the main entrance, and the open lobby was like that of a historic hotel with steps up to a second level—white carpeting, lots of mirrored surfaces, diamond like chandeliers handing from the vaulted ceiling. Venn stood at the tops of the steps, waiting.

"I thought it best, Mr. Cruz, to meet you rather than waste your time wandering through my house. I've never met a street detective who could get the Metro PD to stand by while he went in after a suspect to kill them. Not even the late Wilford G. had that kind of influence, and he'd been a one-man institution of Metropolis for seven decades.

"Do you know you foiled my plans before we even first met or Wilford first brought you into his crusade? I was about to launch my plan when, all of a sudden, Downtown Metro government changed their protocols to scan even active duty personnel at work. You can't replace key people with identical androids if everyone is scanned. I had to find out why. I thought I had been discovered somehow. You were the cause of it, Mr. Cruz. I still don't know why you made them change procedure. One of your many high-profile cases I suppose.

"But that's why I took over the Confidential. To have many, many options to see my plan to the end. No matter what the setback, I could still move forward with the plan. I met Mr. Candy because he tried to blackmail me. It was a trap, of course. I heard about him many years ago and created a sordid double life to make myself an irresistible target for him—publicly, the beloved Metro tycoon, privately and hidden from most, something completely opposite. That's why Wilford despised me long before I made my 'confession' to him. In his seedy little circles that he traveled in as a street detective, he would have known of that sordid double life too. I played my role with Mr. Candy until I knew enough, found out who he really was, then killed him. I became Mr. Candy. He was only interested in greed. He never saw the full potential of the Confidential that I did—to have access to the richest and most powerful of Metropolis at your fingertips. If you're planning to destroy a supercity, then such a Rolodex is essential.

"You're being very quiet, Mr. Cruz."

"I'm going to kill you, Venn."

He smiled; his eyes watched me through his red shades. "G. should be dead by now."

"He's been dead before, but you, on the other hand, will never be coming back."

"Are you sure, Mr. Cruz? Daemon is immortal."

I dove for cover as he shot a laser right out of the palm of his hand, and the entire interior went dark.

"Where are you, Mr. Cruz? Fascinating. I don't see you. How can you evade my eyes? If I didn't know better, I'd say you had an Up-Top cloaking suit. Have you been stealing things from the spacemen and Martians that you shouldn't have, Mr. Cruz? Come out, please. You and Wilford have caused me so much trouble. I'm not interested in having you chase me for the next 50 years."

He heard the noise—the sound of gunshots.

"Thank you," Venn said.

The phrase made me swallow hard.

"Mr. Cruz, I will destroy everything, so there is no possible way you can survive. This entire building is your tomb. Today, both you and Wilford die. That speech I gave at City One was given for your benefit, not theirs. I will destroy Metropolis, not with an army of androids, only one. My plan from the start." Venn wasn't just an android; he was an android weapon.

The noise wasn't me, and the gunshots weren't gunshots at all. I had used them in my first official case, but not since then because I wanted to create a solid, and serious, reputation as a private detective first. I had thrown a handful of Mexican jumping beans. They were silly, but even the silly can be unexpected and effective all at the same time. His robot eyes wouldn't have seen them. When the jumping beans started to pop, they did sound like gunshots. It gave me the time to fire my own death weapon—the nano-mizers.

There was no way Quix or any of his team had casually constructed the weapons. They were military weapons. Which military I didn't know. They shot a stream of programmed nanites—miniature robots—that flew through the air to Venn.

The Venn android's chest and legs were laser emitters that were doing what he threatened—turning the building into my tome. It was no longer dark because his laser had cut and shred the walls and everything in its path. The entire building was crashing down as he kept firing a steady output of seemingly thousands of lasers.

The lasers stopped. Venn looked at his arms, and they were starting to decay. He laughed as he walked down the steps to where he saw my body. His body was disintegrating from the invading nanite swarm.

"Mr. Cruz, you have an android body too."

"I do," my android said from the ground. It was a mangled mess, cut to pieces too many times to count by his lasers.

"They've let you into a part of their secret, though wrapped up in a thick blanket of deception. How can we properly kill each other if we're both sending androids in our place?"

"Venn," I said. "Run."

The entire building fell down on top of us. Metro PD were given the green light and fired their missiles at the rumble. They exploded.

"No!" Venn climbed out of the virtual reality chamber as fast as he could. He frantically began pulling at wires but realized he had no time and grabbed a dark hooded slicker, threw it on, and ran for the door.

It was a long hallway, and he ran as fast as he could. He burst through a door and ran down the stairs, level after level, then out onto another empty floor and down a long hallway. When he came through the next door, it wasn't empty but filled with office workers, some wondering how he came out of a sealed door. He ran up the stairs, level after level, and finally burst out onto the street in the rain. He caught his breath, then ran again.

I hit Venn in the Pony traveling at a good 100 miles an hour. He did manage to turn to see my face in the window for the last second of his life. His body flew through the air and crashed to the wet pavement. Since Venn liked to be clever, I set the Pony down, got out, walked to him, and shot him with the omega-gun to make sure.

Exe's Commission revealed the Confidential included over a thousand people all throughout the city's law enforcement, intelligence, judicial, and operations departments and agencies. I knew there were a lot more names than that and the official list they had been allowing me to see was not the "official" one.

The City claimed they didn't know Byzantine had been Venn's android city all these years. They claimed they had no idea he had amassed an android army outside the city. I believed him; the android army belonged to the City and Venn took it from them. I had read G.'s old notes. The city back then was corrupt to the core, but they also genuinely believed that Up-Top had a hand in the Crash and planned to invade Earth. If you don't have enough cops you can militarize, build them.

It was never Venn's plan to destroy Metropolis with one android. Destroying the City was always the ultimate goal, but the means was always changing after being foiled time after time, then moving to the next plot. Wilford had been stopping him for decades, Connie's ex and crew before that, and I was the final one. It hadn't escaped my attention that both the bad guy, Venn, and the good guys had android copies of me. It was Connie's idea to send it in; she said it had been made in an hour and was on loan from Up-Top by special request of the City. I didn't believe that for a moment. My Turing glasses had been made on the fly; such an android—which Venn's android couldn't detect—had been made a long time ago and simply pulled out of an old vault somewhere. I was using a cloaking suit, but he was genuinely surprised to find out it was an android that he was talking to.

Then there was where I had found Venn—in the basement belly of Downtown Metro. I never did understand why it was so important for Wilford to hide until his 95th birthday. It was almost as if they were suggesting, at that age, his identity file would be moved to a new city archive system not accessible by the Daemon AI—he was hiding from the killer AI. But the Daemon AI wasn't in the system; the whole case was to keep it from getting into the system. But if Venn had physical access to the city's system, maybe the CIC itself, then that would make sense. I'd even wondered if Venn, under another identity, worked for Connie's CIC division from the start.

Even the Great Liar, the Devil, will say a few things that are the truth. The Confidential came into being long before Venn was born. The Daemon AI was also created before he was born. He simply took control of both. The ones who really created both would probably never be known by me or anyone else. Metropolis had its secrets to keep.

The great irony was that the great grandson of cyber-terrorists responsible for The Crash with their mastery of digital tech was stopped (in more ways than one) because he was dumb enough to connect with his android using digital tech. I didn't know what Up-Top's version was like, but to us Earthers, digital tech was hackable. That's what Compstat Connie ultimately did. All of Venn's babbling at the castle was more than enough time for her to trace him. It also confirmed something else I had long suspected: Metro PD could track a person by listening to their breathing and heart beat using the bio-tracking tech, probably embedded in listening posts throughout the supercity—another AI. Connie routed the readings to my Pony's GPS locator, and with my own knowledge of City One, I flew straight to Venn.

Technically, Connie was law enforcement, so she was legally required to turn the information over to Metro PD, not a civilian—me. However, she'd been after Venn too for 50 years. But despite the revenge play, I had to make sure it ended, decisively and completely. There was only one way to ensure that. For all we knew, there could be Metro prison guards on another Confidential.

The case was over. We got the bad guy, but I would have gladly let the bad guy get away if it meant Wilford G. wasn't sitting in a black steel box on display in the city's auditorium style hall we all sat in. When I dealt with Venn, I immediately dialed the number on my mobile on my phone.

"Quix, let me talk to G."

There was a long pause. "Sorry, Cruz. He's gone."

I had never felt so devastated in my life.

"He said he knew you got him and that he could move on to the next life. He said you could come join him to work cases any time after your 120th birthday. And make sure to mentor another youngster to take your place. Metropolis needs its famous street private detective."

It was as if everyone knew he wasn't really dead before. There was a funeral for him back then, but not like the one I was at now. Wilford G. had a private one then, but this was an official City funeral. It wasn't only Wil Jr., his wife, and kids in attendance in the front row, or me, Dot, Cruz. Jr., and the grandparents behind them. It was everyone. G.'s ex-wives, Prima Donna, Tiki, (not in his fat ninja outfit, but a proper suit), a sea of police (not androids), practically the entire sports betting community, greyhound breeders and racers, Quix and his crew, Wize Guy and his daughter, Wize Gal. Run-time, Phishy and PJ came because of me, and they brought all their family and friends. All of G.'s friends from the city, 90 years' worth, which meant a lot of people. Since it was a city funeral, the Mayor was also there, with family, the Chief, and his very large family—seven sons, their children, and Exe too.

All the chaos that happened on the steps of City One, was properly replaced by the final call of one of Metropolis's own—the original Metro street private eye, and my posthumous mentor, who I had the honor to meet and work side-by-side as his partner in crime on his last big case—Wilford G. Senior.

Thank you for reading!

Dear Reader,

I hope you enjoyed my **Liquid Cool** cyberpunk detective novel, *A.I, Confidential*.

<u>Can You Write Me a Review?</u>

If you enjoyed ***A.I. Confidential*** *(Liquid Cool, Book 6)*, I'd greatly appreciate an honest review on one or more of the following sites:

Reviews are the best way for readers to discover good books. My writer's motto is simple: "Readers Rule!" Thanks so much.

Always writing,

Austin Dragon

CONTINUE THE ADVENTURE

Get Your Next *Liquid Cool* Books!

- ***These Mean Streets, Darkly*** *(Liquid Cool Prequel Short)*
- ***Liquid Cool*** *(Liquid Cool: The Cyberpunk Detective Series, Book 1)*
- ***Blade Gunner*** *(Liquid Cool, Book 2)*
- ***NeuroDancer*** *(Liquid Cool, Book 3)*
- ***The Electric Sheep Massacre*** *(Liquid Cool, Book 4)*
- ***I, Alien Hunter*** *(Liquid Cool, Book 5)*
- ***A.I. Confidential*** *(Liquid Cool, Book 6)*

- ***Liquid Cool Box Set*** *(Liquid Cool Prequel and Books 1-3)*
- ***Liquid Cool Box Set 2*** *(Liquid Cool: Books 4-6)*

Also by Austin Dragon

See all my books in science fiction, horror, and fantasy at: http://www.austindragon.com/books

ABOUT THE AUTHOR

Austin Dragon is the author of the ***After Eden Series***, including the mini-series, ***After Eden: Tek-Fall***, the classic ***Sleepy Hollow Horrors***, the new epic fantasy adventure ***Fabled Quest Chronicles***, and the cyberpunk detective series, ***Liquid Cool***. He is a native New Yorker, but has called Los Angeles, California home for the last twenty years. Words to describe him, in no particular order: U.S. Army, English teacher, one-time resident of Paris, political junkie, movie buff, Fortune 500 corporate recruiter, renaissance man, dreamer.

He is currently working on new books and series in science fiction, fantasy, and classic horror!

Connect with Austin on social media at:

Website and blog: http://www.austindragon.com

Twitter: https://twitter.com/Austin_Dragon

Pinterest: http://www.pinterest.com/austindragon

Google+: https://google.com/+AustinDragonAuthor

Goodreads: https://www.goodreads.com/ADragon

Other books by Austin:
See all my books at: **http://www.austindragon.com/books**